5|10

One Wish

Dedication

This book is dedicated in memory of R.H.G., my "Papa," the grandfather who didn't yell at me when I put his bass boat in the ditch so that I could sail, and who willingly supplied the lumber for my hang glider so that I could fly.

Thank you for telling me that thunder was giant pumpkins rolling in the clouds, and that you drank coffee with Santa every Christmas Eve. Thank you for buying my drawings (and my mom's jewelry) when I tried to sell them in the hallway. Thank you for old log bridges, apple trees, rose bushes, white gazebos, and grape Chilly Willy's.

You gave me dreams to own and the wings to soar; I am who I am because of you.

One Wish

Leigh Brescia

Published by WestSide Books
60 Industrial Road
Lodi, NJ 07644
973-458-0485
Fax: 973-458-5289

Library of Congress Control Number: 2008911815

International Standard Book Number: 978-1-934813-05-8
School Edition ISBN: 978-1-934813-21-8
Cover illustration Copyright © by Michael Morgenstern
Cover design by David Lemanowicz
Interior design by Paul Sikar

Printed in the United States of America
10 9 8 7 6 5 4 3 2 1

First Edition

One Wish

Chapter

One

Nobody ever asks you if you want to be popular. It's not like buying a car, where you can decide which features you want—leather interior, sunroof, or navigational system. There isn't this option card that like, arrives in the mail just before high school and lets you pick and choose who you want to become. It's too bad, because really, having an on-board navigational system as a sophomore in high school would be so totally awesome.

But no, you can't decide that you want to be pretty—or popular. Things like that are predetermined. Because, if I had a choice, I would be tall, blonde, and skinny. I would be the girl who guys nod at, talk about, and go to parties to see. I would be the head cheerleader...the homecoming queen... I would be "it." I would be the girl everyone *wished* they could become. I mean, who doesn't want that, right?

Unfortunately this is life, and life is cruel—to some of us. So instead of being a tall, cool blonde, I'm short, with the darkest hair and eyes imaginable—oh yeah, and I'm fat. Ironic, huh? So, while fate dealt me a soul that so dreamed to be on the A-List, it dealt me a body more likely to be lost in a sea of "wannabes" who are never "gonnabes."

I should also mention that sometimes my head doesn't exactly listen to what fate blatantly has been shouting at me for like, my whole life.

So that's how I found myself, on a frigid Thursday afternoon, caught in that space between free will and fate, standing at my locker with my hands shaking. It wasn't because of the cold. No, I was trembling because I had somehow agreed to do just about the stupidest thing imaginable for someone who tries to avoid social situations altogether.

It was just after three o'clock in the afternoon, school was out, and I could hardly load my books into my bag. It was such a simple task, and I was seriously screwing it up. The reality of my situation finally nestled itself into my dorky little brain, and as a result, I was no longer functioning normally. I mean, honestly, why did I let people talk me into these things?

"Are you sure I can't watch you try out?" Zoe asked, for like, the millionth time as she slammed her locker door shut.

"No!" I shouted, furtively glancing around to make sure no one had heard my little outburst. I lowered my voice. "I can't do this. It was such a stupid idea."

"Are you kidding me?" she asked. "Wrenn, I heard you. You're amazing. It's totally in the bag."

I inhaled deeply, trying to take her words of assurance and meld them with my emotions—praying it would somehow give me at least a tiny dose of confidence. Zoe is my best friend; she's my rock—the voice of reason in my crazy, mixed-up, teenage world. But really, I was so mad at her at that moment—because it was her fault I even found myself in this predicament in the first place.

The predicament was this…I, Wrenn Scott, was about to try out for the Spring Musical. I, Wrenn Scott, the raven-haired, fat (or big-boned, whichever terminology you prefer) girl that nobody knew existed at Amberson High School, was about to climb up on stage and sing in front of a million people so that in a few months I could get back on stage and sing for a hundred million more. I blamed Zoe because she saw the flier first, and because she thought I was amazing.

It happened just last week, as we passed the bathroom on our way back to our lockers after lunch. I asked her to wait for me. Her attention, however, was elsewhere. I watched as she extended her thin arm and pulled a neon green flier off the wall.

"Look at this," she said. "They're doing *Grease* this year."

I pushed the bathroom door open and found an empty stall. "When?" I asked, only half interested.

"For the Spring Musical," she replied.

"Oh. We should go. When is it?"

"I don't know," she said, pausing for a moment. "This is just announcing auditions. You know, Wrenn…"

At that point I knew what was coming. I'd heard the introduction, and that "tone," so many times…from my mother: "You know, Wrenn, you really should come to the gym with me. You would have such a good time." And from my younger sister, Karly: "You know, Wrenn, you would look so much better if you made an effort. You would be so surprised at what a haircut and a little eyeliner could do for you." And now from Zoe: "You know, Wrenn, you have a great voice. You really should consider trying out."

Even though I couldn't see her face from behind the stall door, I could tell she was serious. I burst out laughing. "Zoe? *What?* No!"

"Why not?" she asked.

Where could I even begin? "Because it's *so* not me. They would never cast me, of all people." The toilet automatically flushed, and I flipped the lock back and pushed the door open. "And besides…"

"Don't say 'I'm fat,' because I don't want to hear it, Wrenn," she argued, "you have such an awesome voice, I know they would give you a part. They'd be stupid not to."

I appreciated Zoe's confidence in me, but drama was *not* my forte. Even my second-grade teacher knew that. When she chose parts for the end-of-the-year play, I was cast as a "flower on the wall." I had to stand in the corner with this huge daisy cardboard cutout on my head and listen to everyone else while they said their lines. I mean, it was symbolism at its best: I was a literal flower on the wall. How lame was that? I never volunteered for another play again.

Now that I was older and able to rationalize such things, I knew that it wasn't the thought of *being in a mu-*

sical that scared me. No, it was more the idea of performing on stage in front of hundreds of people that was so terrifying. That, I just *could not* handle.

"That's okay, maybe some other time, Zoe." I turned on the water faucet and began to wash my hands.

"Some other time? Wrenn, you can't be serious. These opportunities only show themselves once in a lifetime. I mean, this could be your moment. If I could sing, I would *so* try out!" she retorted.

"Well, why don't you, then?"

"Because I can't carry a tune," she reminded me. "That's why. But you...you're amazing, and you know it."

I couldn't believe she was going on like this. Usually when I said no, she dropped the subject. "What if I make a complete idiot of myself?" I asked.

"Highly unlikely. Besides, you need to do something to break this lack-of-self-confidence streak you've got going on."

I stared at Zoe in the mirror as I dried my hands. "And trying out for the school musical will help me break this so-called 'streak'? Which I don't, by the way, have," I threw in.

She shook her head. "Sure you don't. Whatever. But honestly, what have you got to lose?" she asked.

I let out an exasperated sigh. "When are tryouts?"

Zoe handed the flier to me. It was so Microsoft Publisher—with an outline of a girl in a poodle skirt, and various pieces of fifties clip art (milk shakes, records, etc.). Several music notes outlined the word *Audition*.

"They're this Thursday after school," she said. "You

know I'll wait for you. Just tell your mom you have to stay late for a study group or something if you don't want her to know about it."

According to the flier, I could audition with the song of my choice, which was certainly an advantage. "I don't know. I'll think about it," I said, just to shut her up.

"There's nothing to think about, Wrenn. You would be so perfect. This is right up your alley," she chided.

Right up my alley or not, there was a lot to think about. I mean, you don't just up and try out for a musical without seriously weighing the pros and cons. Well, maybe some people do, but not me. I couldn't just "jump into" something like this; it wasn't like me.

What if...seriously...WHAT IF I forgot my lines, or passed out in front of everyone? Or worse...what if I threw up all over the stage? That would be so completely embarrassing—utter humiliation. You could never live down something like that. You'd be destined to walk around school halls for the rest of your academic career with a nickname like "Vominator" or "The Hurler." You'd never recover, like, not ever.

There's more to this musical thing than just passing out and puking, though. I've just kind of made it a habit to keep my distance from things like stages, spotlights, and costumes because truthfully—whether Zoe wants to admit it or not—I'm fat. Okay, if you insist on using politically correct terms, I'm overweight. The doctor reminds me to eat healthy, my mother begs me to go to the gym with her, and my sister treats me like some unearthly being from another planet. Chubby, chunky, big-boned...whatever you want to call me...I'm fat, and it seriously bothers me.

When I was in the fifth grade, we were sitting in class when our teacher decided to reward us...with candy, of course. It was closing in on lunchtime, and I was starving, so I was absolutely elated when she began to pass around her bucket full of chocolates. I mean, who doesn't like chocolate, right? So when the bucket came to me, I searched through the candy for a moment, trying to make the best decision. I was pulling out a miniature Mr. Goodbar—a delectable combination of peanuts and milk chocolate—when I heard someone snorting in the background. I tucked the piece of chocolate close to me, hiding it from view, then passed the rest on.

Mindy Carter, whose unrelenting snobbiness I won't even begin to go into, reached over and carefully placed her piece of candy on my desk. "Here, Wrenn," she said loudly. "You can have mine. I'm trying to watch my figure, but since you're not...." She smiled, and tossed her perfect blonde hair over her shoulder, her blue eyes sparkling. The entire class erupted in laughter, and I could hear those snorts in the background. Oink. Oink. It seemed like forever before the teacher quieted them down. Meanwhile I sat there—staring at the pencil groove carved into my desk, which someone had colored in with blue ink—trying to keep from bursting into tears. I may have been slightly overweight, but that didn't mean I had thick skin. Fortunately, I had learned at an early age to keep my feelings to myself. It was one thing for people to make you *want* to cry, but it was an entirely different thing to let them *know* they upset you. During lunch I hid in one of the bathroom stalls—the first of many such lunches—and ate my piece of chocolate (and Mindy's, too). Mindy Carter didn't have to say it outright, but her message was clear: I was *never* going to be like her—beautiful, popular, and thin. I was a nobody, and probably always would be.

"I think I'm going to throw up," I informed Zoe.

"It's just nerves," she said. "You'll be fine. Are you positive I can't just sit in a dark corner and listen to you audition?"

"No."

"You won't even know I'm there."

"Zoe!" I cried.

She threw up her hands in exasperation. "Fine! Fine! I'll be waiting for you in my car, and after you tell me how fantastic you did, we're going to Andy's to celebrate with orangeades." She reached out and touched my arm. "Don't worry. You're going to blow them away."

"I'm going to blow chunks," I exclaimed.

"Okay, Wrenn, that's just gross," she replied, her nose turned up in disgust as she began to walk away.

Despite the fact that my stomach was in complete chaos, I smiled. If Zoe wasn't my best friend, I would so hate her. Why she chose me for a friend I'll never know. She didn't walk; she floated. My 5'2" had nothing on her 5'8" and still growing. Crowds separate when she needs to pass. I have to push and shove my way through. Nobody ever sees the short fat girl.

Fortunately, I didn't have to push my way through any crowds on this particular afternoon. The halls were still and silent. And for some reason, the long walk to the auditorium was shorter than usual. Perhaps it was my rapidly growing desire to turn and run away from what lay beyond those protective walls.

How did I manage to get into these situations anyway? Why did I even let Zoe talk me into this? It was absolutely ridiculous! I thought to myself, as I pulled open one of the heavy, metal doors.

The room was dark, save a few spotlights that lit the stage area, and it was absolutely huge. At that moment I was sure it held a thousand people or more, and just the thought of that many warm bodies filling a room to watch me perform made my stomach rumble even more.

For now, it was mostly empty. A few dozen students sat scattered across the room, each with a certain amount and type of talent (singing, dancing, acting) that Zoe had led me to believe that I, too, possessed.

I shuffled down the long aisle, each step bringing me closer to the stage, where a man holding a clipboard was standing. He scribbled notes between giving orders to those around him. As I approached him I struggled to find my voice. "I'm here to audition?"

"What?" he asked sharply, removing his headset.

"I'm here to audition," I said, a bit bolder this time.

"What's your name?" he asked as he flipped through the pages attached to the clipboard.

"Wrenn Scott."

"What was that?"

"Wrenn Scott," I repeated.

"Okay, Miss Scott. You're on the roster. Find a seat and we'll call you when we're ready."

I turned on my heel, and found myself face-to-face with a younger version of the man I'd just spoken to. He was decked out in a flannel shirt, and also boasted a clipboard and a headset. I stepped to the side, trying to get out of the way. He stepped with me, and we went back and forth, in tandem, until he laughed nervously.

"Sorry," he said, moving aside.

Not responding, I brushed past him and lowered my head for the duration of the walk to my seat. My face flushed as I thought about my clumsiness, and I prayed that no one else had noticed.

The auditorium was buzzing with conversation, and I briefly wondered if they were talking about me. They very well could have been, because when you're just over five feet tall and overweight, there's always the possibility that someone is talking about you.

"Steven, I need you at the front," the man called from the stage. I turned my head and watched as the guy in the flannel shirt jogged away from the sound room. He was tall, and his curly brown hair hung close to his eyes.

I recognized him from my lunch period. He always sat close to the exit with a group of guys—weird guys, if you wanted to be honest. They're the kind of guys who believe in parallel universes and play games that require alter-egos and stuff—guys who just weren't my type. Guys who weren't *anyone's* type.

"Okay people," the director called, trying to quiet the room.

It was time. My heart began to pound. My hands were sweating and I was shaking like mad. The auditorium was freezing, and that made me feel even worse.

One by one, names were called. Guys and girls performed their audition pieces. I recognized some of them as classmates, and others from the hallway...but I didn't know anyone personally and I knew they didn't know me, either. I'd always kept my distance.

Some of them were, without a doubt, guaranteed to get a part. Others I was sure I wouldn't have to worry about. And before long I made the fatal mistake of actually feeling confident in myself and my abilities.

I could do this, I realized. And then I smiled. I smiled until...

"Bree Donnelly," the man with the clipboard called.

My eyes darted toward the other end of the auditorium, where Bree stood up and began walking toward the stage.

No. Freakin'. Way.

"What are you singing, Bree?"

She tossed her blonde, wavy hair over her shoulder. "'Memory.' From *Cats*," she said with an aura of assurance that I could only dream of having.

"I know what it's from," the man replied. "Whenever you're ready."

But as soon as I heard those familiar notes, I flipped.... *She is singing my song!* The blood completely drained from my face. *I can't do this. I am not auditioning in front of her.*

I pulled myself up and quickly walked down the aisle. I didn't stop until I had pushed my way out the double doors and reached the lobby. What was I thinking? It was so stupid of me to actually believe I could pull this off.

Bree Donnelly was the most popular girl in school. She was gorgeous. She had a perfect body, and perfect hair, and unnaturally straight white teeth and a stellar smile. Bree Donnelly was the Mindy Carter of high school. She was everything I *wished* I could be, but would never, ever, in a million years, become.

Not only was she popular, but she was also dating *the* hottest guy on earth: Chase Cunningham. But it gets better. Not only was she dating Chase, but the buzz from Christmas break was that they were "pre-engaged."

I had only seen the ring from a distance, and I knew the diamond was smaller than one on a normal engagement ring, but it was a diamond no less, and it meant that Bree and Chase would be together forever. Engaged at eighteen. Bree Donnelly was so incredibly lucky.

Which, of course, was why I couldn't audition in front of her. I mean, there are standards, right? I wanted to be popular as much as the next person, but I was not, I repeat, NOT going to subject myself to that kind of humiliation. Sing the exact same song as the most popular girl in school? No way! I would look like such a loser.

I closed my eyes, and leaned against the window of the lobby. *If only I were thin, and beautiful,* I thought. *If I were tall and graceful like Zoe, and beautiful like Bree, and had a boyfriend as incredible as Chase Cunningham, I would be so popular.*

"Wrenn Scott?" A muffled voice broke my train of thought. I paused for a moment, and wondered if I'd imagined it; had I even heard my name at all?

"Wrenn Scott?"

I *had* heard my name. They were asking for me. It was my turn to sing.

My knees weakened, and my feet remained planted as if cement had hardened around them. I definitely could not move.

"Wrenn Scott?"

My head began to spin with all kinds of crazy thoughts. *Come on!* I told myself. *You can do this. You're good! Just walk back in there and sing!*

"Last call for Wrenn Scott."

Go In There! Just DO It!

I took a deep breath, turned around and opened the door. "I'm here," I called. "I'm sorry."

Everyone in the room turned around to look at me. Some of them snickered. So much for not calling unnecessary attention to myself. I kept my eyes on my feet as I shuffled toward the front.

"What are you singing?" he asked as I sat down at the piano.

"Um, 'Memory,'" I stated.

The man sighed in exasperation. "You're going to have to speak up."

"'Memory,'" I repeated.

He scribbled something on his clipboard, then looked at me expectantly. "Okay. Whenever you're ready."

I walked over to the upright piano and the music teacher reached out to take my music.

Leigh Brescia

I knew the song by heart; I loved it, and I sang it often. My voice wanted to waver, but by concentrating on the right notes and words, everything else escaped my mind. I imagined that I was alone in my bedroom, playing on my own piano, singing whatever was in my heart to sing.

It was my destiny. Even my father, who died not long after I was born, knew I would have a beautiful voice. He was the one who named me Wrenn, after the tiny songbird, and I lived to prove him right. If there was one thing on earth I'd gotten right, singing was it.

Before I knew what was happening, the song was over and I was stepping off the stage. A quiet applause rippled across the crowd, and I couldn't help but smile. Mission accomplished.

Then I walked out of the room as fast as my legs would carry me.

Chapter

Two

The cold winter air stung my face, breathing life back into it as I walked toward Zoe's car, one of the few still left in the parking lot.

"So how did it go?" she asked, as soon as I opened the door.

"Well, I didn't blow it, if that's what you mean," I replied.

"Whoo-hoo! Wrenn's gonna be a star!" she cried.

I threw my book bag onto the floor and removed that morning's Burger King bag from my seat. I tossed it onto the floor where it joined the other bags, empty cups, and balled-up Croissan'wich wrappers, representing at least a week's worth of breakfasts. Zoe's parents were vegans. Burger King kept her alive.

Zoe cranked her old Volvo several times, trying to coax it to life. "Not a word," she said, knowing I was mentally scolding her for the mess.

"Did I say anything?" I asked.

For me, someone who organizes the shirts in her

closet by color and sleeve length, Zoe's car is completely uninhabitable. I can't stand a mess, but it didn't seem to bother her. Not long after we became friends, we were forced to establish a rule if we wanted to remain that way: she can't destroy my property, and I can't clean up hers. It's a win-win situation for everyone involved.

"So tell me what happened," Zoe begged after we'd pulled onto the highway.

I shrugged. "Nothing. I went in, I sang; everything was fine."

I was so glad the audition was over. I felt like this huge weight had been lifted off my shoulders. The pressure I'd felt for the last week had finally disappeared. It was a good feeling, too—knowing I'd done well. And I didn't even pass out...or throw up. But those were just the bonuses.

"Bree was there," I continued. "We sang the exact same song."

Zoe rolled her eyes in disgust. "Please tell me she tripped as she walked on stage."

I shook my head. "Nope, sorry."

"Well, then tell me that your version kicked her butt."

"I don't know," I replied, shaking my head. "She did really well. I'm sure she'll get a lead role."

Zoe flipped on her turn signal, then pulled into the parking lot of Andy's. "Well, do you think you'll get a part?"

"I don't know. I'll probably end up being a flower on the wall or something."

She rolled her eyes. "Honestly, Wrenn, that was like, eight years ago. It's time to let it go."

We climbed out of Zoe's car and headed toward the familiar glass door. Andy's was *the* hangout for Amberson Heights teenagers. Their orangeades were miraculous, and Zoe and I practically lived for them. At a buck fifty apiece, we had spent a small fortune on them since we became friends two years ago—but they were so worth it. No matter how stressful our day, no matter what kind of anguish we were going through, orangeades made all of our problems disappear...at least temporarily.

"So when do you find out if you made it?"

"The results are supposed to be posted tomorrow afternoon. That's what I heard anyway."

"Really? That soon?"

I stared at her in astonishment. "Are you kidding me? That's like, forever," I informed her. Of course, she wasn't the one who had to suffer through the next twenty-four hours, wondering and waiting, analyzing every note and chord, replaying the entire audition over and over in her mind.

The staff greeted us with friendly "Hellos" as we walked inside and made our way toward the red leather bar stools at the counter.

"Hey, what can I get you two?" the waitress asked. She looked our age, with her brown hair pulled back in a ponytail, and she was wearing an Andy's baseball cap.

"Two oranageades," Zoe replied, then, turning to me, asked, "Eres listo para el examen de espanol el lunes?"

"What? Zoe, you know I hate it when you speak Spanish."

"I asked if you were ready for the Spanish test on

Monday. At least, I think that's what I said. It's what I meant, anyway."

"I wouldn't have known the difference," I confessed.

"Wrenn, you have to learn to speak this stuff!"

The waitress set our drinks in front of us, then headed to a table of students.

"I have a B in Spanish, thank you," I reminded her. "Besides, I can translate it perfectly on paper."

She rolled her eyes. "What good is knowing how to write in Spanish if you can't understand it when it's spoken? I mean, what happens when we're backpacking across Europe after graduation and you can't find a bathroom in Spain?"

"I'll just say: Where-o is el bathroom-o," I stated. I took a sip of my orangeade. "All I care about is passing," I informed her. "Yes, it's my worst class, but since I have a B in it, there's hardly cause for concern, but thank you for it, anyway."

"Whatever," she replied. "Do you have time to stop by my house before I drop you off?"

"Sure. Mom thinks I'm conjugating Spanish verbs with you and some other people in our class anyway."

Zoe let out a snort. "You mean your mom actually believed you when you told her you were going to study…in a group…with other people?"

My eyes narrowed. "You're really hilarious, do you know that? And I told her it was your idea. Of course she thought it was brilliant."

"Ha! Muy bien!" she replied. "Anyway, I finished 'La Gente Confusada' last night, and I figured you might want to see it. Since, you know, you saw it in progress."

"The confused people. See? I totally understand Spanish when it's spoken," I remarked.

"La Gente Confusada" is a painting Zoe has been working on for the last few weeks. It's beautiful, even if I can't make out a single person. Zoe is into abstract art, just like Picasso and Pollack. She uses vivid colors, and strategically strews them across the canvas. In this particular painting, the colors represent people, confusion…and, according to her professor mom, "the struggle of women in a masculine society" or something to that effect.

Truthfully, it took me a while before I was finally able to "get" and appreciate Zoe's creations, but to me, her paintings are beautiful and she is so awesome at what she does. My attempts at art consist of stick figures and fluffy clouds. Music was always my thing, so while Zoe and I were both artists in our own way, I avoided all art beyond finger painting.

"Is it hanging yet?" I asked.

"No, I need Gene to help me get 'Las Mujeres Frescas' off the wall first."

I smiled. Ah. Yet another representation of feminine affliction. There were no people in that one, either.

Zoe has a rotating gallery in her room. Her walls are stark white, and there's track lighting. Her most recent efforts all have Spanish names, thanks to our teacher's request that we make the language "part of our everyday lives." Like many others before it, eventually "La Gente Confusada" would rotate out of Zoe's room and head to its final resting place: the attic.

I asked if she was satisfied with the now finished painting, and when she said that she was, I tried not to laugh. She was happy with it all right, but only until she began the next one. Painting is the only thing that Zoe is even remotely obsessive about. To her, there's always a way the objects could look more intriguing; always a new technique waiting to be tried or developed. Zoe is complacent about a lot of things in life, but art isn't one of them.

We finished our orangeades on the way to Zoe's house. When we pulled into her driveway, she didn't even bother shutting off the engine. "This will only take a minute," she explained. I smiled, knowing that it would take more than a minute, and that Zoe just didn't want to have to fight with her car to get it started again.

I followed her through the garage and into her house. Her parents, both artists and professors at the local university, were out and the house was quiet. The large rooms were clean, pristine…and *livable*.

But we had to force open the door to Zoe's room, on the other hand. Clothes, magazines, and books were strewn from one end to the other. Underneath this chaos, her carpet was actually blue, but I couldn't see it or find a safe place to step.

Unphased by the chaos, Zoe marched across the floor toward her easel. A plastic tarp lay underneath, ready to catch any drops of paint that threatened the carpet. She was always armed with more canvases, so I rarely saw the easel empty. There was always something on it waiting to be finished. Art was a constant, just like brushing teeth and talking about a crush on the phone before bed is for any other sophomore girl.

"I can't believe you actually live in here," I said, tiptoeing toward her unmade bed, and trying not to stumble over anything important.

"That's not fair! I never say anything about your room, so you can't say anything about mine."

"My room isn't hazardous to your health," I told her.

She glared at me. "Are you kidding? Alphabetizing books and color-coding socks is in no way healthy."

I opened my mouth to protest, but she had already removed the sheet that hid her latest painting.

"What do you think?"

It was full of dark grays and blues, with occasional splashes of yellow.

"Amazing!" I marveled. "What did your mom say?"

"I still haven't shown it to her or Gene," she replied. "But I think they're going to like it."

I'm still not used to calling Mr. and Mrs. Martin "Gene and Claire," though they keep insisting. And I doubt I'll ever be comfortable with Zoe referring to them by their first names rather than Mom and Dad. It was one of the many twists in Zoe's unconventional, post-hippy-era upbringing. The other amazing twist was that, while she was naturally beautiful, the fact didn't phase Zoe one bit. Be young. Be free. Don't obsess about appearances. Of course, this made life even worse for me. There's nothing like having a best friend who's gorgeous and doesn't even know it yet.

"It was too late when I finally finished it," she continued. "Claire was still awake, but she was in her studio, so I didn't want to bother her."

Like Zoe, Claire is a painter. She and her daughter are very much alike: wild, spontaneous, and opinionated. Gene, on the other hand, balances them out. A potter, he's organized and introspective—the member of the Martin family I could relate to the most; to me he was a breath of fresh air compared to his housemates.

"I think it looks great. So what's next?" I asked.

"Oh, I don't know," she said. "I've been neglecting landscapes and watercolors." Zoe ran her fingers across the dry paint. "I want my portfolio to be well-rounded enough to get into the best art schools in the country by the time I finish high school."

"Or Europe," I added, helping her drape the paint-splattered sheet back over the painting.

"Europe would be nice. Walking the same streets as the masters, seeing what Van Gogh saw...."

"And soon, with a few more paintings, you'll be able to speak Spanish fluently," I teased.

She rolled her eyes. "Shut up. But since we're here..." she let her thought trail off, and that mischievous sparkle filled her eyes. She bolted toward her computer.

"Ugh. Not again," I sighed, plopping down on the edge of her bed. "You are so obsessed."

"It's just for a second. He should be home by now." Zoe quickly typed in her username and password. "We had such a great conversation last night. It was about dream states and Van Gogh's and Monet's works. It was amazing."

"Um, okay. I missed everything you just said," I informed her.

"Whatever. It was a great conversation anyway."

Her inbox popped up. No new messages. "He should have emailed me by now," she said, checking her watch.

"He" was a guy Zoe met in a local chat room. According to her, it began when he noticed her screen name, "Artchick," and struck up a conversation. They hit it off and have been emailing and IM'ing each other since before Christmas. Now, all I hear is "Sk8trGuy" this and "Sk8trGuy" that.

"Oh, but Wrenn, he is so sweet!" she exclaimed the week after they first connected. "We have so much in common! And the best part is: he's local. I could be brushing past him in the hallway every day at school and not even know it's him."

"Well, if you didn't notice him in the first place, he probably isn't worth noticing at all," I told her. But the truth is, I am so jealous. The fact that Zoe has a potential Romeo emailing her every night drives me crazy. I want a boyfriend *so* bad.

We returned to Zoe's car, and a few minutes later, she dropped me off in front of my driveway. The first thing I did was head to my bedroom and change into my favorite sweats. They were such a reward. There's nothing like coming home and putting on something comfortable—and with an elastic waistband—after suffocating in denim all day long at school. Unfortunately, the jeans that were a perfect fit before Christmas break had now become a size too small. It really was my own fault. I adore holiday sugar cookies, and I eat way too many every Christmas. Now, with these pants so tight, I still couldn't bring myself to go to the mall and buy a larger pair. Call it denial if you want.

After changing, I immediately sat down at my digital piano and turned it on. There was a stack of papers lying nearby, each scribbled with thoughts and rhymes, with chord names above each phrase. I played the chords and began to sing the words that were scrawled across a piece of notebook paper.

Then I stopped. Nothing. Zero inspiration. It always worked like that for me. I never finished any of the songs I tried to write. I always composed a few good lines, a couple of great chords; a great verse to one song, an awesome chorus on another, but I could never seem to fuse them all together. It was like I was destined to stay a cover artist forever, always singing other people's songs instead of ever writing my own.

At this point I must have had hundreds of half-written songs stuck in notebooks and scribbled on various sheets of paper. It's like I have musician's block or something. Words don't flow freely, nothing else sounds right, and then I get frustrated and stop. Forget trying to write songs. It just wasn't happening.

Instead, I pulled out some sheet music and put six years' worth of piano lessons to good use. My thoughts drifted to an afternoon a few days ago, when Zoe and I sat in my room, fishing through the same music, trying to decide which song I should sing for the audition.

"What about 'Bridge Over Trouble Waters'?" she'd asked. "That's a classic."

"Too whiny."

"'Somewhere Over the Rainbow'?"

"That's a possibility," I replied. "Let's make a pile of all the 'maybes' so we can narrow them down."

She rolled her eyes. "Of course, a pile. Why didn't I think of that?" she said, her words laced with sarcasm. Ignoring her, I continued flipping through pages of music.

"Oh! 'Unchained Melody'! I love that song!" Zoe began to sing, totally off key.

"Ew! Spare me. If I walk in there singing like that, they'll shoot me to put everyone out of their misery."

"Ha, ha," she retorted. "I was just kidding anyway. That's not how I really sing."

"Sure it's not," I replied. "'Unchained Melody' is okay, that's a maybe." We spent the next few hours sorting through the music to every song I'd ever sung, trying to determine the ideal piece for my range.

My mom arrived home from work shortly after six and knocked on my door.

"Hey, Zoe, Wrenn. I was just thinking about dinner. Anything in particular you want?" she asked.

"No. Whatever you feel like cooking is fine," I told her, knowing she preferred to keep it simple. And by simple, I mean ordering Chinese takeout, or boiling a pot of spaghetti.

"Zoe, you're welcome to stay if you'd like."

"I have to be home soon, but thanks anyway," Zoe replied.

Mom stared at the large pile of music on my bed. "You aren't alphabetizing your piano music, are you?" she asked, crossing her arms.

Zoe burst out laughing and I rolled my eyes. My organizational skills are an ongoing joke between them, but only because they are seriously lacking in that department. They're slobs.

"Actually, I'm going through this mess to see what I have," I informed her.

"She's auditioning for—"

My eyes widened. And I nudged Zoe with my knee. "Zoe!" I hissed. It wasn't like I'd told her beforehand to keep this audition a secret or anything, but I didn't want my mom or Karly knowing. I mean, what if I bombed? The less they knew, the better.

"I'm going through this mess to see what I have," I clarified.

She stared at me, totally disbelieving. "Okay, well, let me see what you have." Mom walked toward my bed and began sifting through the "maybe" pile. "You're such an old soul," she remarked as she examined the titles. "If you're going to an audition, theoretically speaking, of course," she added, "why don't you try something more modern? Something hip."

"Mom," I muttered.

"Something people would recognize?" Zoe offered.

"Exactly," she replied.

"Because I can sing these songs. And, if I *do* decide to try out," emphasizing that no, I hadn't made up my mind yet, "I'm only there to impress one person: the director. And if he's never heard of 'Ebb Tide,' then I'm not so sure he's cut out to direct...anything," I stated, refraining from using the word *musical.*

Zoe coughed. "I've never even heard of 'Ebb Tide.'"

"It's a classic. The Righteous Brothers. And you are seriously missing out," I replied. "But you aren't the director, so it's irrelevant."

"Personally, I've always liked 'Memory' from *Cats*," Mom stated.

I stared at the sheet and notes for a few moments. "I'm not sure," I said. "It might be a little too much."

"But it would definitely showcase your ability. If you can pull off 'Memory,' you can sing just about anything, right?"

"I suppose," I replied, thinking about this. "I guess I'll rehearse some of these and sleep on it. I mean, it might not matter, I haven't made up my mind if I'll even audition."

Zoe stood. "Okay. Well, I guess I'll see you tomorrow, then."

We all said goodbye, and then Mom and I were alone in my room. Not knowing what to say, I began to rearrange the piles of sheet music on my bed, thinking that alphabetizing them might not be such a bad idea.

"Wrenn, I'm really glad to see that you're trying new things," Mom finally said, breaking the silence that had fallen between us. "Auditioning for—whatever it is you have planned—it's very brave of you."

Why? I wanted to ask. Because I'm fat? And a loser? And because a person like me would never do something like this in a million years? Instead I replied, "I haven't made up my mind."

Now, as I sat in my room, thinking back to the audition, I realized that I wasn't exactly being honest with Zoe or my mother at all. Yes, getting a part in the musical was a good opportunity and a great way to try something new, but it was more complicated than that. Because the way I saw it, if I did get lucky enough to land a part, then some drastic changes were in order. The way things stood at the moment, if I walked on stage right now, I'd get laughed right back off—good voice or not. Maybe this musical was what I needed to start trying to lose a few pounds—a few inches off my waistline—and eventually a few pants sizes.

Until now, I'd always preferred to stay in the background. I was the "flower on the wall" type; just another plain fish in a gigantic sea of beauties, a puffed-up blowfish in a school of angel fish—fish that I would never be like—unless I got a part in the musical. If I could land a role, and then lose a few pounds, I'd have a chance to become more like Mindy Carter and Bree Donnelly. I could make myself pretty… maybe even gorgeous. Then I'd be more confident around guys, and finally get a boyfriend.

I'd get invited to parties, out to movies and dinner (salads only, of course). The more I thought about it, the better it all sounded. That's when I realized this musical could change my life forever…even if I was just in the chorus. It might be the new beginning I needed.

So, no, I wasn't being completely honest. But my heart was in the right place, even if my head had ulterior motives.

Chapter

Three

The following day at school, I checked the bulletin board by the office after every class. It looked like the director was going to wait till the last possible minute to post the cast list from the audition. I was a nervous wreck, and Zoe wasn't helping the situation. She was annoying me to no end, asking if I'd heard anything, then complaining that they were taking so long.

"You *do* realize that if they don't get around to posting it today, you'll have to wait until Monday, right?" she asked.

"Don't even go there," I snapped. I was dying inside aiready; listening to her only made matters worse.

Before the last period of the day, I walked once more toward the office. This time there was a crowd of at least a dozen or so kids swarming around the bulletin board. People pushed their way to the front, some leaving with clearly rejected faces, while others were jumping up and down excitedly. There were high fives going on all around. It was finally posted: The cast list.

This is it, I realized.

Not one to throw myself into the middle of a celebration that might not include me, I stood back and waited until the crowd thinned out before I walked over and peeked at the bright sheet of paper. The late bell rang as I began reading, starting from the bottom of the page. I scanned the dancers, the chorus, and the smaller parts. No Wrenn Scott. *I probably didn't make it anyway*, I thought to myself, sucking in my breath and continuing toward the top, my hands shaking by now.

Suddenly I recognized the string of letters that formed my name. There it was! Right with the main players. I followed the dotted line across the page.

Rizzo.

I covered my mouth, stifling a scream. *I got a part! I'm playing one of the leads!* My heart nearly pounded out of my chest. The part of me that thought I was crazy for even trying out was now overshadowed by the part that was leaping with excitement. I felt another scream welling up.

Then I read every name on the list—again.

By now I was a good five minutes late to my science class. I headed for the empty seat beside Zoe. She moved her bag so I could sit down.

"You're tardy, Miss Scott," Mr. Thompson informed me.

"Um, it was an emergency?" I replied. It really was more of a question than a statement. But Mr. Thompson, an older man who should have retired a hundred years ago, was easily one of the most even-tempered teachers in the school. I let him decide what "emergency" meant, and even though he shook his head, he never reached for his grade book to pencil in that I was late.

"Well," Zoe whispered, "what happened?"

"I got a part," I replied. She squealed quietly and began slapping my arm.

"Ow!" I cried, giggling. The antics were enough to draw Mr. Thompson's attention, and he glared at us to be quiet. We immediately sat forward, donned serious expressions, and settled down.

I unzipped my book bag and pulled out my science notebook, opening it to a blank page in the back. I wrote RIZZO at the top in big bold letters, underlining it half a dozen times.

Zoe drew a smiley face in response, followed by the word AWESOME.

I tried to sit still for the next forty-five minutes but it was nearly impossible. Yes, understanding the theories of human genetics was important, but Mr. Thompson just did *not* understand. I was Rizzo! I was going to be in a musical!

The realization hit me like a Mack truck. I was going to be in a musical. THE Musical. On STAGE. There was so much to do. There would be lines and songs to memorize, and lots of rehearsals. And my promise! If I was going to do this, it would have to be done right. No more fattening foods, no more late-night snacks. And no more chocolate! I'd have to exercise every day...no more chocolate? Just the thought made me want a piece, or the whole freakin' bag.

Leigh Brescia

No, I decided that this was too important to screw up.
I had just over three months to transform, so that by the
time the show rolled around, the Wrenn Scott everyone
knew (or thought they knew) would be a thing of the past.
I had no alternative—I had to go for it.

After the final bell rang, Zoe bombarded me with
questions. "So who else made it?" she asked as we made
our way to our lockers.

"Well, Bree is Sandy, of course."

"Of course," Zoe replied, rolling her eyes. "She's the
lead in everything. I'm sure dear old Daddy hooked her
up with the best acting and voice coaches money could
buy."

I shrugged my shoulders. "Well, playing Sandy is a
huge deal," I explained. "She was amazing. I'll never be
as good."

"I don't believe you. Wrenn, you're Rizzo. You're in,
like, the number-two role. How could you say you'll never
be as good as Bree? I mean, you already are! You'll be
standing next to her at the curtain call. How much closer
could you possibly get?"

So maybe I was kind of tired of always being overshadowed by everyone. But Zoe was right; for never having been in a musical before, landing the part of Rizzo was
pretty amazing.

"Who else got a part?"

"I didn't recognize some of the names," I told her.
"But guess who is going to be Danny."

She never tried to guess. "Who?"

"Tad Owens."

"Tad Owens? Are you serious? He is so hot!"

Tad was in a study hall with us last year. While Zoe was able to carry on extended conversations with him, I'd admired him from afar. He was a senior, and so incredibly popular. He was right up there with Chase Cunningham.

"So, when's your first rehearsal?" she asked.

"Tomorrow night. The handout said we were getting together for pizza. I think it's more of a 'get to know each other' type thing."

As we approached our lockers, I could see Bree Donnelly at the end of the hall, standing with her friends, sharing an animated conversation. They were, no doubt, congratulating her on being picked for the lead role in the musical. She closed her locker and began walking in our direction, her long blonde curls bouncing with every step. She smiled at several people she passed.

As she drew closer, our eyes met. She didn't smile, but she didn't look away, either. She just…stared at me. It was uncomfortable, but I couldn't look away. Everything seemed to be happening in slow motion.

Was she going to stop and talk? Congratulate me? Freak out and cause a scene? Did she even know who I was?

At this point I could have reached out and touched her. She raised an eyebrow, and then looked away, brushing past me. I turned and watched her saunter out the side door, followed closely by her entourage.

I turned back to my locker. "You are not going to believe this, but Bree Donnelly just totally stared me down," I whispered.

"You're imagining things," Zoe replied, stuffing her biology book into her bag.

"I'm not. She walked by and wouldn't stop staring."

"Yeah, I was wondering how well the two of you would get along—since she's your deity and all."

I rolled my eyes. "Shut up. She's not my deity. She's popular. I just…respect her."

Zoe let out a sarcastic laugh. "You respect her because she's popular? Wrenn, c'mon and wake up already!"

My mouth clamped shut. I love her to death, but Zoe did *not* understand my infatuation with popular people. That's because she's gorgeous and talented—and doesn't need or want to be popular. If she decided tomorrow that she would like to get with the in-crowd, she'd so be there. I, on the other hand, have never wanted to be anything else. There's something totally awesome about being popular. You're beautiful, funny, people love you, and you can have any guy you want for a boyfriend. And not just *any* boyfriend, but a *popular* boyfriend. And if you're completely lucky, you can snag an older guy from another school. That's the ultimate.

"I don't get you at all," Zoe continued. "How many times have I told you that Bree Donnelly isn't God's gift to the universe? She is a label—a stereotype—and nothing more. Underneath all that makeup she has zits, and if she didn't wear deodorant she'd reek, just like everyone else." She slammed her locker shut with a bang.

My nose wrinkled in disgust. "Zoe, that's so gross."

"Well, zits or not, you'll be on a first-name basis once

this play is over because you're going to be spending a lot of time together."

Zoe was right. What would she think about me? I mean, what if I made a complete idiot of myself? What if she thought I was a loser, or disgusting or...fat?

"I'm going to be a nervous wreck," I decided.

"Wrenn, please, don't start this yet. I'd like a few weeks of peace before you begin freaking out about rehearsals and opening night. Audition day was bad enough."

"This was your idea, you know," I reminded her, throwing my bag over my shoulder and heading toward the door.

By the time Zoe dropped me off at my house, my younger sister, Karly, was already home, raiding the kitchen for some form of chocolate.

"How was school?" I asked, trying to make conversation. Unlike me, Karly was popular, one of the most popular girls in her class, in fact. She was the "Bree Donnelly" of middle school. Pretty impressive for a fourteen-year-old. So, while I tried to make conversation, I was also genuinely interested. As a popular person, there was always some sort of drama going on in her life.

"Well, if you must know, today was absolutely psycho. I'm so glad it's Friday, it's not even funny." She grabbed a handful of Oreos, poured herself a glass of milk, and sat down on one of our bar stools. "A girl can only take so much, you know?"

"What kind of middle-school crisis are you enduring this time?" I asked.

She wrapped her long, dirty-blonde hair on top of her head and stuck a pencil through it. Somehow, it held. I chewed on my lower lip. Even when she wasn't trying, Karly managed to look good. Even when her hair was a ratty mess on top of her head, it worked. I hated that about her.

"Sherie Conner spread a vicious rumor that I had the hots for William Merritt, and that I was going to ask him to the Valentine's Dance next month."

"And this is bad because…"

"Because William Merritt is such a nerd. I mean, hello. He's like, a seventh grader," she retorted. "Eighth graders just don't go out with seventh graders—not unless it's the guy who likes the younger girl. I mean, that's okay, but not the other way around. It just doesn't work that way."

"Oh. Well, maybe everyone will forget about it by Monday."

"Ugh, I hope so. Sherie Conner is *so* dead." Karly dunked an Oreo into her milk and crammed the entire thing in her mouth. "So how was your day?" she mumbled.

"Obviously not as fascinating as yours," I replied.

She rolled her eyes. "Whatever. Are you hanging out with Zoe tonight?"

"No, it's Art Friday," I informed her. One Friday of every month, all the art galleries downtown had show openings. Mr. and Mrs. Martin, when they weren't showing their own work, made the rounds, supporting their students and other local artists. Zoe always went along—it was their family tradition. Kind of like "movie night" or "game night" for any other family.

"And you aren't going with her?" Karly asked.

"No."

"I so don't get you. As soon as I turn sixteen I'm like, never going to be home."

"I'm not sixteen yet," I reminded her.

"Well, two months is practically nothing. You might as well go ahead and say you're sixteen. It sounds so mature." She shook her head in disbelief. "As soon as I can get a boyfriend, or even just a friend who drives, I'm so out of here."

Karly and I are nothing alike. We're polar opposites, even. I think it has a lot to do with the fact that our fathers were such different men. First of all, Mom was actually married to my father, even if it wasn't for very long.

I inherited everything from my dad. My voice, my dark features and olive skin, my height (or lack thereof), and my build, for which I still haven't forgiven him. I also blame my compulsions on him. I'm not sure if my father was as obsessed with organization as I am, but I do know Mom, and it isn't anywhere in her genes.

And it isn't only the physical differences that set us apart—Karly and my mother have long, lean bodies and blonde hair—we are different in every way. The two of them are completely disorganized, which always drives me nuts, and they can eat whatever they want and never gain an ounce. They're both airheads at times, and they are both so melodramatic. There is always some sort of "Sherrie-Conner-type" drama going on in their lives.

With my mom, it usually was about her job: personal assistant to Mitzi Monroe, Channel 8's weekday morning talk-show host. She gave us the local gossip and interviewed "important businessmen" between the traffic update and *Good Morning America*. Mitzi was a celebrity in our town, and while she looked like a genuinely nice, happy person, I knew better from Mom. Having worked with Mitzi for two years straight, Mom has a growing collection of Mitzi Monroe horror stories.

I watched in amazement as Karly stuffed another Oreo into her mouth. If it was me, that crumbly chocolate cookie would travel straight to my butt and camp there forever. I fought the urge to reach over and grab one from the package. But no. No way. I was officially on a crash diet. And that meant no chocolate whatsoever.

"How many of those things are you going to eat?" I asked as she rummaged through the bag and pulled out another handful.

"As many as I want," she informed me.

"Well, Mom is going to kill you when she gets home and realizes all of her Oreos are gone."

"I had a difficult day. Mom understands that completely," she replied, matter-of-factly.

I headed toward my bedroom. "I'm sure she does," I called.

Chapter

Four

It was nearly seven o'clock before Mom stormed through the front door. "You would not believe the day I had," she said, yanking her scarf from around her neck and tossing it on the edge of the couch.

I pretended not to hear.

"Mitzi has some nerve. I swear, I don't know how much more I can take." The smell of Chinese takeout slowly permeated the room.

Unfortunately, this is nothing new. "I can't stand Mitzi Monroe" conversations dominate much of what is said in our household. That's why we eat takeout on a regular basis. Mom has Chop-Chop's number on speed dial and they know her by first name. Bad Mitzi days equal Chinese takeout. Thankfully, I've grown to love sweet and sour chicken. But developing an aversion to Chinese food might not be such a bad thing. At least it would eradicate half of my monthly caloric intake.

"What else is new?" I asked. "You only say that every other day." I picked up her scarf and coat and hung them on the coat rack by the door—where they belonged—and followed her into the kitchen.

"Well, maybe it's time to do something about it." She removed the takeout containers from paper bags that read "Chop-Chop: Chinese to You."

"Sure," I said.

"Sure nothing. I'm serious. I'm going to start making some changes in my life."

"I believe you," I said, opening the containers. "So what happened this time?"

"Oh, it's just the same old stuff. You can't make that woman happy. You'd think she was the Queen of Sheba." She let out an exasperated sigh. "Please tell your sister dinner is here."

I set the rice carton down and walked to Karly's room. I could hear her talking to someone on the phone so I knocked lightly on the door.

"Hold on a minute," I heard her say. "What?" she practically shouted. I opened the door and poked my head inside.

"Mom is home and dinner is here. It's Chinese, so beware."

She put the phone back to her ear. "Anyway, Sherie is *so* going to wish she'd never said my name. I mean, I can't let my reputation be ruined just because she's jealous."

Karly looked up and glared at me, her blue eyes flashing. "Do you mind?"

"Sorry." I pulled my head out and shut her door behind me. I don't know why I was so interested in her middle-school drama.

When she finally appeared at the kitchen table, Mom and I had already begun eating. I'd made up my mind to take much smaller portions than usual, and there was no way that I'd go for seconds tonight. No freakin' way!

"How was school?" Mom asked us.

I opened my mouth, ready to tell her all about my being cast as Rizzo in the play. But before the words came out, Karly jumped in and relayed the entire Sherie Conner incident. I don't know why I expected otherwise. I never contribute to family conversations. The reason I don't is because I never have anything going on in my life. It's always dull at best, lacking any real excitement. At least until now, that is.

When Karly finally finished talking, I opened my mouth to tell them my good news. But this time my mother stole the scene. I began to pick at my chicken teriyaki. *Was I ever going to have a voice in this family?* I wondered. And this time I actually have important things to say.

"Well, my day was unbelievable," she began. "First, Mitzi claimed I didn't buy the right coffee, even though I wrote her order down. French Vanilla Nut with a shot of Mocha Delight; the words came straight from her mouth. Then she misplaced her morning paper, so it was up to me to go out and buy another one. She missed her 12:30 appointment and blamed it on me, even though it was clearly written in her day planner, and between running to and from the copier, and answering a hundred email and voice-mail messages, I had to schedule a six-month teeth cleaning, a doctor's appointment, cancel her weekly pedicure, and move up her massage." She crammed a piece of steak in her mouth with her chopsticks.

I have to admit, as disorganized as she is, it's a miracle that Mom lasted even this long working for Mitzi.

She's done just about everything you can do without a college degree: answered telephones, peddled makeup, worked in boutiques, telemarketed, sold herbal supplements—and those were the places she stayed at long enough to take home more than two paychecks. The same scenario plays out every time she gets bored with a job. On a particularly bad day she will become fed up and quit on the spot, only to go out the following day and apply for some equally pathetic position. Channel 8 holds the record for "longest job worked," and she's complained about it since day one. Fortunately, Mitzi can't keep personal assistants for very long, so it means regular pay raises for Mom, not to mention a stable job.

"Well, I'm definitely going to start making some changes," she continued. "You know, I've always wanted to start my own business. My friend Phil from work thinks I'd be a great entrepreneur. He says I have wonderful micromanagement skills."

The rice between my chopsticks fell back to my plate. My interest was definitely piqued, but not because someone thought my mother had organizational skills. "What? Who's Phil?"

She brushed it off as nothing. "Oh, he's just this guy I know from work. We've been going to lunch together. He works in the advertising department at the station," she explained.

"Advertising?" I raised an eyebrow. "You mean he gets on the phone and harasses people all day?"

"He does more than that, Wrenn," Mom said.

I rolled my eyes. Advertising. Yeah. And what kind of a name was Phil anyway? He sounded like a loser; a used-car salesman for sure.

"So, is he cute?" Karly asked.

"Yeah, I think he is," Mom replied. "He's a bit younger than me, so that's kind of intimidating, but he knows I have two teenagers, and well..."

She trailed off, pausing for a moment, as if trying to figure out how to phrase what she was about to say next.

"Well?" I repeated.

"He wants to meet you," she blurted out.

I nearly choked on the food I was chewing. "What? He wants to meet us?"

"Of course! I mean, I've told him all about you, and I think now is a good time to get acquainted. So...I've invited him over for dinner tomorrow night."

Karly and I fell silent, not knowing how to respond to this...this little announcement of hers.

"Well, don't sound so enthused," Mom commented, looking back and forth at us.

"No, it's not that," I began. "It's just that I have plans for tomorrow night." Here was my chance. I could finally tell them my news.

Mom smiled. "Honey, I'm sure Zoe'll understand if you cancel. I'd really like you to be here to meet him."

"Why does everyone assume that I don't have a life outside of Zoe?" I cried.

I mean, an evening with Phil, the used-car salesman…excuse me, "advertising executive"? What a blast *that* would be. "Actually, I have a rehearsal tomorrow night," I said, nonchalantly. "Thanks for asking."

Mom's and Karly's mouths fell open simultaneously, as if they couldn't believe what they'd just heard. "What? You got a part?" Mom cried.

"Who are you?" Karly asked.

"Rizzo. We're doing *Grease*."

"Rizzo? Sweetie, that is so wonderful!" The surprise in her voice was evident. She was clearly impressed that her chubby, nobody daughter had enough talent to make the cut and be on stage. I had to admit, I was just as astonished about it myself. "I thought you hadn't made up your mind to audition," she noted.

"Well, I decided to go for it," I confirmed, picking at the food on my plate.

"Well, that is amazing, but I really wanted you to be here tomorrow night," she continued. She bit her lower lip and I could tell she was thinking—trying to formulate a plan. "What time do you have to be at school?"

"7:30."

She exhaled a sigh of relief. "Well, that's not a problem at all, then. I told Phil to be here at six. That'll give us plenty of time."

"We're having pizza at rehearsal," I informed her.

"You can eat with us, can't you?"

I took another bite of rice. I didn't want to be the only one not eating pizza. If I passed it up people would think I was too embarrassed to eat, and then they'd remember I was fat and think that was the reason. "Why can't Phil come another night?"

"Because we already made plans. I can't change them."

"So you want me to rearrange my schedule to meet a middle-aged mcdia salesman?"

"It isn't that difficult to compromise, is it?" she asked. "You can eat with us, and you'll still have plenty of time to get to the rehearsal."

I could *not* believe her. I picked up my plate and carried it to the kitchen. "Fine, whatever. Why don't you just make my plans for me next time, too, since I don't have a life." It was true—I didn't, but that was beside the point.

Mom jumped up and followed me. "Wait, Wrenn. Please? It's just one night. All I'm asking is that you come to dinner and be nice to him. I really think you'll like Phil, and he's been looking forward to getting to know you."

Honestly. Meet the children? How long had they been seeing each other anyway? "Fine," I muttered. "I'll be the perfect daughter. But if he makes me late for rehearsal, I'll kill him."

"You won't be late, I promise." She leaned down and kissed me on the forehead. "Thank you so much."

I began to rinse off my plate. *How manipulative was she?* I thought to myself.

"You know, I've had a rough day. Why don't we forget about the dishes and have a girls' night instead?" she suggested. "I could really use one of those right now."

A girls' night? Ugh. I hated girls' nights. They always meant exfoliation and makeup, both of which I detested.

"I'll get my makeup and face creams. Karly, you can get your manicure kit," she continued.

"Actually, I have some homework to do, so I think I'll just skip it this time."

Mom stared at me in disbelief. "Homework on a Friday night? Wrenn, you are not my daughter."

"Well, I have a Spanish test on Monday and my teacher went over tons of new stuff this week. It isn't my strongest subject, so I really need to study."

"Not your strongest subject?" Karly stated with a snort. "What is that, like an A minus?"

"Shut up!"

"Studying is what Sunday night is for," my sister informed me.

"Which is why I'll have another semester on the honors list to look forward to and you're barely making a C average," I retorted. That was the only downside I could think of to being popular: no time or interest in academics. Still, I could totally sacrifice grades if it meant riding in the same car as Bree Donnelly and Chase Cunningham.

"No, I've made up my mind," Mom interrupted. "We're having a girls' night…all three of us."

Chapter
Five

I tried to prolong cleaning the kitchen, hoping that they'd begin without me. Maybe then I could sneak into my room without being noticed.

"Come on, Wrenn!" Mom finally called. "Save the rest for later."

"I haven't swept the kitchen floor yet!" I replied, as I wiped down the counters.

"I'll do it later!"

I threw the dishrag into the sink and trudged into the living room. Reluctantly, I took my place on the floor. There were bottles and tubes everywhere. It looked as if Clinique had bought out our living room to use as a store-front. *Okay*, I thought, *let the horror begin.*

"First, the face cream." Mom handed me a white tube of soap and instructed me to wash my face. Not like there was a purpose—there was nothing to wash off, since I did-n't use makeup.

And there's a good reason for it, too. I tried to wear makeup once, when I was thirteen. My mom had given me permission, and I had experimented all weekend, using fashion magazines for guidance. I looked great when I left for school that morning, because eyeliner really does wonders for the eyes. For once, I knew my classmates would see a pretty face instead of my fat rolls.

By lunchtime, I could feel people staring. And in math class, when I was called to the board to work out a problem, someone from the back of the room "meowed" like a cat. I instantly knew what they were referring to. People began to snicker, and the moment class let out I ran to the bathroom and wiped the makeup off as fast as I could. So except for the random "girls' nights" my mother insisted on having, I haven't worn makeup since. It just wasn't worth getting laughed at again. I'd much rather go unnoticed instead.

"Ouch!" I looked over at Karly, who was peering into a handheld mirror, tweezing her eyebrows; yanking them from their roots one by one. Mom was doing the same thing, only she wasn't as vocal.

"I could do yours, too, if you'd like," she told me when she saw me staring. "They look like they could use some shaping."

They look like they could use some shaping because I'd never let anyone come near them. I tried to pluck them once, and gave up after one measly hair. It just wasn't worth all the unnecessary pain. "That's okay," I said.

"Wrenn, if you were half as obsessed with your appearance as you are with organizing your closet, you'd be much better off," Karly taunted. "Ow!" she cried again.

I ignored her, leaning my head against the couch and

letting the green avocado mask harden on my face. Mom finished her own tweezing and grabbed the manicure kit from the table. "Here, let me see your toes," she said, grabbing my foot.

She began pushing the cuticles back. "Ouch! That hurts!" I complained.

"You really need to start taking better care of your feet," she informed me.

"I take care of them," I mumbled.

"Well, it looks like they need serious help to me."

"There is nothing wrong with my toenails."

"No? Look at them." Mom held up my foot for me to see. "They are pitiful. You've picked them to nubs."

"I get bored."

"Well, try not to get bored enough to torture your fingernails that way." She clipped and filed and began applying a coat of pink polish.

"See?" she said, as soon as she was done painting. "A little polish goes a long way. Now you're ready for sandals."

She must have forgotten it was the middle of winter and barely pushing forty degrees outside. It would be a good four months before it was finally sandal weather.

"Now go wash off your mask. I'm going to give you a makeover."

"No, thanks," I told her. "The facial is enough. I don't need makeup."

Karly snickered. "This from a person who doesn't know the difference between curling mascara and lengthening mascara."

I rolled my eyes. Like there was any difference.

"Anyway," Mom continued, "you have pretty eyes. We could really play them up. Please?"

It was as if her only happiness in life was to give me a makeover. I hated that I was always so easily persuaded (read: manipulated). "Fine," I muttered as I stood up and walked to the bathroom. I let the water heat up before I attempted to wash off the thick mask. By the time I finished, my face was flushed bright pink, making it appear even fatter than usual. I stared at my reflection in the mirror. How on earth was I going to be popular when I looked like this?

As I returned to my spot in the living room, I noticed Mom busily lining up all the products she planned to use on me. I felt like some sort of a lab rat.

"First, let's see what color foundation you need." She began dabbing various colors on my cheek. "No, that's still too light," she commented. "I'm so jealous. This is the color I use in my peak tan season. Here it is the middle of winter, and it's still too light for you."

I sat still for the next twenty minutes, sucking in my cheeks so she could apply blush, looking at the ceiling so she could apply eyeliner and mascara, and puckering my lips for lipstick.

"Perfect!" she finally exclaimed, handing me a mirror. "You know, Wrenn, you should wear makeup more often."

"For real," Karly added, as she wiped a shimmery eye cream across her lids.

Now that we were finished, and Mom's excitement

over our stupid girls' night had faded, Mom looked around the room, searching for something else to fill the void. "You know, all of a sudden I have a serious craving for an orangeade. What do you say we run out and get some dessert from Andy's?"

"No!" I practically shouted.

She stared at me, a confused expression crossing her face. "Why not?"

"Because I can't go out looking like this."

"You look great. What's the problem?" she asked.

"It's late," I lied.

Mom looked at her watch. "We have plenty of time. It's just a quick run. Go change into something presentable."

My thoughts began to race. I had to think of something fast. "Um...why don't you go pick something up and I'll clean up this mess?" I suggested.

"Wrenn, please. It's just for a little while. It's good to get out of the house every now and then. You obviously need some fresh air."

Defeated, I walked to my bedroom and flipped on the light. My worn blue comforter was draped perfectly across the bed. There was nothing on the floor. It was pristine. Immaculate. Just the way I liked it. I grabbed my jeans from their drawer and slipped out of my favorite sweatpants. They were so comfortable. Part of me wished I could wear them to Andy's. But no, I was supposed to change into something "presentable." It was Mom's way of saying that sweatpants made me look fat.

For the next five minutes there was a huge struggle to

get my jeans pulled over my butt, and I finally resorted to lying on my bed and sucking in my stomach until they zipped. I glanced at my reflection in the mirror before leaving the room. Mom did a great job on my makeup—I had to give her credit. Still, I was uncomfortable. I felt like I was trying too hard, using the makeup on my face to hide the fat on my belly. It seemed so transparent. I thought people would see right through me.

"Come on, Wrenn. We're ready to go!" Mom called from the living room. I grabbed my jacket and followed her and Karly out to our old gray Cutlass. I could see my breath smoking in the cold air. It was freezing out; the perfect night to stay indoors. Why my mother needed dessert now, I had no idea.

By the time we pulled into the parking lot, Andy's was packed. And I remembered why I wanted to stay home in the first place. My entire high school was there, crowded in the booths. And here I was, out with my mom and kid sister on a Friday night. I was such a loser.

I kept my head down and my eyes focused on the floor as we filed past tables of popular people. I guess what ran through my mind was, "If I can't see them, they can't see me." I don't know what I was thinking, going along for this ride.

Mom found us an empty table—right in the middle of the restaurant—and ordered our desserts. My mind wandered. I thought about being fat—the fattest girl on stage and the laughingstock of the school. When our order came I resisted the urge to inhale my orangeade. Mom and Karly took their time, clearly enjoying this opportunity to be social. The minutes slowly ticked by, and it seemed like forever before they finally finished their drinks.

"Oh, Mom! There's Angie and her boyfriend. Can I go say hello?" Karly begged, breathlessly.

She nodded and Karly bolted across the restaurant, leaving the two of us alone.

"So," Mom said, crushing the ice in her drink with her straw. "I'm really excited about tomorrow night. I really think you're going to like Phil."

"I'm sure I will," I replied, watching as an entire group of people surrounding my sister laughed and hung on her every word. How did she do it? I mean, how did she end up with all the "cool" genes? I completely missed that boat.

"...don't you think?"

I snapped back to reality. "Hmm?"

"I said, if everything works out, maybe we can have him over more often. Don't you think that would be nice?"

"Sure. That would be nice," I said, agreeing with her.

"So are you excited about the musical?" she asked, changing the subject.

I sloshed the leftover ice in my cup. "Yeah. I'm kind of nervous, though."

"Of course you're nervous, but I'm sure you'll have a great time." She paused for a moment. "You must have nailed your audition piece, then."

"I did."

"What did you finally decide on?"

I checked my watch, wondering how long Karly planned to socialize. "'Memory.'"

"Good choice. I always loved that song."

"Apparently so does Bree Donnelly. That's what she sang, too."

"Oh? Who is Bree Donnelly?"

I slouched in my chair. "Only the most popular girl in school. She's playing Sandy."

"Wow. Is she one of your friends?"

"Not hardly. She doesn't even know I'm alive," I muttered.

"Well, maybe this musical will change things."

"Doubtful."

"Wrenn, you shouldn't be so negative. You're a very bright and charming person. I'm sure once this girl gets to know you, she'll realize that."

Like it was that simple. Oh, of course. The most popular girl in school will want to be best friends with me as soon as she realizes how "bright and charming" I am. Yeah, right.

My mother's eyes scanned the room, then moved to the clock on the wall—where Elvis's hips were busy gyrating back and forth. "I guess we should probably pull Karly away from her fan club," she stated.

We stood, pushed our chairs under the table, and managed to grab Karly on the way out of the restaurant. Finally, the exit sign was in plain view and I could bolt. In seconds I would be outside and on my way home. I could almost feel the warmth and comfort of my favorite sweatpants again.

But instead, as my mother reached out to open the

door, it suddenly swung open for her. A cold breeze blew into the building...and there he was. The hottest guy on the planet: Chase Cunningham. His brown hair was hanging in his absolutely perfect brown eyes. His black leather jacket hung perfectly on his tall, muscular frame. I felt my breath catch in my throat. Chase Cunningham was so–so–perfect. I nearly melted on the spot.

Chase shook his head ever so slightly, just enough to get the strands of hair off his face. We caught each other's eye. Ohmigod! Chase Cunningham was looking at me. *Act Cool.*

My mom, having no clue who this amazing piece of eye candy was, walked right through the door without a care, offering a polite "thank you." Karly was right behind her. Then it was my turn. *No big deal. You know how to walk. Just go through, smile, and say thank you. Everything will be fine.*

I approached Chase, but instead of following my initial plan, I completely chickened out, and averted my eyes to the ground. That's when I hit something...hard.

"Excuse you," a voice cried.

I couldn't manage to stammer an apology. I could only turn and watch as Bree Donnelly sauntered through the door, limbs like a gazelle, her khaki miniskirt wrapped tightly around her tiny body.

Chase stared as the door between us closed, separating me from everything inside. It was a symbol of my boring, uneventful (read: pathetic) life: as usual, I was being left out in the cold—literally.

As I walked to the car, everything suddenly became clear to me. I just ran straight into Bree Donnelly. I mean, I made this klutz move while her hottie of a boyfriend watched, no less. I buried my face in my hands and tried to keep from screaming. I was so totally humiliated.

The moment I reached my bedroom, I peeled off the jeans and slipped into my pajamas. Then I reached for the phone and dialed Zoe's number so I could tell her how totally mortified I was.

"I can't even believe I did that!" I whined. "I am such a loser. I can't face her at the rehearsal tomorrow night, and there's no way I can go to school on Monday. Seriously. I need to lay low and hide for a while."

"Will you relax?" she said. "They probably didn't even know who you were."

"It doesn't matter. You didn't see his face. It was like his entire expression screamed 'You poor, ugly, fat girl, you are so clumsy!'"

"You're being irrational. I seriously doubt that's what he was thinking."

"But you didn't see his face!" I pointed out.

"Please, Wrenn. What do you want me to say? That Chase Cunningham thinks you're the biggest loser ever? That the whole school will know what a moron you are by Monday morning?"

I buried my face in a pillow. "I think I'm going to die."

"Well, it's over now, so there's no need to dwell on it. I mean, they've probably already forgotten about it anyway."

"Whatever," I said, knowing she would never understand how completely humiliated I felt. I sighed. "Anyway, Mom had a terrible day at work. She came home with Chinese food and demanded that we have a girls' night."

"Yuck," Zoe replied, knowing how I felt about them. Claire would never subject her to a girls' night. I mean, honestly. Claire didn't even believe in wearing a bra.

"I know, and apparently she's seeing some guy from work."

"That's cool."

"Yeah, it's awesome," I replied, with more than a hint of sarcasm in my voice.

"I guess it's not cool, then."

"Um, no. It's not. For starters his name is Phil."

"What's wrong with that?"

I twirled the phone cord around my fingers. "I don't know. I just don't like the idea of her gallivanting around town with a guy named Phil, is all. He sounds like a middle-aged geek with a beer belly and bad hairpiece."

"Or, he could be a nice guy," she suggested.

"I seriously doubt it."

"Well, anyway, guess what?"

She never gave me enough time to answer whenever she asked me this. I mean, what's the point of asking someone to "guess" when you're not actually going to let them?

"Sk8trGuy wants to meet me!" she said excitedly.

I nearly fell off the bed. "Meet him? Zoe, you have no idea who this guy is! You've been talking to him for what? Two months?"

"But I feel like I've known him forever," she proclaimed.

"So? What if he's a serial rapist or something?"

"That's not possible," Zoe informed me.

"Oh, isn't it? What if he's some old pervert who stalks people he meets in chat rooms?"

"That's not possible either."

"What if he's ugly, or a complete loser? What if he isn't who you thought he was?"

"I don't know," she replied. "I'll worry about that later. Wrenn, we have a connection. I think I'm in love!"

"*Eww*, Zoe. You've never even seen this guy!"

"I know!" she cried. "But if I don't find out soon, I'm going to go crazy. Don't you think I should at least meet him?"

"Really? You think? What's his name then?" I asked.

"I don't know."

"How old is he?"

"Eighteen, but he just turned eighteen," she quickly added. "He's still in high school."

"Are you sure?"

"Yes."

"How do you know? He could be lying."

Her demeanor did a complete 180. I was right and she knew it. "Okay Wrenn, you've made your point. Gene and Claire would probably kill me anyway," she added, sulking.

"Oh, that's a good way to look at it. Sure. Your *parents* will kill you."

She sighed. "So, what are your plans for tomorrow?"

"Relax, meet the middle-aged ad salesman at dinner, go to rehearsal. You?"

"Absolutely nothing," she muttered.

"You'll thank me for this later, trust me."

"I'm sure."

We wrapped up our conversation and said goodbye. I let out all my pent-up frustration in one breath as I placed the phone back in its cradle, then let my head hit the pillow.

Chapter

Six

By five o'clock on Saturday evening, my mother was running around the kitchen in a state of utter panic. I could hear cupboard doors slamming and pots and pans banging. Every now and then she would let out a little shriek, just to let everyone know that her entire world was falling apart.

Annoyed, I walked into the kitchen and asked if she needed help. I didn't really have to ask, because I could see that things were not going as planned. The oven was turned on, ingredients were strewn across the counter, and her hair was still in rollers.

"Phil is going to be here in less than an hour and I'm not even ready yet! It's this stupid roast!" she cried, slamming the oven door closed. She ran across the room and pulled a few cans of green beans from the pantry.

I don't know why she was making such a big deal about this. It was just dinner. She should have ordered Chinese takeout. It was rude to pretend she was a gourmet chef when the last time we'd eaten roast was…well, the last time we had dinner at my grandmother's.

I opened the dishwasher and pulled out a clean pot. "Go get ready. I'll take care of this," I told her, taking the cans from her.

She let out a sigh of relief. "Thank you, Wrenn. You are such a lifesaver." Then she disappeared behind her bedroom door.

I looked around the room, examining what I had to work with. It was a disaster area. The main course was in the oven, but that was the extent of what had been accomplished so far. I knew I needed help.

When I opened the door to Karly's room I saw her lying across her purple bedspread, the phone in her hand.

"What are you doing?" she wailed.

"I need you in the kitchen. Get off the phone," I said with as much authority as I could possibly muster.

"I can't. It's Joy. It's an emergency."

"Did her parents die?" I asked.

She eyed me strangely. "Um, no."

"Is she in the hospital?"

"No."

"Then it isn't an emergency." I walked forward and yanked the phone from her hand. "I'm sorry, Joy, but Karly is going to have to call you back later." I spoke into the mouthpiece, then carefully placed the phone back into its cradle.

"I can't believe you!" she yelled. "Mom! Wrenn just hung up on Joy!"

"Karly, do whatever your sister says," came her muffled reply.

She glared at me. "You are totally psycho. We were trying to come up with a good way to get back at Sherie."

"And *that* was your emergency?" I asked incredulously.

"Are you kidding? I have a reputation to save here. Seriously, I suggest you shut up."

"Seriously, I suggest you get out the broom and sweep the dining room floor. Then set the table with something nice, like a...a tablecloth."

"Do we even *have* a tablecloth?" she asked.

I rolled my eyes. "I don't know. Just use the best stuff we own. For some reason, this is important to Mom." I walked back into the kitchen and began peeling potatoes.

In less than forty-five minutes, a chocolate pie was thawing on the counter, the meat was cooling, the beans were simmering, mashed potatoes were ready, and biscuits were in the oven. The counters were clean and wiped down. The table was set; candles were lit. I'd managed to accomplish in less than an hour what it had taken my mother the entire afternoon to only begin. So much for her "micromanagement skills." She emerged from her room, adjusting an earring, at precisely the right moment.

"This is so beautiful!" Mom cried. "Thank you both for helping. I owe you big time."

I handed her a spoon for the mashed potatoes, then took off my oven mitt and left it on the counter. "You're welcome. But now I only have ten minutes to get ready," I complained. "Take the biscuits out of the oven when the timer beeps." I headed out of the room, but stopped at the last minute. "And I'm not talking about the smoke detector...biscuits are usually ready *before* the fire alarm goes off," I chided.

As quickly as possible, I jumped into the shower and washed my hair. And even though Mom hated wet hair at the dinner table, this time she would have to get over it. Maybe it would teach her to order Chinese the next time she had the brilliant idea to invite a guest to dinner. I pulled on a sweater and piled my hair on top of my head in a twist.

The doorbell rang just as I shut the door to my room.

"Okay, girls," Mom called. "Please be on your best behavior tonight."

I rolled my eyes. Yeah. Like we were four-year-olds prone to temper tantrums.

I listened to her as she opened the door and greeted Phil. He'd arrived right on time and brought flowers. So predictable.

"Wow. You look terrific!" he exclaimed as he walked into the room. My mom giggled nervously. I tried not to throw up.

"Well, hello, you must be Wrenn." He came toward me, his hand outstretched. I shook it. He squeezed my fingers—hard. Obviously, there is significance to the whole "importance of a good, firm handshake" thing, but this was overkill. My hand throbbed painfully. "Your mother has told me so much about you."

Did she mention that I look nothing like her? Or would that explain the disconcerted expression on your face? I forced a smile. "It's nice to meet you, too," I replied. "Mom has told us the nicest things about you."

"Really?" he asked. I swear he was blushing.

No, not really, I thought to myself.

Okay, so Phil didn't look exactly like I had pictured him. There was no sign of a potbelly—that was good. He wasn't short, but tall and lanky instead. Not completely bald, though he did have a noticeably receding hairline, and the thin glasses he wore made him look, well, for lack of a better description, nerdy. All in all, he wasn't *terrible* looking, but he was definitely *not* Mom's type.

"Dinner smells terrific," he continued.

"Thank you," Mom replied. "It was nothing, really."

I rolled my eyes and tried to stifle a laugh. *Yeah, Mom. Go ahead and take credit for my dinner. Phil, my friend, you have no idea what you are getting yourself into.*

We sat down together at the table and began to fill our plates.

"So, Wrenn," Mom said, about midway through the most boring meal I'd ever endured, "tell us about the rehearsal you'll be going to tonight."

Ugh. How contrived did this sound? We might as well have been using cue cards. "Well, Mom," I began, playing along. "As far as I know, we're going to order pizza and read through the script. I'm not sure what to expect, since this is the first musical I've ever been in."

Mom cringed a bit, but smiled.

"That's terrific! Kerri didn't mention you were in a musical," Phil said.

I felt the pink undertones creep to my cheeks. "It sort of just happened yesterday," I said.

"What musical?" he asked, genuinely interested.

"Oh, they are doing *Grease* at her high school. Wrenn will be playing the part of Rizzo," Mom supplied, taking a bite of mashed potatoes.

"That's terrific! I admire that. In college, I was a drama man myself. Although I did more 'behind the scenes' work than acting on stage."

I offered a half-smile. *No kidding.*

He cleared his throat. "Thank you for this, Kerri. It's so nice to sit down and have a home-cooked meal," he continued. "I don't get them very often. I'm more of a microwave dinner kind of guy."

I bet you are, I thought. *There's nothing like sitting in front of the television watching* "Jeopardy" *in your underwear while eating Hungry Man Dinners, is there?* Ugh. Just the thought of Phil wearing only his underwear made me shudder. Those long, skinny legs—Gross.

The second hand on the clock seemed to be moving in slow motion. *When was this dinner going to end?* I wondered. That's when Phil began to talk about his antique lunch-box collection. I propped my head up with my hands and played with the leftover food on my plate—the food I wouldn't eat because A, I was on a diet, and B, I still had another meal to eat at rehearsal.

I wiped my sweaty palms on my jeans as I climbed out of Mom's car.

"Call me when you're finished," she reminded me.

"Goodbye, Wrenn," Phil said, waving. "It was a pleasure meeting you."

"Likewise," I replied, before slamming the door shut.

I hurried to the front doors of the school, trying to get

as far away from Phil and the word *terrific* as I possibly could.

It was dark inside. I tried to remember the last time I'd seen such a large place so empty. There was just something about being at school after hours that was seriously creepy. The only light came from the glow of the Exit signs at the end of either hallway, and I was almost too scared to venture any further.

My watch read 7:30. I was right on time. Where was everyone else? I crept across the lobby toward the auditorium. There were no lights on, but I peered through the tinted glass anyway.

"Are you looking for someone?" a voice called.

My heart leapt into my throat, and I must have jumped a foot into the air.

I struggled to catch my breath. "I—I'm in the musical," I stammered, turning around.

"Oh, yeah. It's Wrenn, right?"

"Right." I cocked my head to the side, examining the features hidden in the shadows. Did I know this guy?

"I'm Steven," he supplied. "The cast is meeting in Room 109. I was just heading that way."

We began walking together. "So are you in the play, too?" I asked.

Steven let out a laugh. "I can't really sing—if you know what I mean. I'm stage crew; Mr. Pike's right-hand man."

"Mr. Pike?"

"The director. You remember, the day of auditions? That was Mr. Pike."

"Oh, we never officially met," I replied.

He paused for a moment. "You were great, by the way. At the audition, I mean. I was really impressed with your voice, and the song you chose."

We turned down a hallway that was fully lit. "Thank you." I began to blush, but managed to steal a glance Steven's way. I recognized him immediately. He was the guy I'd practically tangoed with the day of auditions. He brushed a strand of his shaggy brown hair off his face.

"Well, here we are," he said, stopping in front of 109. "And congratulations on getting that part. You deserved it."

Unable to look him in the eye, I tucked a stray piece of my dark hair behind my ear and thanked him again. We walked into the room together. All of the desks had been pushed aside, and everyone was sitting on the floor. Boxes of pizza were stacked on the teacher's desk. Steven and I stepped around various bodies as we made our way toward the front.

"What would you like to drink?" asked a cheery blonde holding a 2-liter bottle.

"Um, Mountain Dew is fine," I said, picking up a paper plate. Ugh. Sugar and mega-calories. Why did I not think to bring a bottle of water? From now on, water was the only liquid I would consume. Oh, and maybe an occasional orangeade. If, you know, it was an emergency.

"I'll have the same," Steven added.

One slice of pizza was all I took; Steven grabbed three. Technically, I'd already eaten dinner, and for someone who was supposed to be on a diet, things weren't going very well so far. Pizza was a definite no. Tonight was the last night I could splurge—ever—so I would eat my one piece and enjoy it—while it lasted.

"Okay, my budding stars and starlets," Mr. Pike sang out, clapping his hands together. "I'm going to pass around your scripts. Your assignment for this weekend is to high-light and begin memorizing your lines or solos if you have them."

He handed someone a stack of white booklets, which then made its way around the room. I took one off the top and passed the rest along. Flipping through the pages, I paid careful attention to anything marked "Rizzo."

Mr. Pike continued. "Tonight we're only going to lis-ten. Notice that there are no chorus people here. Their re-hearsals don't begin for another few weeks. The purpose of this rehearsal is to get you acquainted with the songs and your lines. Hopefully, you are familiar with this mu-sical—it's a classic, as you probably know. If not, I suggest you buy the movie or get it from the library and watch it. Or at the minimum, get the CD and listen to it. Even if you're already familiar with it, I suggest you watch or lis-ten to it again."

Halfway through his spiel, the door opened and Bree Donnelly sauntered into the room. She was fashionably late—fifteen minutes at least—and was snapping her gum loudly.

"Miss Donnelly, how nice of you to join us," Mr. Pike said sarcastically, as he tossed a script her way.

She caught it mid-air. "No problem."

"Let me use this opportunity to inform you that tardiness is unacceptable." He stole a glance in Bree's direction, as she took a seat on the floor, completely oblivious to the warning that was, in fact, aimed directly at her. "I also will not tolerate absence. If you have an emergency, you must inform me immediately. I recommend that you evaluate carefully what you consider to be an emergency, before picking up the phone or coming to me with an excuse," he added. "If you can't be here to rehearse, you can't be in the show."

Steven leaned in closer, and whispered in my ear, "Don't worry. He's all bark and no bite. He gives this same speech every year. It's practically verbatim." I felt a prickle on the back of my neck.

Mr. Pike turned his back toward us, and I made myself comfortable on the floor as the music began.

Two hours later, I was standing outside in the freezing cold, waiting for my mom. "I swear, as soon as I'm sixteen, I'm applying for the first job I can get, and then I'm buying myself a car," I muttered. My breath turned to smoke in the January air, and I rubbed my arms vigorously to keep warm. The door to the building opened behind me. I heard voices and laughter.

"Oh, I didn't know anyone was still here," someone called. I turned around and watched as Steven and the blonde girl who was pouring drinks earlier walked toward me.

"You can wait inside, you know. The building isn't locked," she continued.

"I know," I lied. "My mom should be here any minute, though. So I was just waiting out here."

She stuck her hand out. "I'm Frenchy, by the way. Well, my real name is Tabitha, but until April, I'm Frenchy."

"Rizzo," I replied.

"Oh. You're Wrenn. I saw you at the audition. You were amazing," she said with a sense of awe. "I mean, you were really great."

My eyes instantly fell to my feet and I began to blush. "Thank you," I whispered. For someone who was supposed to be a budding starlet, I wasn't handling my newfound attention very well. "I'm kind of new at all this," I said with a shrug.

She waved her hand. "Don't worry, you'll get used to it," Tabitha said. "When you're on stage for the first time, it's such a rush. You'll never want to leave the spotlight, not ever."

I gave her a half-hearted smile. "I never really wanted to be *in* the spotlight," I confessed.

"Well, you're going to be there now," she replied, stepping off the sidewalk. "So you may as well get used to it!" Tabitha waved good-bye and crossed the parking lot.

"Bye, Steven!" she called.

Steven answered, then, turning toward me, asked if I needed a ride home.

"No, it's okay—really. My mom is on her way." I glanced down at my watch. "Like, any minute now."

He shrugged his shoulders. "Well, if you ever need anything—a ride to rehearsal or something—I'd be glad to pick you up."

I smiled at him. "Thanks. That's really sweet of you."

Steven pulled out a sheet of paper from his clipboard and a pen from the pocket on his flannel shirt. I recognized the headlights of my mother's car fast approaching.

She pulled beside us and slowed to a stop, just as Steven handed me the piece of paper. "This is my address, phone number, and my email address. I'll be glad to take you to and from rehearsals if your mom ever gets tired of it. I know mine sure did."

"Okay," I agreed, as I opened the passenger side door. "Thanks."

As soon as the door was shut and I was safely buckled in, my mother let the questions fly. "Who was that? What's his name? Do you like him?" And more importantly, "Does he like you?" Notice that she wasn't at all concerned for my safety as I waited in the dark, but wanted to know all about my love life. Those were her priorities. She was almost as concerned with my love life as she was with my weight—and that was way concerned.

"His name is Steven; he's in the play. I hardly know him."

"Well, what's the piece of paper he gave you?"

"His number."

"His number?" she repeated. "As in his phone number?"

I rolled my eyes. "No, his Social Security number. Yes, it's his phone number."

"Well, you're going to call him, right?"

"Um, no, I wasn't planning on it. He said to call if I ever needed a ride or something."

She looked over at me. "Or something? Wrenn, I

think he likes you." She spoke in hushed tones—like this was some huge, amazing secret.

"Likes me? Please, Mom. I don't even know the guy."

"All I'm saying is that you should call him."

I watched the lights in town roll past. "I don't have a reason."

"Oh, I can give you a reason."

There was a funny look in her eyes—that twinkle—and I hoped it was from her "terrific" evening with Phil and not from whatever little ideas were now running through her simple mind.

"Don't even think about it," I threatened. "After tonight, you owe me big-time."

Chapter

Seven

On Sunday afternoon, I was rolling around on the floor in agony, barely halfway through one of my mother's exercise videos when the phone rang. Drenched in sweat, I answered it, every muscle in my overweight body aching.

"Hello?"

"Hey, it's Zoe. You will never, ever, in a million years, guess who I just talked to on the phone!"

"Who?"

"You're supposed to guess!" she cried.

I rolled my eyes. Oh, so *now* she wanted me to guess? "You just said I'd never guess in a million years," I pointed out.

"Fine. Get this—I talked to Sk8trGuy!"

"On the phone?" I asked, panting.

"Yes, on the phone. We were online, and he asked why we hadn't talked on the phone yet, and I said I didn't know, and he asked if he could call me, and I said yes and gave him my number," she explained.

My mouth fell open in shock. "You gave him your number?" I seriously thought we had discussed this.

"Yes, but that's it. He still doesn't know my name or any other personal information." She paused for a moment. "What is wrong with you? Are you dying?"

"Huh?" I asked.

"You sound winded."

I sat up on the floor. "I'm working out," I explained. "So, yes, in a way I'm dying. Hopefully, it's only temporary. So what did you talk about if you couldn't give specifics?"

"Art. It's always art," Zoe said, breathlessly.

"And you don't even know his name?" I asked.

"No, and he doesn't know mine."

"So you just call him Sk8trGuy, and he calls you Artchick?" I asked, propping my sweaty head up with my free hand.

She thought about this. "We don't really address each other by name. We just…talk."

I rolled my eyes. "Whatever. So was it the most enlightening experience you've ever had?" I asked, my voice laced with sarcasm.

If Zoe noticed, she didn't let on. "Of course it was! I'm so in love," she added with a giggle.

"How can you be in love with a guy you barely know, and still haven't seen?" I asked.

"Because I *do* know him. That's the thing. How many boyfriends and girlfriends talk as much as we do? Seriously. It's because it isn't about looks…or popularity. It's about who we are as people."

80

"But you don't know anything about him," I pointed out.

She let out a huge sigh. "I know how he feels about 'Starry Night.'"

"In the grand scheme of things, 'Starry Night' barely registers," I informed her.

"That's just because you're not an artist. You'll get it one day, I promise. When we go to Europe after graduation and you see it in person...you'll understand. So how was rehearsal last night?" she asked, changing the subject.

"Fine."

"Just fine?"

"It was fine. We didn't rehearse or anything. We just listened to a recording of the show." I hesitated a moment before continuing. "There was this guy named Steven there, and he gave me his phone number."

"As in, he wanted you to call him sometime?"

"Well, yeah, I guess so. I mean, if I ever needed a ride or anything," I explained.

The concept practically astounded her. "He offered to give you a ride?"

"Yes."

"And you talked to him?"

"Yes. He sat with me at rehearsal."

"Wrenn, are you serious?" I could picture her on the other end, staring into the receiver, completely disbelieving every word I was saying. No guys ever volunteered to sit beside me. Not even nerdy guys.

"Yes. I'm serious," I said, my jaw tightening.

"I bet he has a crush on you."

I rolled my eyes. "Not even. Zoe, that's not possible."

"Not possible? That a guy could actually like you for who you are? Girl, have a little faith."

I had faith. But if Steven really did have a crush on me, the only logical conclusion I could come up with was that he had fallen in love with my voice, and not with me or my looks.

"Come on. When was the last time a guy was interested in me? You don't have to think too hard, do you?"

"So? That was then, this is now."

"But nothing's changed. Face it; I'm just not girlfriend material."

"You aren't going to go into your whole 'I'm so freakin' fat no one will ever like me' rant, are you? Because I had a really good afternoon and I don't want it ruined by having to listen to it all over again."

"Well…."

"Well, nothing, Wrenn. How many times do I have to tell you? You are *not* fat. You're within the bracket of the ideal weight for your height."

"I'm on the upper end of that bracket, Zo," I reminded her. "One more chocolate chip cookie and that upper-end-of-my-ideal-weight crap will be out the window."

"I'm not hearing this," she said, and began humming a random tune. "Wait a minute," she said. "You're working out?"

I sighed. "Yes. Anything else?"

"You never work out."

"That's obvious," I groaned, rolling my eyes.

"So why start now?"

"Because my jeans don't fit right and I'm in a musical in three months."

"Your jeans don't fit right and you're in a musical in three months?" she repeated sarcastically. "At least you're doing it for the right reasons. I have to go anyway. I just wanted to give you a quick update."

"That was so kind of you."

"Well, I knew you'd want to hear how great Sk8trGuy was again," she teased. "I'll talk to you later."

"Hey, you aren't going to meet him, are you?" I blurted out.

"Bye!"

"Zoe?"

Silence. I stared at the empty earpiece. Leave it to Zoe to try something stupid, like meeting a guy she barely knows. I hung up the phone and turned the exercise video back on, beginning the agony all over again.

The spotlight burned my eyes, but somehow I managed to read the lines that were highlighted on my script.

"I don't get it," I whispered. "So when you walk over here, I'm going to walk in front of you and say my line, right?"

"I guess so," Bree replied. "If not, we'll find out as soon as Pikey cuts the music and starts yelling."

I giggled, thankful that I'd actually managed to carry on a conversation with Bree Donnelly without sounding like an idiot—even if it lasted only four seconds. Baby steps.

Waiting for my cue, I shielded my eyes with my hand and looked out at the cast members seated in the audience. I could see Steven walking back and forth between the rows of chairs. He was serving as the crew manager, meaning he was overseeing all the prop people, and the sound and lighting technicians. He took his job seriously, waving his arms wildly when pitching ideas to Mr. Pike, or tersely giving orders to his subordinates. He communicated to everyone via headset, and he never left his clipboard unattended.

It wasn't that Steven was terrible-looking. I mean, he was a senior. I'm sure if he got a better haircut and ditched his old, flannel shirts, he'd even be semi-cute. The truth was, well, he was a nerd. Tad Owens made fun of him whenever his back was turned, and Bree made random comments about his quirkiness. It annoyed me when my mother asked me on a regular basis about the status of our friendship, and it embarrassed me when Steven approached me before, during, or after rehearsals. It wasn't about Steven, really. He was a nice guy. He just wasn't my type.

As soon as my scene ended, I walked off stage to the seat where I'd left my purse, my bottle of water, and my pack of gum. I sat down and watched as another group began rehearsing their scene.

Hot and out of breath, I took a swig of water. My stomach growled in response. Why on earth had I decided to skip dinner?

"Hey," a voice called. "Great job up there."

Of course. I turned to see Steven, who sat down directly behind me. He leaned forward and propped his elbows on the chair in front of him.

"I don't know how you remember all those lines and moves, but I guess that's why I'm stage crew and not the star," he continued.

I took another swallow of water. "Thanks, but I'm no star. And we're still using the scripts, so I don't have to remember lines yet. I don't know how well I'll do once we give them up."

"You'll be just as great. It'll be second nature. By the time these things are over, even I've memorized everyone's lines." We watched Tad and Bree rehearse together, and I tried to ignore the uncomfortable silence that had fallen between us.

"Um, you're doing a good job, too," I finally stammered. "You know, keeping everything in order and stuff." I had to say something.

"You think so? No one really pays attention to the stage crew. I enjoy working behind the scenes. It's a challenge," he said. "But you—you were meant to be on stage. I can't believe you haven't done this before."

There was no time to respond. I heard a buzz coming from his headset. "Okay, I'll be right on it," he said. "Spotlight trouble," he informed me as he rose to his feet.

I smiled politely. "No problem."

As Steven walked away, I glanced at my watch. It was almost nine, which meant rehearsal would be ending soon. It was also Saturday, which meant Mom and Phil were out on a date...again. Tonight I was relying on Zoe for a ride.

"Where have you been?" she asked as I climbed into the passenger's side of her car, once again pushing the trash onto the floor.

"Sorry, but it's not my fault. Mr. Pike kept us late."

"It's okay, I'm not mad. I was just making sure you weren't flirting with Steven."

"I wasn't flirting with Steven," I confirmed.

She put the car into gear and pulled out of the parking lot. I heard her inhale sharply "Okay. Wrenn? Please don't kill me."

"Why would I kill you?" I asked.

"Because, I know you, and you're going to want to kill me, but you can't because you are my very best friend in the entire world. Don't forget that when I tell you what I'm about to tell you."

I glared at her, a scowl planted across my face. "Zoe, what have you done?" I demanded to know.

"I haven't done anything—yet."

"What are you *going* to do, then?"

She scrunched her face. "Please don't yell at me," she begged.

I threw my hands up in exasperation. "How can I yell at you when I don't even know what's going on?"

"Okay, okay." Zoe took a huge breath, then let it out: "We're meeting Sk8trGuy."

"What? What do you mean, *we*?"

"I mean, that I'm meeting Sk8trGuy tonight at Andy's and you're going with me."

"You cannot be serious!" I shouted.

She wrinkled her nose. "You said you wouldn't yell."

"Zoe, you don't even know who he is! Why would you want to meet someone you don't know? It's not safe!"

"But I *do* know him. I know he's a good guy. You have to believe me. And that's where you come in anyway. You're my protection."

I laughed sarcastically. "Oh, *I'm* your protection? Good thinking, Zo."

"Yes. There's safety in pairs. We're a pair, we'll be in a public place; there's absolutely nothing to worry about."

"What about Mom and Phil?"

"You can tell them rehearsal let out late. You can call them on my cell phone. Or you can say we stopped at Andy's for an orangeade. You know your mom won't mind."

I shook my head in disbelief. "What if *I* mind?"

"You're my best friend. Please, please, please, please! Just do this one thing for me and I swear I will never ask you for anything ever again. I *swear*."

I rolled my eyes. Like I could believe *that*. "Give me your phone," I demanded.

"What?"

"Just give it to me."

With one hand on the steering wheel, she dug into the depths of her purse, eventually pulling out her cell phone.

I punched in a few numbers. "I'm holding this, and I'm programming 911 on your speed dial. I swear, if anything happens. If this guy is a pervert, or a twenty-, thirty-, or forty-something-year-old loser, I'm calling the police."

"Fine."

We walked into Andy's and sat down on the bar stools closest to the register.

I couldn't believe she had resorted to this tactic to get me to go with her, though I'm not sure why it surprised me. This stunt had Zoe written all over it. Of course, as soon as she realized that I wasn't going to kill her, Zoe had instantly become a nervous wreck, asking me questions every ten seconds: "Do I have anything in my teeth?" "How does my hair look?" "What if he doesn't like me?" And so on.

"Look, I'm shaking," she said, showing me her hands. "I can't do this."

I stood to my feet. "Great, then let's go."

She grabbed my arm. "No! Wait! I'm fine, I promise." I sat back down.

"What time is it?" she asked.

"9:35."

"Is it really 9:35? Or is it 9:33 and you're rounding up? Or maybe it's 9:37 and you're rounding down? Some people do that you know. Or is it really 9:37, and you're just trying to make me feel better about Sk8trGuy being late?"

"It's 9:35 and thirty seconds," I stated, matter-of-factly.

This quieted her. "Oh."

Between her repeated questions about the time, Zoe told me that she and Sk8trGuy had made these plans the night before. They would meet at the counter at Andy's at 9:30 sharp. Zoe would be with her best friend, which was where I came in, and she'd be wearing a royal blue sweater. I must say that she had taken great pains to look good, and I could tell she had spent extra time in the bathroom agonizing over mascara and eyeliner—so totally unlike her.

"What if he came in already and thought I was hideous or something?" she asked.

"Not possible. Besides, according to you, it isn't looks you two are attracted to—it's personality," I reminded her.

The door to Andy's swung open and in walked a guy: a cute guy. Zoe sat straight up and stared at him, anticipating a return of his gaze. Instead of walking toward us, however, he picked a booth on the other side of the restaurant. Moments later he was joined by a girl and another couple.

"Guess that's not him," I supplied. Zoe took a sip of her drink.

"What time is it?"

Honestly, she was killing me. "It's 9:38."

A group of guys walked in but they also found a seat elsewhere. They were followed by another couple.

At 9:45: "Well, he obviously isn't coming," Zoe said. "Let's get out of here."

She was completely bummed out. "Maybe he's stuck in traffic or something," I suggested, trying to make her feel better. She didn't respond. "I mean, something could have come up…like a family emergency. His great aunt could be dying in Vancouver," I offered.

"I guess I'll never know," she muttered.

I rolled my eyes. "Don't be so dramatic, Zoe. Go home, sign online, and ask what happened. I'm sure he has a valid reason."

We hopped off our bar stools and pushed them under the counter. "Let's just pay for this and get out of here. I have a painting to work on anyway."

As we waited in line at the register, someone else walked into the restaurant. Zoe and I turned around in tandem.

"Look! It's Chase," I whispered, grabbing Zoe's arm.

Sure enough, Chase Cunningham had entered the building. He stepped in line directly behind us.

"I see him," she replied. I turned around to look at him again, and forced myself to keep from drooling.

He smiled at me. "You're Wrenn, aren't you?" he asked.

Ack! Was he talking to me? He said my name! Chase Cunningham was talking to me!

"I'm Wrenn," I repeated, turning to face him. "How did you know?"

He ran his fingers through his perfect brown hair. "I put two and two together. You're in the play with Bree. I've seen you around at rehearsals."

"Yeah. I'm Rizzo."

"Cool. So how is everything coming along? With the play and all."

"Good," I told him. "Bree is just amazing."

"Yeah, she's into that sort of stuff. I'm just picking up dinner. You guys got out late tonight."

"It was a long night," I confirmed.

Zoe turned to look at me. "Are we going or what?"

"Oh, sorry." I handed the waitress my ticket.

"I'm Chase," he said, looking at her.

"Zoe," she replied.

"I've seen you guys around school."

"That's not unusual. It's highly likely, even, since we go to the same one and all," she retorted as I pulled a dollar and a few quarters out of my purse. When I handed them to the waitress, one fell, clinking loudly on the tile floor. It rolled and finally wedged itself under the counter. I leaned down to pick it up, accidentally bumping into Zoe in the process. It was completely stuck, and I knew I looked like such an idiot with my monstrous butt up in the air. Defeated, and now completely embarrassed, I stood back up and took out another quarter.

Immediately my face flushed. Of course this would happen to me...making it the *second* time I'd utterly humiliated myself in front of Chase.

"Well, tell Bree I said 'Hello,'" I said, as Zoe and I prepared to leave.

"Sure."

We walked out of the restaurant. Or Zoe walked, rather. I bolted. "This always happens to me," I whined. "It never fails. Every time I see him I end up making a total moron of myself. It's like the entire world spins on its axis just to keep me looking like a reject. How does this keep happening?"

"This bites!" Zoe shouted.

"Tell me about it. His amazing brown eyes...."

"Would you shut up about the eyes? I'm not talking about Chase. Why didn't Sk8trGuy show up?" Zoe was on the verge of tears.

"I told you. Anything could have happened," I offered, but truthfully, I was relieved that he didn't show. It just reinforced my belief that you shouldn't try to meet Internet strangers face-to-face. Sk8trGuy was probably some forty-year-old convict chatting with Zoe from death row. That's if death-row inmates are even allowed to chat. "Just wait and see what his explanation is before you assume the worst," I continued.

Zoe put the car into gear and pulled out of the parking lot; only the sound of the radio broke the silence. She dropped me off in front of my house. Between Mom's car and Phil's car there was no room in the driveway for hers. I thanked her for the ride, then stepped onto the curb and into the wet grass.

The lights were out in the living room, but I could see the television was on, glowing and flickering with each new scene. I trudged up the front walk and used my key to unlock the door.

Mom and Phil were snuggling on the couch when I walked into the room. An old, sappy love movie was playing. I barely managed to control my gag reflex.

"Hey, hon, how was rehearsal?" Mom asked.

"Fine."

"Wrenn, long time no see," Phil joked. I rolled my eyes. I'd just seen the man yesterday. "How has your weekend been?"

"Fine."

"That's terrific!" he replied.

Ugh. I had only known Phil for a few weeks, but that was long enough to know that he was just plain weird. He was nice, too nice. I mean, really. How can everything be "terrific"? Didn't he ever have a bad day? Work was terrific, sales were terrific. Last night's *Jeopardy* winner was terrific. Ugh! Terrific, terrific, terrific.

Mom and Phil were going out every weekend, and he had already eaten at least a dozen meals with us. I honestly had to wonder about a guy in his late thirties who had never been married. When I pointed this out to my mother, she claimed he just hadn't found the right woman yet.

In my opinion, he probably scared off every female he'd ever dated just by talking about his retro lunch-box collection. He joked that he had so many he'd lost count after two hundred. I found that extremely hard to believe—not that he had over two hundred lunch boxes, because, quite frankly, that didn't surprise me at all. No, what surprised me was that he "lost count." He was too meticulous for that. Not only did he know which ones he had, he probably kept a file cabinet filled with information about them: where and when he bought them, how much he paid for them, how much they were worth and "personal comments," like, an essay on what each box meant to him.

"You should love that, Wrenn," Zoe said after I told her this. "He's organized; a man after your own heart."

"Oh come on," I replied. "I'm not that eccentric."

"Don't be so sure."

Since that moment, I've made a concerted effort not to be so obsessed with organization. I even purposely mixed up the shirts in my closet. I was in the process of reinventing myself in a major way. That meant that there was no longer any need to keep clothing arranged by sleeve length and color. I was *not* going to end up like Phil.

"There's pizza in the fridge," Mom said, interrupting my thoughts. "We saved a slice for you."

My thoughts drifted to that very morning, when my mother's bathroom scale showed that I'd already lost several pounds. I also noticed recently that my favorite sweatpants weren't quite so snug—and even my jeans were going on easier, but not right after they were washed, because everyone knows that jeans don't really fit until the second or third time you wear them. "Thanks," I replied, "but Zoe and I grabbed a bite to eat at Andy's on the way home. That's why I was late."

It wasn't a complete lie. We did stop at Andy's. She didn't have to know I skipped dinner. My stomach growled, as if on cue.

"I'll be in my room," I said, turning to leave.

I walked into the kitchen and opened the refrigerator. The aroma of pepperoni pizza permeated my senses. It smelled so good. I forced myself to shut the door. No temptation; tonight it was all about the cardio.

Chapter

Eight

"What on earth were you doing last night?" Karly asked.

I opened the refrigerator door and pulled out a bottle of water. "Working out. Why?"

"Are you kidding me?"

"Would I lie?" I asked, taking a swig.

She shrugged. "Sorry, it's just that I didn't peg you for the 'work-out' type. I mean, how long has Mom been trying to get you to go to the gym with her? What's gotten into you?"

I walked across the kitchen and sat down on a bar stool beside my sister. "I'm just trying to make a few changes, that's all."

"So you're bouncing all over your room every night and skipping meals. And you call that changing?" she asked.

"What are you talking about?"

"Wrenn, please. It's obvious. And don't think that Mom hasn't noticed, either."

I narrowed my eyes. "What are you saying?"

"I'm saying if you're trying to lose weight, that's your business. But you can't expect Mom not to say something when you start shedding pounds because you're not eating. It's not healthy. Even I know that."

"I'm eating. I'm just not eating as much. And I'm not missing any meals," I lied. "I just go out with Zoe and people from rehearsal."

Karly stood up from her seat and snickered. "Whatever. All I'm saying is that you need to watch out. You know Mom would freak out if she knew."

"There's nothing to freak out about," I said, my voice rising in anger.

She threw up her hands. "Okay, fine. Whatever you say. So what's with this sudden change?"

"I just want to change. What's wrong with that?"

"Nothing. I'm glad. No offense or anything," she quickly added.

I fingered the white cap on my bottled water. "I know I'm not the coolest person in the world, Karly. I never pretended to be."

"Then why start now?"

"What?"

"Why are you so concerned with being cool now? Is it a guy?" she asked.

"No, there's no guy."

Karly headed toward the refrigerator and pulled out a bottle of ranch dressing and some carrots, then grabbed a bag of potato chips from the counter. "Wrenn, please. There's always a guy involved."

"There's not a guy. Not specifically anyway. I don't know," I said, taking another swig of water. "I'm just tired of standing in the background. I spent my entire life there, and now I'm ready for some attention. I don't want to be chubby. I want to get noticed. I mean, how did you manage to get so popular?" I asked her.

She eyed me strangely. "How did I manage it? I didn't do a thing."

"What do you mean, you didn't do a thing? You had to have done something. You don't just become popular overnight and not work for it."

"I don't know. I just started hanging out with the right people." She shrugged her shoulders and bit into a carrot. "You don't decide if you're going to be popular; everyone else decides it for you."

"And you just happened to get lucky," I confirmed. It was so typical. Karly had never worked at anything in her life. Of course her popularity would be handed to her, just like everything else.

"I wouldn't call it 'getting lucky.' It's not easy being popular—trust me. The background is a good place to be. You don't have people like Sherie Conner trying to ruin your life."

"Yeah, right. That's so easy for you to say," I said, rising to my feet.

"I'm serious. It's not all fun and games. It's hard work."

I let out a sarcastic laugh. "I feel *so sorry* for you." I picked up my bottled water and left her standing in the kitchen. Hard work to be popular? Please. Like I was going to believe that.

On Saturday evening, Tabitha met me in the hallway at school. "I'm so glad you're early," she said, grabbing my hand. "Come with me." She pulled me along; I could barely keep up with her.

"What's going on?"

"Brace yourself. Chase dumped Bree and now she's locked herself in the bathroom."

My mouth dropped in horror.

"I know," she stated, the surprise evident in her voice.

"Are you *serious*?" Chase Cunningham dumped Bree Donnelly? They were like, *The Couple*; pre-engaged and everything. I could not believe what I was hearing.

"I don't know. She just came in and went straight to the bathroom. We tried talking to her, but she won't answer us. We need reinforcements."

We hurried down the hallway and stopped outside the girls' restroom. Sure enough, when I tried pushing on the door, it didn't budge.

"I seriously think she's messed up," said Erica, a junior who was playing the part of Jan in the musical.

"Bree," Tabitha said, knocking on the door. "Can we talk?"

"There's nothing to talk about," came her muffled reply. It was obvious she was crying. I'd never seen Bree cry before. Until now, I didn't think she cried at all. I figured she'd never had a reason. The idea completely astounded me.

"It's okay. These things happen. So Chase dumped you. It's totally his loss. Really!"

I heard her sniffle on the other side of the door. Tabitha nudged me. "Say something," she whispered.

My mouth opened but nothing came out. What do you say to someone at a time like this? I mean, this was a big deal. You can't just bounce back from being dumped by Chase Cunningham. Even *I* knew that.

"He took the ring back and everything," she wailed.

"Well, you know," I stammered. "Tabitha's right. It's his loss. And if he was a jerk, then you're better off without him. At least now you know. There are so many guys out there who would kill to have you as a girlfriend. Chase has no idea what he's done."

"Wrenn is right, Bree," Tabitha added. "Please unlock the door."

Everything was silent for a few moments, but then the lock finally clicked.

When we pushed the door open, we found Bree dabbing under her eyes, trying to prevent her mascara from running even more than it already had.

Erica stepped around us and grabbed another tissue. "Here," she said, handing it to Bree.

"There was no explanation, nothing. He just said he didn't think we belonged together anymore." Her eyes filled with fresh tears. "What if he found someone else? Someone better than me?"

"Highly unlikely," Tabitha said. "And you know you're going to bounce back in no time. Come on. You're Bree Donnelly. You don't let some guy bring you down."

Bree stared at her reflection in the mirror, then began to finger her blonde curls. "You're absolutely right. He's not going to get me down, because it's *his* loss," she affirmed. "He made a huge mistake. *Huge*."

"Exactly," Erica added. "The biggest mistake ever. He's the loser here."

Tabitha's face lit up. "I know. Why don't we crash at my place tonight? We can have a girls' night—all four of us. My parents won't mind. Then we can bash Chase all we want. What do you say?"

The four of us? Was I being included in this get-together? But why was it always a girls' night? I hated girls' nights!

Tabitha continued making plans. We could use her cell phone to call our parents, and she would drive us all home the following day if we needed a ride. She'd lend us stuff to sleep in....

When I dialed Mom's number, I was half hoping she would say no. Of course, I wanted to hang out with the girls, especially Bree, but seriously, I could do without the facials and makeovers. But instead of saying no, Mom thought it was a terrific idea and told me to have a good time. Karly was staying with a friend, and she and Phil were planning to rent a movie. Everything was perfect. Perfect and terrific.

As soon as rehearsal ended we piled into Tabitha's car. The girls' night was officially underway. It began simply enough, with the car windows cracked and the radio blasting. Even Bree appeared to be having a good time.

Once we were on the other side of town, Tabitha turned down the music. "I'm stopping at the drug store. What do we need for tonight?"

"What do you have?" Erica asked.

"Plenty of snacks, but I was thinking along the lines of hair dye and stuff."

"Oh that would be so awesome! We could give each other highlights!" Erica cried.

"Is everyone up for that?" Tabitha asked.

I was the only one who didn't answer, but somehow no one picked up on it.

Half an hour later, we were dumping out the contents of our shopping spree onto a bed. We'd all chipped in to make Bree's night a little happier.

I looked at the plethora of beauty supplies that were strewn across the comforter. It was almost as bad as one of Mom's girls' nights, with the potential to become much, much worse—especially since permanent hair color was involved.

"Wrenn, would you let me cut your hair?" Tabitha asked.

The color drained from my face. "What? Are you kidding?"

"No. I cut my sister's hair all the time."

I wasn't exactly in the market for a haircut, especially since I had just had it trimmed. Besides, I thought my hair looked fine the way it was.

"Seriously, you would look cute with shoulder-length hair and layers," Bree suggested.

Bree thought I would look cute if I cut my hair. I bit my lower lip, and glanced at my reflection in the mirror. Shoulder-length? That was at least six inches. And layers? What if she messed up? This had disaster written all over it.

"Here, let me show you a picture of my sister," Tabitha said, as if reading my mind. She walked over to her desk and brought over a wallet-sized family portrait. "See? I cut her hair the week before this was taken. She looks great."

"I'll let you cut mine," Erica piped.

"Okay. I'll do yours first, and we'll let Wrenn think about it."

I hoped that cutting Erica's hair would satisfy Tabitha's urge to snip and shape so then I'd be off the hook.

The four of us congregated in Tabitha's tiny bathroom. Bree began opening highlighting kits while Erica hung her head underneath the bathtub faucet.

I looked on, and within an hour, Bree had beautiful streaks in her already blonde hair, and Erica's was cut short and layered.

"Awesome!" Tabitha cried. "I'm so going to do this for a living." She looked in the mirror at Erica. A wave of shock passed over her face. "Guys! Do you know what we're doing?"

"What?" Bree asked.

"This is right out of the musical. I'm serious! It's the girls' night! Look! We have Jan, Frenchy, Rizzo, and Sandy right here in my bathroom. And Sandy is upset about her man. This is like, so déjà vu."

"You're right. This is totally scary," Erica commented.

"Yeah, it's like the play is coming to life or something," I added.

"Great. Well, I know that you're supposed to drop out of high school to go to beauty school and everything, but you're *not* going to pierce my ears," Bree added. "My dad threw a fit when I came home with my second hole. He'd die of a heart attack if I got a third."

"I'm not piercing anyone's ears tonight. I'm just cutting hair. So, Wrenn, what do you say?"

"No, that's okay. I really don't think I want a haircut right now," I told them.

"Come on, Rizzo! You'll look great!" Erica cried. "Live a little."

"I won't cut it too short, I promise," Tabitha said.

I let out a huge sigh. "I just don't know."

"Can I be honest with you?" Bree asked. "I really think you could use a haircut. I mean, you don't want to look like that forever, do you?"

Like what? Was she *insulting* me? At a slumber party where I already believed I didn't belong? My throat constricted, and in a moment I felt as if I might burst into tears. Bree Donnelly had no idea what it was like to hate the way you looked. She had never felt ugly a day in her life. She was clueless. I swallowed the lump in my throat and blinked a few times. I stared at my face in the mirror, my long, straight brown hair hanging lifelessly past my shoulders. No, I decided. I didn't want to look like this forever. I was tired of being plain. I wanted to be noticed. And if Bree thought I needed a new hairstyle, then I needed a new hairstyle. It was that simple.

"Fine," I acquiesced with a wave of my hand. "Cut away." I mean, it was just hair, right? It grows.

Tabitha let out a little squeal. "Wrenn Scott, you will *not* regret this."

I held my head under the faucet while Tabitha washed my hair. Then I sat quietly on the bathroom stool, trying not to cry out every time inches of my hair fell to the floor. Unfortunately, I didn't have long to mourn the loss of my tresses, because moments later....

"Wrenn, have you ever waxed your eyebrows?" Bree asked.

"No." I groaned.

"Well, I swear by this stuff." Before I could even protest, Bree Donnelly had slapped a spoonful of hot wax on my eyebrows, then placed and yanked off the paper strip, pulling out a million tiny stray hairs.

"Ow!" I cried. "What are you doing?" I shouted. My eyebrow throbbed, and in the mirror I could see the patch had turned bright pink.

"It only hurts for a minute," she calmly informed me.

"Wrenn, you have to hold still or your sides will be uneven," Tabitha said.

Again, Bree reached for the wax and prepared to do my other eyebrow. I pushed her hand away.

My eyes watered. "No way! You are not doing that to me again."

"Hold still! You're wiggling too much," Tabitha complained.

I tried to remain seated while keeping an eye on Bree.

"You have to do the other one. You're lopsided," she said.

"Forget it. I'll live."

"Now Wrenn, honestly. Look at yourself in the mirror. Do you really want everyone at school and in the play to see you like this?"

The pain from the first attempt was beginning to subside, and I did look ridiculous with only one eyebrow waxed. Sighing in defeat, I told her to go for it.

A smile crossed Bree's face, and she proceeded not only to remove the excess hair from beneath my eyebrows, but between and above them as well. "You can pluck out stray hairs with tweezers once a week," she informed me.

Yeah right, like I was going to put myself through that any time soon.

Moments later, Tabitha announced that she was done with my hair. I turned my head from side to side, admiring my new 'do. My head felt much lighter, and the cut was definitely more stylish.

"I want to highlight it now," Erica said.

There was no point in protesting. Every time I said no, Bree and everyone else talked me into doing whatever it was that I didn't want done in the first place. Besides, I was two for two so far. My hair looked great and my eyebrows looked great. What could go wrong?

I sat still while Erica pulled strands of hair through the holes in the plastic cap, then watched as the hair lightened before my eyes.

It was after midnight. We were all wearing borrowed T-shirts—mine just a little too snug—and sitting on Tabitha's bed. While the other girls gossiped and bashed Chase, I thought about how incredibly lucky I was to even be sitting in the same room as Bree, the most popular girl in school. I felt better about myself already—like I actually could belong here—with these popular people. Between the haircut and the highlights, I hardly even recognized myself. I had to refocus every time I looked into the mirror.

"So who do you think the hottest guy in the play is?" Erica asked.

"Tad Owens, without a doubt," Tabitha answered.

"He *is* cute," Bree stated. "I always thought that if I wasn't dating Chase, I'd like to go out with him."

"I think you'd make a great couple," Erica said. "But what about that guy in the chorus? John something-or-other? I think he's hot."

"I know who you're talking about. That brown-haired guy in the front row. He *is* cute," Tabitha agreed.

"No, I've got it," Bree said. "The absolute hottest guy in the play is Steven James." Everyone began to laugh, and even I cracked a smile.

"Steven is just—Steven," Tabitha said. "He's totally harmless."

"That headset of his just drives me crazy," Bree continued, ignoring her.

"Oh I know. And he's always trying to act ultra-important. I think he thinks he's the director or something," Erica said.

"Wrenn, isn't he, like, a friend of yours?" Bree asked.

"No," I replied, almost a little too quickly.

"I didn't know. I mean, he's always talking to you at rehearsals."

"No, we aren't really friends, but he does like talking to me for some reason."

"Uh-oh. Steven has the hots for our Wrenn!" Erica cried.

I smiled and began to blush. "I don't think so."

"Oh, come on, it's obvious. We need to set you up with someone so he'll leave you alone," she continued. "Who can we set Wrenn up with?"

They began spouting off name after name—none of whom interested me. The only names I wanted to hear were Tad Owens or Chase Cunningham. I knew Chase's name wouldn't come up, and Bree had already claimed Tad. Who was left?

"It definitely needs to be someone involved in the play. That way they know how talented you are," Erica stated.

What, you mean so they don't notice my fat rolls? I silently wondered. *I'm working on those, you know.*

"What about John, the chorus guy?" Bree suggested. "We all agree he's cute."

"He'd be perfect! We talk all the time, so I can work on him for you. You know, build you up," Erica continued. "He'll be eating out of the palm of your hand by Valentine's Day, I promise."

I smiled. It sounded like the perfect plan. I mean, John the Chorus Guy was cute, even if I preferred Tad. I'd have to make an exception, especially since it would almost guarantee my plans to become popular.

Of course their plan was going to work — Bree and I were friends now. She wanted to set me up with a cute guy. I was *so* on my way.

Chapter

Nine

"What on earth did you do to your hair?" my mom asked the next morning, the moment I walked through the front door. My clothes were dirty and felt completely attached to my skin. I desperatcly needed a shower.

"The girls cut and highlighted it last night," I informed her. She walked toward me and began running her fingers through it.

"I like the length," she continued. "But the highlights look orange."

"Orange?" I repeated. "They're blonde." I looked at my reflection. The hallway mirror showed a girl who was tired and unfortunately sported odd-looking highlights.

"They just look brassy, that's all," she stated.

"What? They looked great last night!" I cried.

"Don't panic. It's okay. The dye wasn't left on long enough but it can be fixed. Let me call Denise to see if she can squeeze you in this morning."

Mom walked into the kitchen and picked up the phone. I continued to stare at myself in the mirror. *They didn't tell me my hair was orange,* I thought. I had to won-

109

der if they had done this on purpose. I mean, why give the fat girl a decent dye job? Maybe they thought that anything was an improvement. For all I knew, Bree and Erica and Tabitha could be laughing at me this very moment.

"Yeah, it's not that bad. It's just that her hair was so dark," I heard Mom say. Silence. "Okay, we'll see you in a few."

She returned to the living room. "Denise can work you in now."

"Can I get a shower first?"

"No, if we are going to get there before the rush, we have to leave now," she said, grabbing her purse. Sighing, I turned to follow her out the door. I was tired. I was hungry, and I wanted my favorite sweatpants.

"So how was last night?" Mom asked as soon as we were on the road.

"It was okay. I didn't plan on getting a new hairdo or having my eyebrows ripped out at the roots, but it's all good."

The car swerved to the right, kicking up gravel from the side of the road.

"What are you doing?" I yelled, my heart racing.

"You let them tweeze your eyebrows?" she asked with surprise.

"No. They waxed them." I turned to look at her, showing off the thin line—all that was left of my once substantial eyebrows.

"I am so upset! What made you let them do it and not me?" she asked.

"Peer pressure," I blurted out. "I didn't really have a choice. They practically wrestled me to the floor."

She only nodded. We drove in silence for a few minutes. "So what's with this whole change you're undergoing?" she finally asked.

I played dumb. "What are you talking about?"

She smirked. "Don't tell me there's nothing going on."

"Seriously. There's nothing going on."

"I can see it, Wrenn. Ever since you got that part in the musical. You're exercising; you cut and dyed your hair. You let your new friends wax your eyebrows...."

"You make it sound like it's a big deal," I replied.

"No, it isn't a big deal, and you are such a beautiful girl. I'm glad you're taking better care of yourself. I just want to know what is behind this sudden change, that's all."

"I don't know. I'm ready to try something different," I said with a shrug. "I'm going to be on stage in front of people in a couple of months. . . I just want to look like I belong there.

A smile crossed my mother's face. "What's his name?"

I rolled my eyes. "There's no guy, if that's what you mean." I stared out the window. Out of the corner of my eye, I could see my mother glance at me.

"Don't tell me there's no guy. They're usually the driving force behind these changes. I remember the first time I cut my hair for a guy. I was in the ninth grade. I forget his name, but he was a sophomore, and oh, so fine. All the girls adored him."

I laughed. "Speaking of guys, what's going on between you and Phil?"

Her cheeks turned bright pink. "Don't think you can just change the subject. We're talking about you."

"Yes I can, and I'm asking what's going on."

She peered over her shoulder and veered to the middle lane. "We're just dating. Nothing serious, yet."

"Yet?" I repeated. "So now you are officially dating?" The thought completely grossed me out.

"Yes, we're dating."

"And you like him?"

"Would I date him if I didn't like him?" she asked.

Probably not, I decided. The realization that my mother was smitten with Phil the balding lunch-box collector slowly began to sink in.

"We understand each other," Mom continued after a few moments. "We're both at a time in our lives when we're looking for something, you know, permanent."

"Ugh. Tell me you aren't thinking about marrying him already."

"No. I'm just saying we have a lot in common, that's all."

I couldn't believe that Mom would actually consider marrying someone as nerdy as Phil. "He's not really your type," I pointed out.

"Okay, well, what exactly is my type?" she asked.

"I don't know."

Then there was silence. That thick, heavy, foreboding silence where seconds pass like hours.

I opened my mouth, ready to comment on the terrible weather we were having, when Mom spoke. "In case you haven't noticed, I haven't had much luck with men. There were dozens of guys, and then your dad, and Karly's dad. Then half a dozen more. I just want some stability, that's all."

"You can't help that my dad died," I told her. "That wasn't a bad choice on your part."

She continued to stare straight ahead; her eyes were glazed over, as if she was lost in another world.

"I like Phil," she affirmed. "And he likes me. And we're going to continue to see each other until one of us feels otherwise. I deserve to be happy, too."

I didn't press the issue, but it hurt me to think that just because she didn't have a husband, her life was the pits. What about me and Karly? Shouldn't we count for something? Maybe we didn't get along all of the time, but I liked to think that the three of us were doing just fine without the testosterone — what little of it Phil might have, that is.

When we finally pulled into the mall parking lot, it was still early and relatively vacant. Because the shops weren't open yet, Denise met us at the side door. She had been our stylist for as long as I could remember; a good decade of shampoos, haircuts, and perms. I smiled when I saw her. She would know exactly what to do.

"I love the cut," she said as she draped a cape over my shoulders. "It makes your face look thinner, and it brings out your eyes."

"Thank you."

"So who cut it again?"

"Just a girl I know from school," I told her, shrugging my shoulders. "It was the result of a girls' night."

"Love those," she replied. "Here's what I'm going to do. I need to color your hair light brown to take off this brassiness, then go back over the highlights with blonde. It should lighten easier, and a wash will take out any brassiness. Your hair is really dark."

I bit my lower lip. "But you can fix it, right?"

"No problem. It will be a drastic change, though. Are you ready for this?"

I smiled at her. Drastic changes are good, I decided as I sat back in the chair, making myself comfortable.

I closed my eyes and listened while my mother and Denise talked about work and their love lives as if I wasn't even there. For a good hour and a half, it was Phil this and Phil that, and "I hate Mitzi Monroe." But when it was all over and I opened my eyes, a completely different person stared back at me.

Denise had not only colored and highlighted, but she cut my layers even shorter, giving my once lifeless hair more body.

I watched the girl in the mirror shake her head back and forth; her hair was light, soft, and bouncy. The guys at school were *so* going to die when they saw me. A new look, a few more pounds off my waistline and I wouldn't even need Erica's help snagging John the Chorus Guy. I'd be able to get him on my own.

Trying not to burst with excitement, I thanked Denise while Mom wrote a hefty check to cover finishing what my new friends had started.

"Let's head down through the mall for a few minutes," she suggested. "There's a new store I want to look in while we're here."

I followed her into a trendy shop and began flipping through the racks.

"Oh, I love this!" Mom held up a black halter dress with an asymmetrical bottom. "This would be gorgeous on a night out with Phil. Find something so we can try them on together."

"I don't see anything I like," I told her.

"Well, just grab something. You never know what'll look good on you."

I glanced around the shop. None of this stuff would look good on me. These clothes were made for girls who were 5'9" and stick thin.

The far wall held shelves filled with jeans. Those were the safest bet. At least now I could see how much weight I'd really lost. I walked over and picked out a pair; a size smaller than I would normally buy.

"This looks terrible on me," Mom said after less than a minute behind the dressing room door. "Come out and look." I zipped up the jeans with no problem, then met her outside in front of the three-way mirror.

"Wrenn, those pants are adorable!" she cried. "The boot cut makes you look taller." I told her what size they were, a size I hadn't been since I was like, 11. "You're kidding! Let me see the butt." I turned around and showed her the seat. A perfect fit. "We're buying them," she declared. "Meanwhile, this dress looks awful on me."

"It doesn't look bad," I told her. "It's a cute dress."

"I know, it just doesn't look right on me."

She stared at her reflection for a moment before returning to the dressing room. Seconds later she threw the
black dress over the wooden wall and into my area.

"Here, try this on," she instructed. I picked the dress
off the floor.

"What? I can't wear this," I informed her.

"Just try it. Some things look better on different people."

"I can't wear your clothes."

"This dress was made bigger. Please? I want to see
what it looks like on you."

I rolled my eyes and slipped the dress on.

As I emerged from the dressing room I decided it was
tight in all the wrong places.

"Wrenn, you look amazing!" Mom cried. "You're
hardly the same you! I can't believe it!"

I studied my reflection in the mirror. I could stand to
lose a few more pounds, but overall the dress did look
good.

"I like it," I decided.

"Wouldn't it be so cute with some strappy black sandals? Especially if you were on a date or something." She
looked me over. "Did you want to try a bigger size?"

"Um, no. It fits okay." There was no way I was buying a larger size. I would just lose the extra weight so I
could wear this one comfortably.

"Is there anything special coming up? A dance at
school, or a party or something?"

I don't know why Mom was even asking me. I'd
never attended a party (unless Zoe's birthday parties or my

own counted) or any type of social function at school—dances or otherwise.

"No, I don't think so," I told her, thinking she didn't want to pay for a haircut, jeans, and a little black dress. "I'd rather have the jeans anyway." I shut the door to the dressing room and changed back into my street clothes. We got in line and Mom was preparing to pay when she suddenly headed back to the dressing room. When she returned, she was holding the black dress.

"There's no need to waste a perfectly good dress," she told me. "Besides, it's on sale, and I still owe you for helping me with that dinner for Phil."

I smiled at her. New hair and new clothes. I couldn't have asked for a more amazing day.

Chapter

Ten

Zoe's mouth dropped in astonishment. "What have you done?" she asked, as I walked toward our lockers. I did a little twirl.

"Oh, do you like it?" I asked, a huge smile sweeping across my face.

She stared at me, her mouth gaping. "Um, yeah! It looks great. Different—I mean, I hardly recognized you."

I smiled. "Trust me, *that* is a good thing." The five-minute warning bell rang as I began switching books from my book bag to my locker and vice versa.

"Are you wearing eyeliner?" she asked, leaning closer and peering at my eyes.

"Yeah, does it look okay?"

She stood back. "It's fine, but what's with all the sudden changes?"

I pushed a strand of highlighted hair away from my eyes. "It's a long story," I confessed.

"Well, I hope you have time to tell it."

"There was a girls' night on Saturday."

"Your mother did this?"

"No, it wasn't my mother. It was more like…Bree's idea."

"*Bree Donnelly?*"

"Yeah. Chase apparently dropped her and she was upset…I mean, like, really upset. So Tabitha suggested we have a girls' night to make her feel better."

"Tabitha from the play," she confirmed.

"Yes. So we went to her house and Tabitha thought she should cut my hair, Erica highlighted it—sort of, Bree thought my eyebrows needed waxing, and well, I'm almost sixteen, so I thought it was time I started wearing makeup."

"But you never wear makeup," Zoe informed me.

I frowned. "And I thought it was time to change that. It doesn't look bad, does it?"

"No, it looks good."

"Okay then," I replied.

She paused for a moment. "But you hate girls' nights."

This wasn't the reaction I was expecting at all, and I was beginning to feel annoyed. "I did. I mean, I do. But you know, this one wasn't so bad."

"But look at you."

I slammed my locker door shut. "Honestly, Zoe, you act like I've made some huge mistake or something. It's hair dye and makeup. If it offends you that much I'll wash it off."

She looked surprised. I'd never raised my voice at her—ever. Until now, I'd never had a reason. I was the fol-

lower; the flower on the wall. Voiceless. "N-No," she
stammered. "It's not a mistake. It's just really different.
You look good. Really."

"Well, I feel good," I replied as we began walking toward homeroom. "I'm eating better and I'm exercising.
I'm actually a size smaller. Can you believe it? I just want
to look as good on the outside as I feel on the inside."

This seemed to appease her.

We walked in silence for a moment, watching as
everyone hurried toward their classrooms.

"So Chase dumped Bree, huh?"

"Yep."

"That's crazy. They were like, pre-engaged and everything."

"I know. What do you suppose happened?" I asked.

She pushed open the door to our homeroom and first
period math class. "Bree happened, that's what. He probably wanted someone who wasn't so high-maintenance.
She probably drove him nuts."

"Bree isn't that bad," I muttered as we found our seats
at the back of the room.

A look of surprise crossed her face. "Tell me you
aren't serious," Zoe admonished.

I dropped my bag to the floor, and lowered my voice.
"I've spent time with her. She's really not that bad."

"Not that bad? Wrenn, she is completely wicked."

"You don't even know her," I hissed.

Zoe's eyes narrowed. "And you guys are best friends
now? You've known her for what, five minutes?"

"I've known her long enough to know that she isn't

wicked. You should have seen her crying over Chase. It was like she was about to die."

Zoe rolled her eyes. "I'm sure her life is completely over, now that she's been dropped."

I smiled. "Not even. We're going to hook her up with Tad Owens."

"We?"

"Yeah. Me, Tabitha, and Erica."

"So you guys are all tight now, is that it?" she said with a laugh.

"No," I said, tucking a piece of stray highlighted hair behind my ear. "It's just that we spend a lot of time together. We see each other several nights a week. We have a lot in common."

"Do you do any work at these rehearsals?"

I stared at my best friend in disbelief. Was she serious? She had no idea how hard we were working. How hard *I* was working! How badly my arms and legs hurt after hours of dancing at rehearsals and workouts at home. Sure, we had fun sometimes, but it was a brutal schedule and a lot of exhausting effort! How could she say something like that? She was absolutely clueless!

I leaned over and unzipped my book bag, then pulled out my algebra book. "Trust me. Despite what you may think, it's not all fun and games," I stated, flipping to the day's lesson. The teacher began to call roll.

"I didn't mean to imply that you weren't working," Zoe whispered.

"Well, it sure sounded like it," I shot back.

"I'm sorry. I didn't mean it that way."

I turned my head and began reading up on the Pythagorean theorem. "It's fine," I mumbled.

There was no way I was going to let Zoe rain on my parade. This was all her idea anyway. Getting a part in the musical was the most exciting thing that had ever happened to me. I was having a blast, and things were finally changing for the better. As far as I was concerned, Zoe was just jealous.

"Hey, what's going on?"

I turned around just to be certain that the voice was addressing me and not someone else. "Oh, hey, Steven. Not much, what's going on with you?" My heart sank. Why is it that the only guy who paid attention to me was a complete loser? Why couldn't it be Chase, or John the Chorus Guy?

"Nothing. I wanted to check and see if you needed a ride to rehearsal tonight."

I continued loading my book bag. "No, my mom is going to take me. But thanks for the offer."

He held onto his bag and looked down at his feet. "Okay. I just wanted to check," he repeated.

I smiled and went back to work, but Steven continued to stand beside me, watching my every move.

After a long pause, he cleared his throat. "I also wanted to say that you look really great. You know, with your haircut and all. I almost didn't recognize you this morning."

I looked at him, wrinkling my nose. "You saw me this morning?"

"Yeah. My locker isn't far away, and our homerooms are near each other and all."

"Oh." I had no idea.

He readjusted his backpack. "Well, you look really good."

"Thank you." I stuffed my science book into my book bag and zipped it closed. More silence fell over us. "Okay, well I should go. Zoe is waiting for me," I told him.

"No problem, I have to get home anyway. I'll see you tonight, though."

"Okay."

As Steven walked away, I let out a huge sigh and shut my locker door.

"Hey chica," Tabitha said as she came toward me. "Wow, they did a number on you."

I swept aside my bangs. "Oh. It was my mom. She said my hair was too dark and dragged me to her stylist to even it out."

"Well, it looks awesome! Anyway, I just wanted to let you know that a group of us planned to hit Andy's this afternoon. Are you interested?"

I looked out at the parking lot, where Zoe was sitting in her car waiting for me. "Um. My best friend is driving me home, do you mind if she comes?"

"The more the merrier," she replied. "I'll see you there."

"Okay."

Tabitha took off and I began walking toward the exit,

staring at my reflection in the window. Already my face looked thinner. I mean, I could almost see cheekbones. My strict diet and exercise routine were finally taking effect, and I decided that the end result would be so worth it. I was getting there.

"What took you so long?" Zoe asked as I opened the car door. I removed that morning's Burger King wrapper from the seat.

"Steven stopped me," I told her.

She laughed. "He is so cute! And he has it so bad for you."

I rolled my eyes, finding the concept hard to believe. No one could have a crush on me. Not yet, anyway, and especially not a senior.

"Zoe, please. He's just being polite," I remarked.

It wasn't that I didn't want anyone to have a crush on me. It's just that I preferred it to be John the Chorus Guy. Bree, Tabitha, and Erica were trying so hard to set me up with him. And the more I thought about it, the more I liked the idea. I mean, he had to be at least a junior. And he was so cute. If people saw us together in the halls...I would be so freakin' popular.

I cleared my throat. "Did you want to stop for an orangeade this afternoon?" I asked.

She thought about this for a moment. "I guess we can. I hadn't planned on it," she said as she pulled out of the parking lot. "I have a painting waiting for me when I get home."

My face fell. "Oh, it doesn't matter. It's just that Tabitha said that a group of them were going to Andy's. She invited us."

"'Them' as in people in the musical?"

"Yeah. She said you could come along."

"Gee, thanks," she replied sarcastically.

I leaned back in the seat and folded my arms across my chest. "We don't have to go. It's not a big deal. I mean, I'm not the slightest bit social, anyway."

She sighed. "No. It's okay. We can go for a few minutes. I don't mind."

In my head, I let out a cheer "Cool. Thanks," I said, nonchalantly.

By the time we pulled into the parking lot, the others had already arrived. They were sitting at a huge table in the middle of the restaurant.

Tabitha immediately waved me over. "Hey! Pull up a couple of chairs."

"I'll order our drinks," Zoe said, as she walked over to the counter. Scales and calorie counts flashed through my mind, but I didn't stop her. I figured I'd just have a sip or two.

I grabbed two chairs from another table and sat down.

"So, Wrenn, which cartoon character do you think Mr. Pike looks more like: Wimpy or Mr. Wilson?" asked Tabitha.

"Mr. Wilson, definitely," I told them.

"See? That's what I said!" Tad Owens shouted. "No one else agrees with me."

"I agree with you," Erica began, "but that's just because I have no idea who Wimpy is."

"He was in 'Popeye,'" Tabitha said. "Didn't you watch cartoons as a child?"

"I'm sorry. I didn't watch cartoons about sailors. I was more into 'Winnie the Pooh,'" Erica retorted. "Still, I can't imagine that either character is flattering to Mr. Pike."

"Um, that's kind of the point," Tad offered.

Everyone burst into laughter as Zoe came to the table with our orangeades and sat down beside me.

"Thanks," I said. "Guys, this is my best friend, Zoe."

There was a round of "Hey's" and "How are you's."

"So, what do you think about Wrenn's new 'do?" Tabitha asked, to no one in particular.

I stole a glance in the direction of John the Chorus Guy. He was sitting by Erica, not paying me a bit of attention.

"Um, it looks good," Tad stated. "What did you do?"

"It was the result of a girls' night at Tabitha's," I explained.

"Tabitha cut my hair, too," Erica interjected, tossing her head from side to side.

"Glad I missed *that*," another one of the male cast members commented.

"Tell me about it," Tad replied.

My shoulders fell. Okay, so they weren't as impressed as I'd first hoped. But they were guys. Guys were clueless, I resolved. I took a sip of my orangeade, wondering how many jumping jacks it would take to burn off the calories.

"I hope Pikey doesn't make us do the school-yard scene again tonight," Erica commented, changing the subject. "Remember the Hemorrhoid Convention?"

126

The entire table burst into laughter again except for Zoe, who of course had no idea what was going on.

I fanned my face, trying to calm down. "Zoe, it was so funny. We were rehearsing this one scene, and the guys were just standing there with these looks on their faces." I burst out laughing again, and tried to finish. "Mr. Pike started waving his arms and cut the music, then shouted something about them looking like a Hemorrhoid Convention."

Zoe just stared at me, not amused in the least.

"You know, because obviously people at a Hemorrhoid Convention wouldn't be happy to be there. Pikey said it looked like the guys were in pain."

"Now we can't do that scene without laughing," Tabitha added. "It was absolutely hilarious. I will never forget that, like, ever."

"And anytime someone starts frowning or looks bored, we yell 'Hemorrhoid Convention!'" Erica cackled, waving her arms for effect.

I continued to laugh. "It was so funny. I thought I was going to die."

Zoe let out a polite chuckle, but it was obviously an inside joke. You just had to be there to appreciate it. I exhaled slowly.

Zoe was clearly uncomfortable. This just wasn't working for her. It was like trying to unite two completely different worlds. Zoe was my best friend, but I had new friends now, too. And I liked spending time with them. Still, it was pointless trying to mix the two. Sometimes life doesn't work that way. Zoe had no business at our table.

"I need to get home," I said, standing to my feet. "I have to be there when my little sister gets home."

"We'll see you tonight," Tabitha told me. "And it was nice meeting you, Zoe."

She smiled. "It was nice meeting you, too."

Everyone said good-bye and I swear I heard Tad say "Catch you later." *How amazing was he?* I let out a scream on the inside.

We left the building and headed toward Zoe's car. "They seem nice," she commented.

"Oh, they are. We have so much fun. But it's still hard work," I quickly added.

"I know," she replied. But there was that "tone" in her voice. That's what led me to believe she felt otherwise.

Chapter

Eleven

On Friday I watched as Karly and her best friend, Joy, jumped off the school bus.

"Joy is staying the night," Karly informed me as she walked into the kitchen. "Mom said it was okay."

I opened the refrigerator door. "Does it look like I care?" I asked.

"I was just saying." She began to raid the cabinets, and eventually pulled out a bag of potato chips and a box of chocolate chip cookies.

"Oh that's healthy," I taunted, with more than a hint of sarcasm in my voice.

"It's salty and sweet," Karly replied. "Eat a few potato chips, wash them down with cookies."

"Salty and sweet. Are you serious? Do you even know how many calories are in those things? Eat a handful of each and that's it. You've already maxed out what you're supposed to eat in one day. And let's not even talk about the salt and sugar."

"What are you? A walking nutritionist?" she asked. "We have fast metabolisms."

I looked at Joy, who only shrugged her shoulders. "Sounds good to me," she said, brushing off my warning.

"Okay, whatever." I continued searching the refrigerator for something that was actually good for me. No way was I falling prey to Karly's "salty-and-sweet" theory. The extra pounds would reappear overnight.

"Your hair looks great," Joy stated, looking in my direction. "What did you do to it?"

"Cut and colored," I replied.

"And your face—it looks thinner."

"Oh, yeah," Karly broke in. "She's lost like, an obscene amount of weight via jumping jacks."

Joy's mouth fell open in amazement. "Really? I thought you looked skinnier. Not that you were big to begin with or anything, because you weren't," she quickly added.

"It's okay. I just decided it was time for a change, that's all."

"Well, you look good."

Karly snorted. "She freaks me out. I mean, she actually wears makeup now. It's like some alien has taken over her body. At night I hear her jumping up and down. I'm surprised the entire floor hasn't caved in with her working out so much."

I rolled my eyes, preparing to toss a verbal dart, just as the phone in the kitchen rang. Had I known what was coming, I wouldn't have answered it.

"Wrenn, honey, I'm so sorry, but I'm going to be late tonight," Mom's voice came through the phone. "Today was just awful; Mitzi is driving me completely up the wall. I really need to stay here and get some work done. Are you okay for dinner?"

I frowned. "Yeah, we can handle dinner, but I have rehearsal at seven, remember?"

"I know, I'm sorry. Can you give Zoe a call? It's just this once—I promise."

"Zoe is going to a play with her parents," I informed her.

"Well, what if I called Phil? I'm sure he'd be happy to pick you up."

"No, that's all right," I quickly stated. A ride from Phil? I'd rather die. "I'm sure I can find a ride from someone. I'll make a few phone calls."

"Thanks, Wrenn. Just make sure Karly eats real food for dinner, okay? Is Joy there?"

"Yes."

"Okay. Well tell them I'll be home no later than 8:30, and not to open the door for anyone. Do you think you can get a ride home, too?"

I let out a huge sigh. "I suppose."

She seemed relieved. "Thank you. It's only this once, I swear."

When I hung up the phone, I relayed Mom's message. "She'll be home at 8:30. Don't open the door for anyone and eat real food for dinner. That means your salty-and-sweet trick won't cut it."

I walked back to my room and picked up the phone. Zoe was the first person I called. She confirmed that she was going out with her parents. I tried Tabitha next, but there was no answer. I didn't know Erica's number and Bree's was unlisted.

I could skip rehearsal, but would this constitute an emergency? No, and there was so much to do. I couldn't bail, not tonight. Who else could I call? Mr. Pike, maybe? My nose wrinkled in disgust. No, that would be way too weird.

With rehearsal starting in an hour, I threw myself on the bed, defeated. No one on earth could pick me up. A car and a license. Why were those two things so hard to come by?

I began to rationalize. I could call Phil...but honestly, I'd rather miss rehearsal than ask him for help, even though I knew he would think it was just "terrific!" Yuck.

I stared at the ceiling and tried to see shapes in the texture. There was one other option, but I would never live it down. No. If I called Steven, he'd think I liked him. At school I spent the entire day trying to dodge him. Was he really my only hope? I thought about this for a moment before deciding. Ugh. My life was officially over.

I rolled off the bed and began to dig through my purse. I finally found the phone number Steven had given me a million hours ago. Reluctantly, I dialed his number. When his mother picked up the phone, she seemed pleasantly surprised to hear a girl's voice on the other end. Of course she was. What girl in her right mind would call Steven?

"Can I speak to Steven, please?"

"Of course. May I ask who's calling?"

"It's Wrenn. We're working on the musical together," I explained.

"Okay, hold on one second."

I sat patiently while his mother called him. I heard them whispering, and seconds later a breathless Steven picked up the phone.

"Hello?"

"Hey, Steven, it's Wrenn." *I would never live this down.* "My mom is working late tonight and I was wondering if you could pick me up on your way to rehearsal."

"No problem. Where do you live?"

I gave him the directions, and to my utter dismay learned that he lived only a few blocks down the road; it was a mere five minutes away, if that.

Not wanting to make small talk, I got off the phone as soon as I could. After hanging up, I hurried into the bathroom and began touching up my makeup.

For the record, my mom practically freaked out when she saw me rummaging through her makeup stash in her bathroom. She gave me whatever I wanted—foundation, eyeliner, lipstick. She seemed so pleased when she first saw me wearing mascara. Like, maybe I was her daughter after all. She even threw in a ten for new lip gloss. Amazing, right?

I was still running sections of hair through my flat iron when the doorbell rang. I checked my watch. *Of course Steven would be early,* I thought to myself.

I let him inside, saying, "I'm not finished getting

ready, but you can watch TV or something. I'll only be a few minutes."

"That's fine. I just, you know, wanted to make sure I found your place okay," he replied.

I gave him a polite smile and returned to my bathroom, silently cursing my mother for doing this to me. Working late? Please. She could have been home in plenty of time to take me to rehearsal if she really wanted. I'll bet if she had made plans with Phil, she'd have found her way back early. The thought disgusted me.

When I returned to the living room, Steven was watching Mitzi Monroe do a special live report on Channel 8. He stood up.

"You look great," he said, as if we were on a date or something. "I know I've told you a hundred times, but you really do look different, with your hair and all. I mean, you were pretty before, but now you're—" he trailed off, unable to finish the sentence.

I felt those pink undertones creep into my cheeks. What was worse, his words made me feel warm and tingly inside. It was nice to have someone compliment me for a change—even if it was only Steven. "Thank you. That's really sweet."

Neither one of us moved right away. I could feel him watching me, but I didn't dare look back at him. Instead, I pretended to be deeply intrigued by a dark spot on our beige carpet. I rubbed it a few times with my shoe; as if the rubber soles could make it disappear completely—which was what I wanted to do at that exact moment. Honestly, I could kill my mother for abandoning me like this.

134

"Well, I guess we should get going," Steven finally said.

I locked the front door and walked out to his black Jeep Wrangler. I thanked him as he opened the door for me.

"No problem," he said, then walked around to the driver's side and climbed in.

"I really like your car," I said.

"Thanks. My dad bought it for me last year. He's always had a thing for Jeeps."

"So he's letting you live his dream?"

"Pretty much," he answered. "I don't mind though. I love them as much as he does. So what about you? You can't be too far away from sixteen and a driver's license."

"I turn sixteen next month, but I can't get a car until I get a job and save some money."

"I hear you. So when will you actually turn sixteen?"

"On the twenty-first," I replied, staring out the window, watching as the streets of my neighborhood turned into the highway.

"Hmm. I'll have to make a note of that."

I smiled politely.

"So besides singing and acting, what do you like to do in your free time?"

"Um, well, that's pretty much it," I said with a shrug. "I play the piano."

"Cool. I'm teaching myself to play the guitar."

I turned toward him in surprise. He played the guitar? "Wow." I said. "We could start our own band. All we need is a drummer with spiky hair and a lip ring."

He laughed. "That would be awesome." He looked at me, and for a moment our eyes locked.

Ugh! What was wrong with me? I can't go around suggesting things like starting a band with this guy. Steven will think that I actually like him! I can't give him the wrong impression.

I quickly changed the subject, praying that he would forget everything I'd said by the time we reached the school parking lot. Honestly, why did I have to smile so much?

We kept to "safe" topics for the rest of the ride: school, the play, etc., and to my relief, no one saw us arrive together. I'd already hatched a plan in my mind. If someone I knew was in the parking lot, I was going to lean down and pretend I was looking for something in my purse. I could only imagine what Bree Donnelly would have said if she knew that I'd gotten a ride to rehearsal with Steven James. Forget about being popular. I'd never live it down—ever. But I was safe for the time being, so I scurried inside before anyone linked the two of us together.

Halfway through rehearsal, I found myself sitting with Erica. I took a breath and managed to ask how it was going with John the Chorus Guy.

"John the Chorus Guy?" she asked. "Oh, right. He is *so* cute."

"Has he said anything about me?"

"Um, yeah. We've talked about you some. I really think you should go over and talk to him, though."

I watched him rehearsing on stage. "But I don't know what to say," I confessed.

"Stick to what you know. You're both in the play, so talk about that," she advised. "I mean, I can only build you up so much. The rest is up to you. His scene is almost over. When he sits down, just go over to him and start talking." She shrugged, as if it were that simple.

I inhaled deeply. "Okay. I can do that."

It was a good idea, I guess. I mean, I watched him constantly, hoping that every time he left the stage he would come to sit down beside me. "This is it!" I thought, whenever he walked in my direction. But each time I was completely disappointed when I discovered that the reason he walked in my direction wasn't to talk to me at all. And it bothered me, not knowing what he and Erica were talking and laughing about all the time. I guess she was right. I had to take matters into my own hands.

After what seemed like ages, Mr. Pike sent the chorus to their seats and called another group to the stage. I took a deep breath and walked over to where John was seated. My heart felt like it would explode as I wiped my sweaty palms on my jeans.

"Hi," I said as I sat down behind him.

He turned around and looked at me. "Hey," he replied. "Wrenn, right?"

"Yeah. And you're John."

He raised his eyebrow, and stared at me for a moment. "Um, it's Jared, actually."

I felt a scream well up inside me. Jared? John the Chorus Guy's name was really *Jared*? And just *how* did that minute detail slip past Erica? I could have killed her, honestly. How stupid did that make me sound? This whole time I thought his name was *John*!

My face turned red with embarrassment. "I'm sorry. It's nice to meet you John...um, I mean, Jared. Sorry." UGH! What was wrong with me?

His attention returned to the people on stage.

"So," I continued, you're really good at this. Have you done it before?"

"A musical?"

"Yeah. I mean, you make it look so easy—like you've done it a million times."

"Oh yeah, well, I'm used to it. I'm in the chorus."

"A community chorus?"

He shook his head. "No. The high school chorus."

"Oh, cool," I said. *My high school had a chorus? How did I manage to miss this stuff?* I wondered. Silence fell between us again. It was obviously up to me to keep the conversation flowing. Apparently he and Erica had more in common to talk about.

"This is my first musical," I confessed.

He turned in my direction. "I'm sorry?"

Ugh. So Jared the Chorus Guy wasn't even paying attention to me. No big deal. "Oh, I just said this was the first musical I've been in."

"That's okay," he replied. "You have to start somewhere."

"Yeah, I guess." I shrank back in my seat.

Mr. Pike cut the music and faced the audience. "Okay people, we're done for tonight."

I muttered a "good-bye" to Jared, who didn't seem to hear me, and walked to the other side of the auditorium. I picked up my purse. How stupid was I? I didn't stand a chance with him now. What were Erica and Bree thinking? No guy would ever like me.

"You ready?" Steven asked, interrupting my thoughts.

"Yeah, I am." *You don't know how ready,* I silently added.

We walked out to his Jeep and climbed in. We were quiet for most of the trip home. I told him that practicing wore me out, but the truth was, I didn't feel like talking to anyone just then.

When we reached my driveway he offered to walk me to the door.

"No, that isn't really necessary," I said.

"Come on, it isn't a big deal." He climbed out of the car and followed me up the walk. Mom was home and Phil was here. I would never live this down. Could my life get any worse?

The porch light blinked on while I was still searching for my keys. The front door opened and Mom greeted us.

"Hey," she said, smiling. "You're back."

I rolled my eyes. "Mom, this is Steven. He gave me a ride to rehearsal."

"It's nice to meet you, Mrs. Scott," he said, shaking her hand.

"Thank you so much for picking up Wrenn. I don't usually have to work as late as I did tonight. Won't you come in for a while?"

I threw her a look. "Well, it's kind of late; he probably wants to get home," I offered.

My mother threw a look back at me; it was a look that demanded that I go along with her suggestion—or else.

I turned to Steven. "You're welcome to come in if you'd like. You know, if you won't get into trouble or anything."

"Sure, a few minutes would be okay."

Of course he would say yes, I thought, rolling my eyes. We followed Mom into the living room.

"Phil, this is Wrenn's friend, Steven."

Phil stood up to meet him. I saw Steven clench his jaw as his hand met Phil's. That signature, finger-smashing handshake. I smirked, even though I really wanted to laugh out loud.

"Terrific! It's nice to meet you," he said.

"Phil works with me down at Channel 8. Can I get you something to drink?"

"Sure, thanks. Whatever you have is fine," Steven replied.

The two of us sat down on the couch.

"Wrenn, your hair looks terrific!" Phil stated. "Your mother told me you changed it, but I didn't realize it was this dramatic. I hardly would have recognized you on the street."

"When I saw her at school, I could have sworn she was a completely different person. She really looks great," Steven added.

I blushed and thanked them both for the compliment, just as Mom returned with our drinks. "So, Steven, tell me about yourself."

"Well, I'm a senior this year, and I've been accepted

to Northwestern. I want to major in communications and broadcasting. I will probably go into production and maybe management. I love working behind the scenes and helping to make things happen."

"You should stop by Channel 8 sometime if you're interested in production," Mom said. "I'm sure you could get an internship this summer." She turned her attention to Phil. "We should check into that for him."

"That would be great. I've worked on plays at school and in the community, but some broadcast production experience at a real TV station would be awesome."

"Well, I will definitely ask around and let you know," she said.

"So how is the musical going?" Phil asked me.

"Good," I replied. "Everything seems to be coming together."

"Wrenn is amazing," Steven supplied. "You should see her, and hear her for that matter. She has the most awesome voice."

My face flushed and my cheeks burned with embarrassment. Why did he have to go on and on about me like this?

A wide smile crossed my mother's face. "Oh, you should hear her sing 'Over the Rainbow.' It's like listening to an angel. I want to cry every time."

I buried my face in my hands. "Mom, please," I moaned.

"I've never heard you sing, Wrenn," Phil commented. "Why don't you sing something for us now?"

"That's all right. I'd rather not."

"Come on. We're all friends here," he replied.

No, we are not, I thought to myself, *and if you do not butt out....* "Actually, my throat is a little sore from singing so much. I really need to rest my vocal cords after all of this rehearsing," I told him, repeating something I'd heard Bree say a few days earlier. This seemed to appease them, and Phil didn't argue.

"Well, I should get going. Thank you for the drink, Mrs. Scott," Steven said, getting up.

"Please, call me Kerri. And thank you for picking up Wrenn," Mom replied, standing with him.

"It was really no problem. I'm right down the road, so anytime you need a ride, give me a call."

"That's so nice of you!" she said, glancing at me.

Not two seconds after she shut the door, a million questions flew, including "Why on earth" did I not like him?

"Mom, please, he's just a friend."

"You don't have any feelings for him?"

"No."

"But he seems so nice," she said. I could almost see the wheels turning in her head. How could she arrange for us to get together? What if she *made* it so he had to pick me up again? What could she plan that would best suit the occasion?

"He's nice, but he's really not my type," I explained.

"Yeah, you've been saying that a lot lately." I knew she was referring to what I'd said about Phil. And she probably also was suggesting that if she could make an exception, so could I.

"He's just a friend," I confirmed.

"Well, I think he's cute."

Even Phil commented on how "terrific" he seemed. He said that Steven reminded him of himself at that age.

I could only roll my eyes in response. Thank you, Dr. Phil. I'll *really* go after him now.

Chapter

Twelve

"So, he said he wanted to meet me again," Zoe informed me, as she dipped a French fry in ketchup.

I picked apart my burger, only pretending to take a bite every now and then. "Did he ever explain what happened the last time?" I asked, completely annoyed.

She thought about this. "No, not exactly. But he called and apologized. He said something came up and he was sorry."

"And you forgave him on the spot, and decided you still wanted to meet him after he stood you up and didn't even give you a valid reason?"

"Well, I didn't forgive him right away," she explained. "I took a few days off and didn't email him. I was almost ready to call it quits," she assured me. "But then I realized I missed him. I missed emailing him and talking online. He sounded really sorry."

"Can I be honest with you?" I asked.

"Not if you're going to tell me you don't think it's a good idea for us to meet."

"I don't think it's such a good idea for you to meet," I confirmed.

"How did I know *that* was coming? Wrenn, we've been through this before. I'll make sure it's safe. You can come with me again. We'll meet in a public place. It's not a big deal."

"But you don't even *know* him!" I cried for like, the millionth time.

"And can I tell *you* something? I do feel like I know him. I know him well enough to know that I like him — a lot."

"So you've said," I replied, sarcastically.

"No, I mean, I feel like I really, really know him. Like he's right under my nose already. I feel like I brush past him in the hall, or see him on the way to school. I feel like he's right there, and that I could just reach out and touch him if I wanted to — if I knew who he was."

I shook my head in disbelief. "Are you dehydrated or something?"

Zoe snorted. "I'm not dehydrated. You just don't want me to be happy."

The bell jingled as the door to Andy's swung open. I sat straight up. My eyes widened. "You'll never guess who just walked in," I whispered.

Zoe turned around in her seat.

"Don't look at him!" I hissed, grabbing her arm. "You're making it too obvious."

"Who is it?"

"Chase Cunningham! I think he's coming this way," I squealed. "Act cool."

I looked down at my plate and began to sip my drink. Chase continued to walk in our direction, slowing only when he reached our table.

"Hey, Wrenn. Hey, Zoe. How's it going?" he asked.

I opened my mouth to respond, but instead of saying, "Fine, Chase, how are you?" I choked on air, and began to cough violently.

"What she means to say is that we're fine," Zoe supplied, as I patted my chest and downed the rest of my orangeade. "How are you?"

"Good. I just dropped in for a minute. Do you mind?" he asked, as he pulled out the empty chair beside me.

"Not at all," Zoe said.

"I can't stay long. I called my order in but it's not ready yet. It's pretty packed in here," he said, looking around.

"Well, you know how Saturday afternoons are," Zoe continued. "I mean, this is like, the only decent place in town to get a burger."

She leaned her elbows on the table, and offered him her typical dazzling smile. I hated her. She looked so completely relaxed. How on earth could she be so smooth in front of Chase Cunningham? The temperature in the restaurant rose twenty degrees when he walked through the door, and she remained cool as ice.

"So how's the musical coming along?" he asked me.

"Oh, it's great," I stammered. "It's really coming along."

"That's good. I don't really have an inside track anymore," he commented.

"Yeah, we heard," Zoe told him. "I'm sorry to hear about you and Bree."

He snickered and leaned back in his chair, interlocking his hands behind his head. "Don't be sorry. It's better this way. Bree does her thing and I do mine." He sat forward again. "So, Wrenn, your hair looks great," he said, changing the subject.

I couldn't believe he actually noticed. I began to blush, tucking a few pieces behind my ear. "Thanks. It was the result of a girls' night. Bree thought I should...." I trailed off, unable to finish the sentence. What a stupid thing to say! I screamed on the inside. What if he didn't *want* to talk about Bree, or hear her name ever again? I'm a walking reminder!

"Bree thought you should change it?" he finished. "That doesn't surprise me. So tell me, did you spend the entire night bashing me, or just part of it?" He nudged me with his arm, smiling.

Was he *flirting* with me? Ack! "We didn't bash you the whole night," I said with a smile. "I mean, I didn't bash you at all," I clarified. "I just listened."

"And you didn't stick up for me?" He brought his hand to his chest, pretending to be hurt.

"Well, it was Bree," I stammered. "She did most of the bashing. If it helps, I didn't believe anything she said."

"It's okay, I'm just teasing," he said. "I have a little sister. I know how girls' nights work."

"That's because he knows how *everything* works. He has *all* the answers," confirmed a voice beside me.

When I looked up, there she stood, her arms folded

across her chest. "Bree," I said nervously, "what's going on?" I'd been so wrapped up in our conversation, I hadn't even seen her come in. She literally appeared out of nowhere. I had to wonder what, exactly, she'd heard.

"I could ask you the same question," she said, her smile forced.

"We were just eating," I began.

Chase stood up and pushed his chair under the table. "It's okay. I'm leaving."

I wanted to reach out and grab his arm, and tell him he didn't have to go anywhere. This *wasn't* a big deal.

"Why the rush?" Bree asked, her eyes narrowing.

"Um, because my order is ready. I just sat down for a minute."

She smiled. "I'll bet. This isn't really your territory, you know."

"Territory? See? That's your problem, Bree. You're a control freak. Well, you know what? Zoe and Wrenn are my friends now, and I'll talk to them whenever and wherever I want. For once in your life, Bree, chill." He turned his attention back to us. "I'll catch you guys later."

Chase picked up his coat and walked away.

Bree glared at Zoe, then turned to me. "Wrenn, we seriously need to have a chat. Can I give you a ride?"

It seemed more like a demand than an offer; there was no room to argue. "Um, sure. I guess," I said, glancing in Zoe's direction. "Is that okay?" I asked her. "I mean, we were done here, right?"

She balled up her napkin and threw it in the red plastic burger basket. "Yeah, obviously."

148

Zoe paid for her meal, then bolted out of Andy's without even saying good-bye. I waited for Bree while she ordered a sweet tea.

"So, what's *her* problem?" Bree asked as we walked toward her red Mustang—a convertible, no less.

"I don't know," I breathed. "She's annoyed with me."

She obviously wasn't interested. "Sad. So, what was going on at the table?"

I climbed into the passenger's side and buckled my seat belt. "I have no clue. Chase just walked over and sat down." I waved my hand for effect, as if this solidified the sheer absurdity of the entire episode.

She put her car in reverse and backed out of the space. "It's so strange. He doesn't even know you." She hardly paused at the end of the driveway before pulling out into traffic. I heard a car horn behind us.

I frowned. "I think he does. I mean, he recognized us a few weeks ago at Andy's. He was picking up dinner for the two of you after rehearsal," I added, hoping it would jog a memory.

"Chase never picked me up from rehearsal, and I go straight home. So obviously he wasn't getting dinner for me."

I sucked in my breath. "Oh. Well, that's what he told us. He said he recognized me from rehearsal. I figured he dropped you off and saw me one day, or you had talked about me to him or something."

Bree snorted, and shook her head. "No. He's such a liar."

"Well, nothing bad was said, I promise. We were just

talking about the musical, and he made a comment about my hair, and I told him that we had a girls' night and you thought it would look good like this."

"What else did he say about me?"

"N-Nothing," I stammered. "That was it. He just said that you did your thing and he did his."

She rolled her eyes in response. "That is *so* typical."

I stared out the window, watching the stores pass by. I couldn't believe that Bree Donnelly was actually giving me a ride. And even though she was technically grilling me, still, I was riding with her in her car. I subtly pinched my leg just to make sure it wasn't just a dream.

"So guess who's taking me out for Valentine's Day?" she said, interrupting my thoughts.

Unlike Zoe, Bree actually gave me the opportunity to guess. "Tad?"

"Yes!" she squealed with delight. "He called me the other night after rehearsal and asked if I wanted to get together. I tried not to sound too excited though, I mean, I've only been flirting and dropping hints since the second Chase and I broke up. It was about time he asked." She glanced over her shoulder and changed lanes.

"That is so awesome!" I cried, genuinely happy for her.

"I know. I adore Valentine's Day. I would have died if I didn't have a date, you know? I mean, who doesn't have a date on Valentine's Day?"

"Oh, I know," I agreed, nodding my head. I thought back to all of my previous Valentine's Days. I'd never gone out on any of them, and unless something drastic happened with Jared between now and then, this Valentine's Day would be no different. Still, I could never let Bree know that.

"So, where do you live again?"

I pointed her in the right direction. She leaned forward and turned up the volume on her radio, the strains of a bouncy pop song filling the air.

"Can you look in my purse and grab my lip gloss?" she asked.

I reached down and pulled up a little brown Prada bag. I unzipped it and began to sift through the contents. It was filled with lipstick tubes, a cell phone, tissues, her wallet, a variety of hair accessories, and a mini-bottle of hair spray. It was like an entire cosmetics counter hidden away in her little leather pocketbook.

"Um, which one?" I asked.

"It's pink. From Sephora," she replied.

I continued to rummage around until I finally found it. I reached over and handed the tube of lipstick to her. As I was closing the bag, something else caught my eye.

I pulled out the white box. "Laxatives?"

"Oh, that's just for emergencies."

"What kind of emergencies?" I asked, checking the brand name and reading the back of the box.

She shrugged her shoulders. "In case I eat too much. What doesn't stay in your body can't make you fat, right?"

I stared at her in disbelief. Was this her secret? Bree Donnelly used laxatives to maintain that perfect little figure of hers? I shook my head, wondering why I hadn't thought of using them before.

I felt completely guilty about leaving the restaurant with Bree when I was really with Zoe, so I made a quick phone call as soon as I walked in the door to make sure everything was okay between us. According to Zoe, it was "fine."

"I'm glad we were able to hang out for a while," she said. "I feel like I haven't seen you since this play began."

"Of course you see me. You take me home every day after school."

"I know, but that's pretty much it."

"Well, once the play is over, things will be back to normal," I told her. I realized that what little life I had during these last few months would completely disappear when the show was over.

"I know. So what's the deal with Steven now?" she asked, changing the subject. "You never mentioned him today."

I twirled the phone cord around my fingers. "Same old, same old. Still stalking me. Ever since I called for that ride he's stopped me like, every day."

"Why don't you give him a chance?" she asked.

"Because he's Steven. Because he isn't my type," I explained.

"And what exactly *is* your type?"

I had to think for a minute. It was one thing to know

which guys weren't my type, but a completely different story to know which ones were. "I don't know. Guys like Tad Owens and Chase Cunningham. Guys who are good-looking and popular."

"How do you know they're your type? You barely know them."

"I just know. I could see myself dating one of them before I could see myself with Steven."

"You mean you'd *rather* date them than Steven," she declared. "Well, I think you should give him a chance. He seems really sweet."

I rolled my eyes. It was so easy for her to say that. She didn't have a geek following her around all the time. If she did, she would feel completely different. "That's okay," I stated. "But speaking of Chase, what was up with him today? I mean, how completely random was that?"

"I know!" she cried. "He just came over and sat down like he'd known us forever. I thought Bree was going to blow a gasket. So what did she say on your little joyride?"

"Nothing. She just asked what we were talking about. She didn't think Chase knew us."

"Well, he doesn't, really," she replied.

I smiled. "Maybe he has a crush on one of us," I suggested.

"I think he was just being nice." My smile faded. That was Zoe…the voice of reason.

I turned myself around in my computer chair. That wasn't exactly the reaction I'd hoped for. This was the second time Chase had confronted us and carried on a conversation. He knew me from the play—he said so himself.

153

And when he came to the table he sat down beside *me*. I knew it was a long shot, but I couldn't help but think to myself, what if Chase actually likes me? By dropping this little hint, I was hoping Zoe would see the same thing, but it was obvious she didn't. I changed the subject.

"So anyway, Tad is taking Bree out for Valentine's Day," I continued.

"That's fascinating," she replied, with more than a hint of sarcasm in her voice.

"It *is* fascinating. I'm glad they're together. She took the whole breakup pretty hard," I supplied.

"She seemed to bounce back quickly enough to me."

"Well, you should have seen her at the rehearsal, after he told her. She was like, freaking out," I explained, re-membering Bree's red eyes and smeared makeup.

"Hence, the girls' night."

"Exactly."

I wasn't even going to pretend to understand Zoe's interest in Bree and the whole girls' night I'd experienced without her. It was true, I had been spending more time with my "play friends" lately, but that didn't mean I was-n't still Zoe's best friend. I don't know why she was being so weird about this whole thing. I mean really, get over it already.

"Look," I began, "if you're worried about my hang-ing out with Bree and Tabitha and everyone, don't. We get along because of the play, that's it."

"Bree Donnelly is the last person I'm worried about," Zoe said, snorting. "I'm more worried about you."

I wondered where she was going with this. "Worried about me? Why?"

"Because you're like, totally smitten with her and her entire life."

I sat up, my shoulders squared. "No, I'm not!"

"Yes, you are. You were obsessed before you even entered her little group. Now that you're there, you're doing everything you can to make sure you stay there. Even if it means ditching those of us who are your *real* friends."

"Hel-lo! I am so *not* part of Bree's group."

"Well, if you aren't, you're working overtime to get there. You don't even look like the same person anymore. Why can't you just be yourself?"

I couldn't believe she was saying this. Of all people, she should have been more supportive. "I *am* being myself," I replied angrily. "You're just jealous because I have other people to hang out with and don't have as much time for you."

There, I'd said it. The truth had finally come out: Zoe was jealous of my new friends. It was that simple.

"I have plenty to do, thank you. And excuse me if I'm being old-fashioned here, but I don't think you should have to change your entire appearance to get people to like you."

I closed my eyes and shook my head, trying to make her understand. "Zoe, they liked me *before* I colored my hair and lost weight. I do have a little bit of talent, you know. I am worth *something*. And for your information, my appearance hasn't changed that much."

"Please. Have you looked in the mirror lately? The hair. The makeup. The weight loss. You are *not* the Wrenn Scott I used to know."

"Look," I said plainly. "I know you don't understand where I'm coming from, but all I've ever wanted is to be pretty and popular. You know how important it is to me. I can't believe that I'm finally making some headway, and you're trying to bring me down. You should be happy for me."

"I'm not trying to bring you down. I'm just trying to figure out what happened to my best friend," she retorted.

My jaw tightened. How do you even respond to something like that? She had it all wrong. I mean, just because I made a few changes didn't mean I was a different person. What was her deal?

"I have to go," I said, after a few moments of silence.

Zoe exhaled into the phone. "Wrenn, I'm not mad at you. I'm sorry that I went off."

"It's fine," I told her. But really, it wasn't. "I'll see you at school." I didn't wait for a response, and just slammed the phone into the receiver.

Chapter

Thirteen

It's safe to say that Valentine's Day is *not* my favorite holiday. Every year the popular girls are showered with cards and flowers, stuffed animals, and red and pink balloons. It was every loser's worst nightmare. Girls even passed around chocolates from heart-shaped boxes, in class, whenever the teacher wasn't looking.

A week had passed since my blowup with Zoe, and things had returned to semi-normal between us. Ultimately, I decided that if she didn't like the new me, then she'd just have to get over it. So far, she was getting over it.

Zoe met me in class, breathless, barely missing the late bell. "You will never guess what I just got."

From her tone and frantic panting, I knew it couldn't be anything from her parents—unlike my own mother, who used to send me things on Valentine's Day just so I wouldn't be disappointed when no one else did.

"What?"

"Roses. Six of them."

I cocked an eyebrow. "Really? Who are they from?"

"That's the best part! They're from Sk8trGuy," she said, a bit too loudly. "I found them at my locker!" The teacher glared at us from the front of the room, forcing us to lower our voices.

"How did he know your name?" I whispered.

"I don't know. But the note said he'll meet me at my car this afternoon. Wrenn, he goes to school here, and he knows who I am!"

"No way!" I exclaimed in disbelief.

Way! Zoe was ultra-hyper for the rest of the school day, and as soon as the final bell rang, she raced to her locker, completely packing her bag before I even caught up with her.

"I am so freakin' nervous!" she cried. "I cannot believe I'm finally going to meet him!"

"So what are you waiting for?"

"I don't know. I have so many butterflies in my stomach right now, it's not even funny."

"Well, you look great, so you should go before he decides to stand you up again."

The smile that was plastered across her face disappeared immediately. "That was so not necessary," she growled.

I laughed. "I'm kidding. He'll be there, and he'll be everything you thought he'd be and more. It'll be a match made in heaven. Now go…but if you're missing when I get out there, I'm not taking responsibility."

"Whatever, I'm going. Just give me a few minutes, okay?"

Zoe took a deep breath, turned on her heel, and walked out the side door.

I took my time organizing my books and cleaning out excess trash from my locker. I checked my watch, rearranged a few snapshots that were posted on the inside of my locker door, and then checked my watch again.

"Hey, what's going on?" a voice called from behind me. I turned to see Tabitha.

"Oh, hey. Nothing much. What's going on with you?"

"Not a whole lot. Just seriously depressed," she said, pulling her hair back into a ponytail. "I think I'm the only girl in the entire school who doesn't have a Valentine."

"Nope, there're two of us," I told her. "But I know what you mean. I was kind of hoping that something would have happened with Jared by now."

She blinked a few times before replying. "Oh. Right. I thought you knew about that," she mumbled, looking uncomfortable.

"Knew about what?"

"Jared a.k.a. John the Chorus Guy. I, um, think he's seeing someone."

My stomach plummeted. "You *think* he's seeing someone, or you *know* he is?" I asked.

"I'm sorry, Wrenn, I thought you knew."

I tucked my hair behind my ears. "It's okay. I mean, he never really paid attention or talked to me."

"I know, but I completely forgot that we talked about setting the two of you up." She sounded sincere and genuinely sorry that it hadn't worked out between us.

"It's no big deal," I replied, with a shrug.

"I'm glad you aren't upset. And you really shouldn't hold it against Erica," she added. "I think it took her by surprise, too."

Wow! So Erica was dating Jared now. The girl who was supposed to be in on the whole "Let's hook up Wrenn and John the Chorus Guy" plan had actually stolen him for herself. Classic. I forced myself to smile.

"Erica is a sweetheart," I lied. "I couldn't hold something like that against her. I mean, when you like someone, you like them, right?"

"Exactly. Anyway, I'm sorry you had to find out like this. I would have told you sooner, only I thought you already knew. He sent her like, two dozen roses. Can you believe it?"

"That's awesome," I told her in the most convincing voice I could manage. I was sure she believed me; I mean, I'd almost convinced myself. And who would have guessed anything was going on between the two of them? They only talked and laughed together all the time at rehearsals. I mean, she didn't even tell me his name was really *Jared*. She actually encouraged me to call him the wrong name. I could have smacked myself for being so naive and dense. I should have seen it coming, and I felt absolutely ridiculous and stupid for not realizing sooner that something was going on between them.

I checked my watch again. I decided that Zoe and Sk8trGuy'd had plenty of time together by now. And I wasn't waiting at this school a second longer. As far as I was concerned, Valentine's Day was so *over*. "Okay, well, I have to run, but I'll see you at rehearsal tomorrow night," I called to Tabitha before heading toward the door.

It was freezing, and it looked as if it would snow at any moment. What an awesome Friday. The guy I liked was dating someone else, and I had no stake in the sea of red and pink flowers and heart-shaped boxes of chocolate; I had no one to plan a romantic evening with. I mean, Mr. Pike had even canceled tonight's rehearsal. Now the only thing I had to look forward to was a night at home, alone.

I crossed the parking lot and headed over to Zoe's car, only vaguely curious about her "mystery man."

When I looked over, I could see her standing close to some guy, but his back was turned. He was tall, and definitely hot from the rear. She smiled as he leaned down to kiss her.

My eyes rolled in protest. Great. As if my afternoon wasn't miserable enough, I had to endure an entire ride home hearing "Sk8trGuy" this and "Sk8trGuy" that, and "I can't believe he turned out to be so and so."

From the way they were practically making out, it was obvious that Zoe found him attractive. Apparently he was everything she'd imagined him to be. Again, perfect. My life reeked in comparison.

As I closed in on them, Zoe pulled away and looked in my direction. When Sk8trGuy turned around, it was all I could do to keep walking straight ahead and not sprawl face-first onto the cold black asphalt of the parking lot.

He looked at me as I approached them. "Good to see you again," he said, smiling.

My body went completely numb, turning into a puddle of mush at the sound of his voice.

I tucked my hair behind my ears. "Hey," I replied, as

cheerfully as I could manage. But what I really wanted to do was run home, throw myself on my bed, and cry until this whole vile day was over.

"Can you believe it?" Zoe cried. "He knew who I was the entire time! I told you I felt like he was close by—and he was. I was passing him every day and I didn't even know it!"

I produced a half-smile. "That's awesome." *Ugh, that was weak.* I tried to brighten my smile, and at least *pretend* to be sincere.

It was the least I could do. Zoe was happy; she'd snagged the guy of everyone's dreams. What were the odds? I mean, seriously. I never expected to be standing there, outside in the cold, on Valentine's Day—by myself—watching my best friend hug Chase Cunningham good-bye. It was like, the *highlight* of my life. Not.

The rest of the afternoon I tried my best not to be jealous, even when it started to rain. But really, Zoe and Chase? How perfect was this? My best friend was dating the first guy of my dreams, Bree had the second, and Erica stole the guy who was *supposed* to be dating *me* right now. A girl can only take so much rejection, you know? And at this rate, I'd had enough to last me a lifetime.

Karly was over at Joy's house getting ready for the middle school Valentine's Dance, and Mom was still at work. So I was stuck at home, alone. A cold mix of rain and sleet was falling outside, and it depressed me even more. I had already raided the kitchen, eating everything from cookies to ice cream, and not feeling the least bit guilty once I'd taken a laxative—relieved to know that all those excess calories wouldn't be sticking around to bother me later.

I was doing great with my diet and exercise. I knew I was burning more calories than I was eating. But there was something about Bree's words that kept ringing in my ears: "What doesn't stay in your body, can't make you fat." She obviously swore by them. Plus, it wasn't like I was using the laxatives all the time; I saved them just for emergencies. And the way I saw it, this afternoon definitely constituted an emergency.

I walked into the living room and turned on the television. After flipping through the channels—twice—I realized there was nothing on but sappy movies and old Valentine sitcom episodes. Those were to be avoided at all costs. Barely tolerable on a good day, they could easily drive me to the brink of insanity on a day like today. And so I settled on the couch in my favorite sweatpants, which ironically were no longer my favorite. Now that they were getting looser, they had a tendency to slip down from my hips if I stood up too quickly. I just hadn't found the time or energy to purchase a new pair.

The TV schedule channel was rolling through another round of listings when I heard the knock at the front door.

I rolled off the couch, temporarily losing my pants in the process, and crawled toward the peephole in the door. A distorted Steven was standing on my front porch.

Ugh, I thought, rolling my eyes. I seriously debated

whether or not I should let him inside. He didn't know I was home. I mean, I have friends. For all he knew, I could be out with them.

He knocked again.

The sleet falling outside pinged off the gutter. *This is ridiculous, I thought. Of course he knows I'm home. It isn't like I have a life or anything.* I unlocked and opened the door.

"Hi," he said.

"Hey, come on in."

"That's okay. I just wanted to give you these." He pulled from behind his back a dozen red roses, tied together with a white ribbon. "Happy Valentine's Day," he said, softly.

My stomach flip-flopped as I reached out and took them. I breathed in their scent and smiled despite myself. It was the first time I'd ever gotten anything from a guy on Valentine's Day—minus the little cards mothers forced their sons to sign for every girl in elementary school. I just couldn't believe it.

"Wow, I'm speechless. Thank you, Steven. You really didn't have to." I stepped aside. "Um, you can come in if you want." I tucked my hair behind my ears.

"No, it's okay. I don't want to intrude."

He looked so pitiful standing outside in the cold. I couldn't let him come all the way to my house and not invite him in—especially since he came out in this horrible weather and brought me roses. "I'm not taking no for an answer."

"Man, you're bossy," Steven joked, walking in and removing his coat.

He followed me into the kitchen. I held onto one side of my pants, praying they wouldn't fall to my ankles, embarrassing us both to death.

"Can I get you something to drink?" I offered.

"No, thanks, I'm fine," he replied. I walked over to the cupboard, pulled out one of Mom's old vases and filled it with water. I set it on the counter and began to arrange the roses.

"So, your mom's boyfriend seems like a nice guy," he commented, looking at the huge arrangement of flowers Mom had received earlier in the week. Leave it to Phil to send flowers *before* the holiday. Yet another one of his oh-so-manipulative romance tactics.

"Phil? Yeah, he's okay."

"You don't like him?"

"It doesn't matter if I like him," I replied. "My mother adores him. Are you sure you don't want anything?"

"I'm fine. So how long have your parents been divorced?" he asked.

"Oh, they aren't. My father died when I was a baby."

"I'm sorry," he apologized. "I didn't know."

"It's okay. It's not like I knew him or anything." *Ugh, there is nothing in this house to drink,* I thought, peering into the refrigerator.

"So…any big plans for tonight?" he asked.

"No, not really," I said. Then I realized what I was really telling him. *Sure, go ahead and ask me out. I'm avail-*

able. "I mean, I'm not a big fan of Valentine's Day," I quickly added. "I'd rather hang out here and watch TV and stuff. The holiday is so commercialized, you know?"

"I don't think you really believe that," he said quietly.

I remained silent, shrugging my shoulders in response.

"Can I ask you something?"

Please, please, please, please, don't ask me out, I silently begged. "Yeah, I guess." We walked back into the living room and sat down on the couch.

"Well, I guess I have to tell you something, rather than ask you."

No need to respond to that.

Steven took a huge breath, and then let everything fly out at once: "Wrenn, I think you're the sweetest, prettiest, most amazing girl I've ever met," he began.

My stomach twisted, and I had to close my eyes for a moment. "Steven, please," I interrupted.

"No, let me finish. I think you're talented and beautiful, and I know a guy like me really doesn't stand a chance, but it's Valentine's Day, and I'm taking a risk. I really like you, and I wish you'd give me the opportunity to prove myself."

He stopped, and I, not knowing how to respond to this…this "confession," just sat there staring at him, unable to find the words—or any other words, for that matter.

The silence was deafening.

"Okay, well, you know how I feel. That's all I came here to say." Steven got up and walked toward the door.

"I think you're nice, too," was all I could manage in response.

"But I'm just a friend," he confirmed, turning to me.

"Well, yeah," I replied, even though I'd never really even considered him my friend. And up to this point, a nuisance would be more accurate.

"Look, I really like you. And even if you don't feel the same way about me, I wish you'd give me a chance. Let me prove to you that I'm a good guy."

I looked him square in the eyes. He didn't have to prove anything to me; I knew he was a good guy. And the fact that he liked me and got to know me before…well, that won him some serious brownie points. But still, how do you explain to someone that he's just not your type? I didn't, however, have a chance to respond.

To my utter surprise, he leaned down and kissed me on the cheek. Hundreds of tiny tingles raced up and down my spine.

Steven pulled away, and when I didn't say anything, he began to squirm nervously. He ran his fingers through his curly hair and let out a nervous laugh. "Okay, well, you can keep the roses, anyway," he joked. "I'll see you tomorrow at rehearsal."

He did what he'd come to do, and now he was leaving. I felt terrible for not feeling the same way about him. He just…wasn't my *type*. Any other girl would be so lucky to have him. He just wasn't the one for me. He couldn't be.

I thanked him for the roses and watched as he cranked up his Jeep and pulled out of my driveway. Moments later everything was quiet, except for the sound of ice pelting the windowsill.

Chapter

Fourteen

If Zoe had annoyed me *before* she found out who Sk8trGuy was, her rapidly blossoming relationship with Chase made me want to scream—or throw things. It's not that I wasn't happy for her. I really was. But now Chase sat with us at lunch, went with us to Andy's for orangeades, and occupied every second of whatever free time Zoe had left.

They were "the couple" and *everyone* was talking about them. Which is why it didn't surprise me when Bree cornered me at a rehearsal. I'd been avoiding her—for obvious reasons. Chase Cunningham was *her* property, and even though she had "moved on" with Tad Owens, it was so obvious that she was jealous. It absolutely killed her to see Chase happy without her—and *with* someone else.

"So how is the duo of the century?" she asked, sarcastically.

I didn't make eye contact, but continued to watch the chorus rehearsing on stage.

"Who?"

She rolled her eyes. "Who do you think? Zoe and Chase. How *are* they?"

"Fine, I guess," I muttered, careful not to sound too enthusiastic.

"What have they been up to?"

I was *not* going to get into this. "I don't know. Nothing, I guess."

"Look," she said, sliding closer. "You don't have to tip-toe around the conversation every time Chase's name comes up. I can handle it. Seriously. I'm so over it."

Yeah, right, I thought to myself. *Then why are you so obsessed with what Zoe and Chase are up to?*

"Wrenn, we're friends, right?" she continued.

I looked at her, surprised. Although I didn't feel like I'd officially been invited into her group, I did feel as if our friendship had been solidified because of the time we'd spent together. Still, I couldn't believe it. Bree Donnelly considered me to be one of her friends? And she said the words out loud? "Um, yeah. We are," I confirmed.

"And you'd never lie to a friend, right? You'd tell the truth no matter how much it hurt."

I thought about this for a moment. "Sure."

"Good, because I need to know something."

"Okay."

Bree took a huge breath. "Were Zoe and Chase seeing each other behind my back?"

I tried not to laugh. "No, why?"

"Because I heard that they had something going on late last year, before we even broke up."

The emails. "Not that I know of," I lied. "Zoe would

never go out with someone who was already taken. She has standards."

She scowled, crossing her arms. "That's funny. I never would have thought that," Bree muttered. "She looks wild. You know, like she'd steal your man in a heart-beat."

I could feel my palms begin to sweat. Technically, Chase *had* cheated on Bree, but that wasn't Zoe's fault. She didn't even know who he was until Valentine's Day.

"No, she's not like that at all. And there was nothing going on. I mean, I'd know. I'm her best friend, right?"

This seemed to satisfy Bree. "Right. Good. Anyway, I'll catch you later."

"Okay," I called as she walked away.

I wiped my sweaty palms on the auditorium chair. I realized I'd been shaking during the entire confrontation. This was *so* not good. I'd set myself up, big-time. And the last thing I needed, now that we were friends, was for Bree Donnelly to find out that my best friend had snagged her boyfriend behind her back.

As soon as I got home from rehearsal, I knocked on Karly's door. "Can I come in?" I asked. I hated that, of all people, I was counting on my little sister for advice. But the truth was, she was the only popular person I could actually ask.

"I guess."

I turned the knob and walked into her disaster of a bedroom. "I need your help," I confessed.

"You didn't wear a hole in your carpet because of all those jumping jacks, did you? Because if you did, you'll have to talk to Mom about it. I'm not getting involved in your 'weight loss/exercise/six-weeks-to-a-better-Wrenn-Scott' experiment."

"This isn't about jumping jacks," I said, pushing a pile of clothing off the bed and onto the floor. "You're popular, so you know how popular people think."

She rolled her eyes. "Wrenn, you aren't serious."

"I *am* serious. This is a big problem."

"Okay, fine," she said with a sigh.

I sat down on the edge of her bed. "It goes like this. Zoe is dating Chase Cunningham, who is like, the most gorgeous guy at school. Well, the thing is that Chase used to date Bree Donnelly, who is the most popular girl in school. Zoe is my best friend, but Bree and I are in the musical together, and we're friends, too."

"So now Bree is holding it against you," Karly interrupted.

"Yes. But it's more complicated than that. Zoe and Chase began talking to each other like, last year. They met online, but Zoe didn't know who he was until Valentine's Day, after he already had broken up with Bree."

"That's not a big deal, she didn't know."

"I know that Zoe didn't know, but Chase did. They were supposed to meet a few weeks ago at Andy's, and we thought he didn't show up, but he did, only he didn't tell us he was Sk8trGuy."

Karly smirked. "Now *that* is a legitimate problem."

"Tell me about it," I told her, rolling my eyes. "So Bree corners me at rehearsal tonight, wondering what was going on between them, because someone told her that Chase had been cheating on her."

"He was," Karly informed me.

"I know he was, but that wasn't Zoe's fault."

"Well, what did you tell her?"

"I told her that I didn't know what she was talking about. Well, in so many words."

"So you lied?"

"Pretty much."

"Why didn't you just tell her that you thought they had talked a few times online, but that Zoe didn't know who he was?"

"Because then she'd know that Chase cheated on her."

"Well, let's think about this. What do you think Bree is going to do when she finds out that Chase *did* cheat on her? You're the first person she'll be mad at because you lied to her."

"How would she ever find out?" I asked. "Nobody else knows."

"Rule number one: Whenever you lie, it always comes back to bite you in the butt; remember that. And think about it, someone already told her that they were seeing each other behind her back, right?"

"Right."

"Then somebody obviously knows something."

"Why can't we just dismiss it as an ugly rumor?"

"Because it's not," she informed me. "If hanging out

with this girl is so important to you, then you'd better come clean with her."

"I can't. I already told her that it was a lie."

She brought her hand to her forehead. "Wrenn, you're giving me a headache," she said, standing up. "If you didn't want my advice, why'd you ask me?"

"Karly, I can't tell Bree that I lied to her."

"Well, that's on you then."

I bit my lower lip. "Okay, fine." I looked around the disarray that she lived in—the clothes on the floor, the movie posters on the wall. So this is what it was like to be popular? I thought. After a brief pause, I asked, "So how's Sherie Conner?"

"What?"

"You know, the Sherie Conner drama, the Valentine's Dance, the ugly rumors," I reminded her.

"Oh. That is *so* over."

"How did you end up getting her back?"

"How did I get her back?" she repeated, clearly not understanding.

"Honestly, Karly, work with me here," I begged, rolling my eyes.

"I don't know what you're talking about."

I shook my head. "Sherie Conner. Spreading rumors about you liking a seventh-grade nerd? Does any of this ring a bell?"

The light bulb came on at last. "Oh, right. *That*."

"Finally," I said, rolling my eyes. "So, how did you get her back?"

"I asked William Merritt to the dance," she replied with a shrug.

My mouth dropped in surprise. "What? But he was a nerd...a seventh grader," I stammered in disbelief.

She looked me square in the eye. "What better way to get back at someone than to show them that they never got to you in the first place?" she said. "Now, do you mind? I have to call Joy."

I shook my head and left the room, shutting the door behind me. I don't know why I thought Karly would be able to help me; if anything, she left me even more confused. Asking a nerdy seventh-grader to the school dance? The most popular girl in middle school going to a Valentine's Dance with a nerd? Who could pull something like that off? What had she been thinking?

I walked into the kitchen to grab a bottle of water. I wanted something more substantial, something like ice cream. Chocolate. Before the musical, I would have had no problem raiding the cabinets for a midnight snack, or eating Oreos and milk in bed. Of course, before the musical, I didn't have problems with Bree Donnelly, either. Before the musical, she didn't even know I was alive.

"So you have what, four weeks until your birthday?"

I nearly jumped out of my skin. "Mom, you scared me." I held onto the refrigerator door for support, trying to catch my breath. "I didn't see you there."

She was sitting at the kitchen table, sifting through a pile of bills. She lowered her reading glasses and stared at me. "Are you okay?"

I stood straighter and opened the refrigerator door. "Yeah, I'm fine," I said, trying to steady my breathing. "You just startled me, that's all. What were you saying?"

"Your birthday," she repeated, returning her attention to her bills. "It's in four weeks."

"Oh, right," I replied, pulling out a bottle of water. "I'd forgotten all about it."

"You forgot you're turning sixteen next month? Are you sure you're okay?"

"I'm fine. Everything's fine." I twisted open the cap and took a swig of the cold water. It instantly left me wanting something more. "It's just that I've been so busy with this show and all."

"I noticed. You're working awfully hard."

I swallowed. "Yeah," I nodded.

She stared at me for a moment and I shifted uncomfortably.

"So what did you have in mind for your birthday this year?" she asked, readjusting her glasses.

"Oh, I don't know. I wasn't really planning on doing anything special." I sat down in the chair across from hers.

"But we always celebrate your birthday," she said. "We could have another girls' night. You know, invite some of your new friends from the play."

I shook my head. "No girls' night. I don't need a party."

"But it's your sixteenth birthday. Why wouldn't you want a party?" she inquired.

"Because it's not a big deal."

"Of course it's a big deal," she replied. "We can at

least have a small get-together. You can invite Tabitha and Steven, Zoe and her new boyfriend. We can get a cake and serve ice cream. It'll be fun."

I rolled my eyes. "Sure, okay, whatever."

Her eyes narrowed. "What *is* your *problem*?" she asked, folding her arms across her chest.

"I don't have a problem," I retorted. "I just don't want a party."

She shook her head. "No, it's not about the party. What's going on with you, really?"

I averted my eyes. "Nothing," I mumbled.

"No, there is something else. Something you're not telling me."

"I had a bad day, okay?"

"Well, what happened?"

"Nothing!" I cried. "It was just a bad day. What's with all the questions?" I stood and carried my water across the kitchen.

"I'm your mother, Wrenn. I just want to know what's going on in your life."

I turned sharply to face her. "Really? Since when?" I shot back.

A look of surprise, mixed with hurt and confusion, crossed her face. "What?"

"You, with all your problems at work, and with your honey, Phil. It's always about you. It's always about Karly. It's never about me. Never! So why worry about me now?" I turned on my heel and stormed out of the room.

"Wrenn!" she called after me.

I didn't stop until I reached the bathroom. Immediately I shut and locked the door behind me, then flipped the water on full blast. After a few moments of rummaging around the middle drawer, I found what I was looking for. My hands were shaking, but somehow managed to pull that little foil packet out of the white box. Then I began to brush my teeth.

Chapter

Fifteen

"Wrenn, I need the potatoes," Karly stated.

I scooped a small portion onto my plate, then passed the bowl to her.

"So anyway, I told Mitzi that she could find her own day planner, that I didn't keep it on a string, and it wasn't my responsibility to keep track of her personal belongings. Yes, I was there to make her work life easier, but I wasn't a babysitter," Mom ranted. "I'll be lucky if I go in Monday and still have a job."

"Maybe it's a good thing," Phil commented, taking a sip of his tea. "You've been working as her assistant long enough. I think it's time to give credit where credit's due."

I watched as Phil cut his roast into small, manageable bites. *What a moron*, I thought to myself.

Phil was a regular at dinner now. I assumed that either he was picking up something on the way to our house, or else Mom was cooking enough for him. So much for his frozen dinners.

"You know, I really think you should work for yourself," Phil continued.

"I don't have anything to offer," Mom replied. "I've worked for other people my entire life. I wouldn't even know where to begin."

"Maybe you could go back to school. Then, instead of taking orders from Mitzi, you could be the one bossing *her* around."

Mom lifted her fork to her mouth. "Hmm. Bossing around Mitzi Monroe. Now *that* would be something."

"You should look into it, Kerri. I think it would be good for you. And the girls are old enough now. They could manage on their own if you took a few night or on-line courses here and there."

I rolled my eyes. Mr. Motivation. I half-wondered if he charged by the hour. I wished that my mom had never met Phil.

"I know. I guess I'll think about it. It would be good timing anyway. Oh, Wrenn," she said, turning to me, "what time do you need to be at your rehearsal?"

I checked the clock. "In an hour. I should probably go and get ready." Happy to find a legitimate reason to abandon this meal, I stood and picked up my plate.

"No ma'am!" my mom practically yelled, her mouth full. She pointed her fork at my chair. "You haven't eaten a bite. Don't think that I haven't been watching you. Now I'm sorry, but if you're skipping dinner to get to rehearsal on time, then you're just going to have to be late."

"What?" I cried.

"You heard me."

"But Mr. Pike hates it when we're late," I told her as I slid back into my seat.

"If I need to walk inside with you and explain to Mr. Pike that you were late because our dinner ran over, I'll be happy to."

Like I needed my mom to walk me to the door. We were *not* going to go there. "Whatever," I mumbled, scooping a small bite of potatoes onto my fork and bringing it to my mouth.

Phil coughed, breaking the silence, and then cleared his throat. "So, Wrenn, how's your friend?" he asked.

Like I had only one friend. Please. "Which one?"

"You know, your guy friend. Steven, was it?"

"Yes, how is Steven?" Mom inquired. "I really need to talk to him about that possible internship this summer."

I rolled my eyes. "Steven is fine," I told them.

"What has he been up to lately?"

Phil, please, I thought to myself. *You're only pretending to be interested.* "Nothing, really. We've been rehearsing nonstop. And there is that little thing called 'school.'"

"Wrenn, your sarcasm isn't necessary," my mother warned.

"It's okay, Kerri," Phil said, trying to smooth things over. "I was a teenager once. I know it's not cool for adults to ask a lot of questions."

We went back to eating our meal in silence; the sound of forks clinking against the plates was grating.

"I really need to get ready now. Is this enough?" I asked, lifting my plate. I felt like a five-year-old, asking if I could be excused; if I'd eaten enough green beans to warrant a trip to my room.

Mom examined my plate. "What did you eat?"

"I ate potatoes, bread, and steak!" I cried.

"Are you kidding? You ate three bites of steak, if that," she retorted.

"Well, maybe I'm not hungry. Maybe I'm full. Maybe I don't *want* to eat steak with you people!" I could feel tears welling in my eyes. Didn't she get it? I didn't *want* to eat steak.

"Wrenn, it's just dinner. Stop overreacting."

"I'm not overreacting!" I cried, my voice shaking. "If I don't get ready, then I'm going to be late. I'm not hungry, and I'm not going to eat another bite!" I folded my arms across my chest and leaned back in my chair, refusing to move.

"Okay, fine. It's fine," Mom said quietly. "Go ahead and get dressed."

"Finally," I muttered. I jumped up from the table and carried my plate into the kitchen, throwing it into the sink. The plate shattered. Bits and pieces of uneaten food mingled with the shards of ceramic. I stared at the destruction, the mess I'd created, surprised at the sheer strength of my anger. Then I turned on my heel and headed toward the hallway, only pausing long enough to wipe my eyes with the back of my hand.

Despite our late dinner, Phil pulled into the school parking lot early. I half-suspected that he'd sped the entire way, if only to prevent another argument. The doors were still locked, so I was forced to wait in the back seat, listening to Mom and Phil discuss classic Rock 'n Roll from the seventies.

I wasn't paying attention to them until Phil asked, "Isn't that your friend?"

I glanced toward the front of the school. Sure enough, there was Steven, peering through the dark glass and pulling on every door handle.

"Roll your window down," Mom said. Phil obeyed. "Steven!" she called.

"Mom! What are you doing?" I hissed.

"Oh, Wrenn, it's so cold outside. Come on. It's just for a minute." She motioned for him to come to the car.

Steven, in his traditional flannel shirt (this one red), stuck his hands in his pockets and walked toward us, his light brown hair falling just above his eyebrows.

"Open your door," Mom demanded.

"What?" I cried.

"Wrenn, please. Just open your door."

I sighed, and pulled on the door handle of Phil's SUV. Steven climbed in beside me.

"Hey, how's it going?" he asked.

"Good," my mom replied. "How've you been?"

"No complaints."

Steven looked at me; I forced a smile.

"I talked to the general manager at the station," she continued. "He seemed interested in my internship suggestion. He was going to throw around the idea at one of his upcoming meetings. I'll let you know how it goes."

"Thanks, that would be great," replied Steven.

I leaned forward and checked the bright green digits on Phil's dash. "Someone should be here by now," I said.

"Patience is a virtue," my mother attested.

I rolled my eyes. I knew that patience was a freakin' virtue, all right? But I didn't particularly relish waiting in a car with Steven and Phil. I mean, what if someone drove by and saw me? I would be ruined.

"I think that's Mr. Pike's car anyway," Steven said.

Sure enough, a decades-old beige Mercedes pulled into the school driveway. The silver-haired man driving could only be Mr. Pike. *It's about time*, I thought, pushing open the door.

"Can I give Wrenn a ride home for you tonight? You know, save you a trip?" Steven asked.

Mom looked at Phil, then back at Steven. "That would be great!" she exclaimed.

What? I glared at the back of my mother's head. How could she do this to me? *How?* My jaw tightened. "But, Mom, you were only going to rent a movie. I didn't think picking me up was a problem tonight."

"Well, now we won't have to stop the movie halfway," she explained. "Steven offered, and it's on his way. I don't see the problem."

"Fine. I guess I'll see you later," I stated through clenched teeth, forming the words slowly.

"Good-bye, Steven," Phil said. "It was terrific seeing you again."

"It was good seeing you both, too," he replied.

I shut my door a little harder than usual, letting Mom know that I wasn't thrilled with her move to pawn me off on Steven, just so that she could have a night alone with Phil. She had a lot of nerve, that's all I'm saying.

Chapter

Sixteen

"She doesn't understand what she's doing to me. I swear, she is absolutely ruining my life," I complained. I threw a tube of mascara into the red plastic drugstore basket I was carrying.

"If it bothers you that much, just tell her you don't want Steven driving you home anymore," Zoe suggested.

"I *have* told her. I've told her a million times. I'm not interested in him. I don't want to date him, I don't even *like* him. It's like she insists on doing everything she possibly can to try and get us together."

She rolled her eyes. "Honestly, Wrenn. I don't see what the big deal is. From what I've seen, Steven is a genuinely sweet person, who by the way has been incredibly nice to you. You aren't even giving him the time of day and he still likes talking to you, offers to take you places and gets you roses for Valentine's Day. That has to count for something."

I walked down the medicine aisle, glancing at the rows of shelves. "Steven is a nerd," I confirmed. "I don't care how nice he is. He's not my type."

I finally found what I was looking for. I picked up a box of laxatives and tossed it in with the rest of my purchases.

"What's that?" Zoe asked, peering into my basket.

My stomach dropped and my hands grew clammy. "Oh, they're for my mom. She asked me to pick some up for her," I said quickly, tucking my hair behind my ears.

"Your mom asked you to buy laxatives from the drug-store with your own money?" she questioned.

I shrugged. "Yeah. I mean, it's something we usually have in our medicine cabinet," I stammered. "We must be out or something, or else she wouldn't have bothered, I'm sure." Yes, I was lying, but the less Zoe knew about my little secret, the better off I'd be. Everything was perfect, and the last thing I needed was her breathing down my neck about this weight-loss thing. I was under enough pressure already.

She eyed me warily. "Okay," she replied. "It's just a little strange, that's all."

I let out a nervous laugh. "It's no big deal—I mean, as long as she pays me back. I'm not paying for it with my money or anything. Oh, she wanted me to pick up some Advil, too." Hoping to distract Zoe, I turned and began to walk away quickly, praying that I actually had enough money in my wallet to pay for all of "my mother's" purchases.

After Zoe dropped me off in the driveway, I let myself into the house and headed straight for the bathroom. I hurriedly tore open the bag I'd knotted shut and began pulling things out one by one and setting them on the counter.

"What are you doing?" a voice behind me said. I quickly swiped my arm across the counter, dumping everything into the top drawer.

"Karly! I didn't think you were home yet," I stated, my voice shaking.

"I'm home," she replied, walking toward me. "Where have you been?" She eyed me accusingly.

"Zoe and I stopped at the drugstore. I needed a few things. It's no big deal."

She raised an eyebrow. "If it's no big deal, then why are you being so secretive?"

"I'm not being secretive," I declared. "You're imagining things."

She folded her arms. "Well, if you aren't being secretive, then you won't mind if I open the drawer."

I backed away from the counter and let her pull the drawer open. She sifted through its contents. "Mascara, foundation. I don't get it. What are you hiding?"

"I told you I wasn't hiding anything."

She snorted. "Yeah, right. You looked like a deer in headlights when I walked into the room."

"Okay, *Mom*," I replied sarcastically.

Karly shut the drawer and walked out of the bathroom. "I'm spending the night at Joy's. Her mom's picking me up after she gets off work."

"Whatever," I replied as I flipped off the light and walked into my bedroom. My heart twisted in my chest. I sat down on the edge of my bed and tried to steady my breathing. First Zoe, then Karly. I was so going to have to be more careful.

When the phone rang an hour later, I was playing the piano and didn't bother answering it. Karly knocked on my door. "It's for you," she called. "It's Mom."

I picked up the phone on my nightstand and told Karly to hang up.

"Hey."

"Wrenn, it's me. I need a favor."

I rolled my eyes. Of course, a favor. When was I *not* doing her favors? "What kind of favor?"

"Do you think you can get a ride to rehearsal tonight? Phil asked me to go out to dinner. It was kind of a last-minute thing."

I could feel the blood in my veins begin to boil. "Honestly, I will be so freakin' glad when I get my license and my own car," I practically yelled. "Then I won't have to worry about finding a ride ever again."

"Wrenn, there's no need to be upset," she said calmly. "It's just one rehearsal. I would have let you know earlier, but he just now called," she explained. "Why don't you give Zoe a ring?"

"Because Zoe has a life," I retorted.

"What about Steven? Or someone else from the play?" she suggested.

I laughed, unable to process the words I was hearing. "I've told you that I don't want to ride with Steven!" I shouted. "I don't like him, I don't want to be set up with him, and I don't want to call him and beg for a ride!"

"Wrenn, you're being irrational. I'm sure Tabitha or someone else can pick you up," she stated.

"I'm not irrational. I'm tired of you people planning my life around yours. Why can't you just meet Phil later?"

"Because I'm an adult, and I make the decisions. Why can't you just work with me?" I could tell she was getting annoyed.

My mind reeled. "Why can't *you* work with *me*? Why do I have to call around to find a ride, just so you can go out with Phil?"

"Wrenn, that is enough," she replied angrily. "You act like I do this to you every other night. I've been very good about chauffeuring you to and from these rehearsals. You have to find yourself a ride tonight. It's a non-issue."

A non-issue? *A Non-Issue?* That depends on whom you asked. Because to me, it sure was an issue. A huge one. I was so sick of her whole "I'd rather go out with my nerdy boyfriend than take my own daughter to her rehearsal" mentality. It was obvious that I didn't even register as a legitimate member of this family anymore. But then I thought about it, and wondered: Had I ever? *"Wrenn doesn't have a life; don't mind her."* It must be what Mom and Karly thought, and now Phil, too. I never had a say-so in anything that mattered. I was voiceless.

"Fine," I said. "Thanks for not putting yourself out."

Without waiting for a reply, I slammed the phone onto the receiver. I could picture my mother on the other end, staring at the phone. I never hung up on anyone—ever, but I liked the sense of control it gave me. It was like, for once, I was in charge of my own life, instead of letting other people run it for me.

But even so, while I was able to put an end to the conversation, Mom had the upper hand. I still needed a ride.

I trudged into the living room and peered through the window. It was March. The days were getting longer, and it got a little warmer each week. The sun was still shining, and suddenly I found myself wanting to get out. Not just out of the house, but completely out of my life. Forget rehearsal; forget school. Forget Mom and Phil and Karly. Forget *Grease*. Just screw it all.

I went to my room where, safely behind my bedroom door, I changed into a pair of shorts I'd safety-pinned tighter and put on an old, two-sizes-too-large T-shirt. I pulled my tennis shoes from the closet floor.

Jogging down the street, I heard nothing but the sound of my shoes hitting the pavement. I exhaled and began to feel my muscles unwind. Finally—I was alone. I really needed this. It was my time to run, relax, and just get away from everyone. And I didn't care if I had rehearsal. I was in charge now, and nothing was going to stop me. I should have done this a long time ago: I needed a break from the entire world.

I ran all the way to the end of my street and turned onto another. When that one ended, I ran down another, with no particular destination in mind. When my side began to cramp, I slowed to a walk.

The sun was just beginning to sink behind the trees, and it was getting colder. As I checked my watch, I realized that I wouldn't make it to rehearsal now—even if I wanted to.

Leigh Brescia

The street signs looked only vaguely familiar, so I turned around and headed back toward my house. One by one, the street lamps flickered to life. Soon it was completely dark, and it became hard to distinguish one house from another. I wrapped my arms around myself a bit tighter, trying to keep warm.

Cars blinded me with their headlights every time they passed, and suddenly, in the darkness, I became aware that someone, or something, could jump out of the bushes and grab me at any moment. My pace quickened, and I searched desperately for something—anything—that would give me some clue as to where I was.

Thoughts played like a movie reel in my head; what I would do if someone tried to attack me, where would I kick them first—

That's when I heard a car behind me. It seemed to be slowing down. Soon it was right beside me, traveling at the same speed as I was walking. *Someone was following me. Should I run? Should I yell?* Something inside me told me to look over at the car. I took a quick glance.

"Hey," Steven called.

I wanted to scream. *Of course* it was Steven. He was driving his Jeep with his top down, and I knew the only place he could be going in that flannel shirt was to rehearsal.

"You freaked me out!" I practically yelled. "I thought you were a—a—murderer."

He laughed. "I was wondering how long it would take for you to look at me."

"It isn't funny," I growled, still walking, keeping my eyes straight ahead.

"I'm sorry," he said, still laughing. "Where are you headed?"

"Home."

"Isn't home that way?" He motioned his thumb behind him. I stopped and looked around. Steven pressed his brakes lightly, stopping just in front of me. "You have no idea where you are, do you?" he said with a smile.

I found nothing even remotely humorous about this situation. "I just went for a run. I lost track of time," I explained.

"And all sense of direction," he added. "Get in; I'll give you a ride."

"I'm not going to rehearsal," I declared, folding my arms across my chest.

He scratched his head, then ran his fingers through his wild, curly hair. "Okay," he said, forming the words slowly. "I don't have to take you to rehearsal. I can take you home instead."

"I can find my way by myself."

Steven nodded. "Yeah. You were doing a great job on your own. You would've been inside the city limits soon. Get in."

I looked around the neighborhood. Seriously, I had no idea where I was. I could continue walking and stay lost, or take advantage of the opportunity to get a ride. I crossed in front of the Jeep and climbed in. "Look who's being bossy now," I pointed out.

Smiling, Steven made a quick U-turn, and headed back toward my end of the neighborhood.

"So, I guess you were on your way to rehearsal," I said, trying to make conversation.

"Yeah. I guess you weren't."

I stared at the road ahead. "Nope, not tonight. I needed a break."

He flipped on his turn signal and came to a complete stop at a stop sign, even though no one was behind us or anywhere near us, for that matter. "Mr. Pike has been really tough on you guys lately," he said. "I hate to say it, but the closer to opening night, the worse he gets."

"It's not just that. I need a break period. From everything." I leaned back in the seat, my legs aching and my side hurting.

"You're much too pretty to be stressed, Wrenn Scott," he replied. "Anything you want to talk about? I might not be able to help, but I'm a pretty good listener."

I shook my head. "No. I'm just tired, that's all."

"Tired from running? Tired of the play?"

"Tired of everything: the play, school, home."

"Is there anything I can do?" he asked.

I glanced at Steven as we drove along, the streetlamps lighting his face each time we drove under one. He was actually concerned, I realized. He cared.

"No," I told him quietly. "There's nothing you can do."

Unfamiliar houses quickly turned into familiar ones, and soon we had reached my driveway. Steven put the car in park as I unbuckled my seat belt.

"If Mr. Pike asks about you, I'll make something up," he told me. "Like, you were feeling bad at school today, or something."

"You don't have to do that."

"No, it's okay. I mean, you really *are* feeling bad. He doesn't have to know the reason why."

Steven was actually going to cover for me. Immediately my thoughts flew to Valentine's Day, and I remembered how I'd turned down his request for a date. He'd brought me roses, and I wasn't decent enough to give the guy one measly date. I was wracked with guilt about all the terrible things I'd said and thought about him; all the times I'd ignored him. *Maybe I should give him a chance*, I thought.

I blinked several times, pushing the idea out of my head. I couldn't deal with this right now. I wasn't in the right frame of mind to make life-altering decisions. "Well, thanks for the ride," I finally said.

"I'm serious. If you ever want to talk, or you know, vent a little, give me a call. There's no need to run to the ends of the earth."

Ugh! Why was he so sweet? Why did he care so much? My throat tightened, and my eyes misted as I offered a smile. *What is wrong with me?* I looked away quickly, so Steven couldn't see my eyes. He wouldn't understand. I didn't even understand. *Why was I so freakin' emotional all of a sudden?* "Thanks again."

I opened the door and climbed out of his Jeep. A sharp pain jolted my side. I grimaced.

"Are you okay?" Steven asked, leaning forward.

I let out a nervous laugh. "Yeah, I'm fine. I just got a cramp from running," I explained, rubbing the affected area. "I'll see you later. And thanks again for the ride."

I practically ran to the front door and let myself into the dark house. As soon as I got inside, I burst into tears. I was embarrassed and ashamed. I felt horrible.

Steven didn't pull out of the driveway right away. I watched him from the dining room window, through my tears. He remained parked, just staring at the house. I wondered what he was thinking; whom he was thinking about. I didn't need an answer because I knew. That made the tears fall even harder. Finally, his headlights flipped on and he drove away.

It was quiet inside the house. Karly was gone, and who even knew when Mom and Phil would decide to reenter reality?

I went into the bathroom, finished my breakdown, and washed my face with cold water. I changed into my new favorite sweatpants, smaller and much more flattering ones, and then took the opportunity to do what I loved most. I began to sing—not to rehearse—but just to sing. I was sick and tired of rehearsing. No more fifties show tunes. I used to adore singing; now I could hardly stand it. Now I actually found myself avoiding the piano and my music, and I hadn't tried to write a song in ages. I missed my music. I missed loving the piano. I missed singing just for myself.

I was surprised when I heard a knock on my door, not long after I sat down to play.

"Who is it?" I asked.

"It's me," Mom replied. "Why aren't you at rehearsal?" she asked, her voice muffled.

I checked my watch. "Why aren't you at dinner?" I replied.

"I asked you first."

I rolled my eyes. "I'm not at rehearsal because I couldn't find a ride," I told her, wanting her to feel bad about choosing Phil over her own flesh and blood.

"Steven couldn't pick you up?"

I didn't even want to think about him right now. "No."

"Did you even call him?" I didn't answer. "Wrenn, open the door."

I rolled my eyes. "It's not locked."

She turned the knob and pushed it open, then took one look at my face. I was a mess. "What is *wrong* with you tonight? Have you been crying? Is it that time of the month?"

"No," I snapped. "I haven't. And it's not."

"Well, why didn't you go to rehearsal?"

"Because I didn't feel like it," I retorted.

Mom walked in and sat down on the edge of my bed. "Is there anything you want to talk about?"

"Why does everyone want me to talk all of sudden?" I asked.

"What is that supposed to mean?"

I shook my head. It was pointless to even try to explain. "Nothing."

She paused. "Come on. I'm cooking a pot of spaghetti. I know how much you love pasta," she finally said.

"I'm not hungry," I said, turning back to my piano.

"Have you already eaten?" she asked.

"Yes, I ate earlier," I lied.

"What did you eat?"

"A sandwich."

"Well, I think you can eat some pasta with me."

"I thought you ate with Phil."

"Um, no. We changed our minds," she said quickly.

I turned and stared at her. "So what were you doing?"

"We just went for a ride, and stopped at a store or two." She stumbled over her words. "We just stayed out for a while, but I wasn't hungry then. I'm starving now, though, so come on," she said, getting up.

"I told you, I'm not hungry." I began playing the introduction to the song I was singing when she stomped over to the digital piano and turned off the power. The keys fell silent.

"What are you doing?" I cried.

"You're going to come into that kitchen and eat a bowl of spaghetti if I have to cram it down your throat myself!" she shouted.

I swallowed hard; my body tensed.

"Don't think I don't see what is going on, Wrenn. I don't like this so-called diet you're on."

"I'm eating right and I'm exercising. What's your problem?"

"I don't have a problem. *You're* the one with the problem."

My mouth fell open and I let out a sarcastic laugh. "Are you serious? You were the one trying to drag me to the gym all the time—dropping little hints about my eating too much. 'Wrenn, I really don't think you should eat that third piece of bread.' 'Wrenn, I really think you should lay off the Oreos.' 'Wrenn, you should come to the gym and go bike riding with me,'" I mocked. "Now I'm finally losing weight, and you're trying to make me fat again!"

"You may be eating, Wrenn. But just barely. You're eating enough to make me believe that you are, anyway. I wasn't born yesterday. And if I have to chain you to the kitchen chair and force feed you, then I'll do it. I'll watch you eat every meal. I'll make you sit at the table until you're finished." She paused for a moment. "Or you can come and eat spaghetti on your own. It's your choice."

I didn't protest. Instead, I followed her into the kitchen and watched her fill a pot with water. When she set a bowl of spaghetti in front of me, I didn't say a word. I ate. I ate every last bite of it. And when I was finished, I pushed the bowl across the table and stood up from the chair. Then, feeling positively wretched, I headed for the bathroom.

Chapter

Seventeen

I was so freakin' annoyed. It was Saturday afternoon. I had rehearsal in a few hours. I wanted some peace. I wanted time to myself. I wanted to relax. And what does my mother do? She'd shoved a shopping list in my face and told me to bike ride to the store up the road. A shopping list—*her* shopping list.

"But Phil is coming to dinner," she said, when I'd told her "No way."

I grabbed a container of shampoo off the shelf and threw it in my basket. When was Phil *not* coming to dinner? I mean, please. And how did she expect me to get this stuff home, anyway? I wondered about it as the cashier rang up my purchases.

It took some finagling, but I managed to tie the bags to the handlebars. Unfortunately, now they prevented me from pedaling. It would take twice as long to get everything back home, eating even more into my time.

When I reached the driveway, I noticed that Phil's SUV was already parked there. I rolled my eyes. Phil. Phil.

Phil. I was so completely sick of Phil. I mean, literally, my stomach hurt every time he came around—which was way too often these days. I dumped my bike in the front yard and climbed the steps to the porch.

My hands were full, so I kicked the door a few times. No one came. I kicked again and waited for a few more moments. Nothing.

"What is wrong with you people?" I shouted, dropping the drugstore bags on the floor and pulling my house key out of my pocket.

I pushed the door open, then leaned down, trying to pick up all the bags. "I mean, you would think that since I did your shopping, you could get the door for me," I snapped.

"Surprise!"

People jumped from the kitchen, from behind curtains and furniture.

"You guys!" I cried, my face flushing and my heart racing. "You almost gave me a heart attack!"

That's when I took everything in: the dark room, the large white sheet cake with a huge "Happy 16th Birthday, Wrenn!" written in bright blue letters. Leave it to my mother.

"Make a wish," Mom said. I walked toward the cake.

The candles flickered, casting strange shadows beneath them. I closed my eyes and made the same wish I'd made every other year.

It was juvenile, really—making wishes as the glow of the flames disappeared into smoke, but I did it just the same, because this year I knew my dream would finally come true. It had to.

Everyone clapped, and someone turned on the music. Zoe and Chase were there; Karly and her friend, Joy; Phil, of course; Tabitha, and Steven. I felt my skin growing hotter when I realized that Chase Cunningham and Steven James were in the same room—for the same party. I could never become popular as long as people like Chase believed I was friends with Steven, and since they were both at my party.... Ugh. I could almost kill my mother for inviting him.

Thankfully, I didn't have to dwell on it for too long, because at that moment Phil came toward me, a camcorder attached to his hand. "This is Wrenn Scott's sixteenth birthday," he stated. "Say hello, Birthday Girl!"

I rolled my eyes. Why did my mother insist on making him a part of everything? I tried not to look directly into the camera, hoping he would go away. "Come on, Wrenn," he urged. "Tell us what it's like to be sixteen."

"It's about time," I muttered.

"When are we going to get our license?"

"First thing Monday morning."

"Monday afternoon," my mom interjected.

Phil immediately turned the camera toward my mother. "And here we have Wrenn's beautiful mother, Kerri Scott," he continued. Mom offered a cheesy smile. She was smitten. I felt my gag reflex kick in, and when I pointed my finger down my throat, Zoe giggled.

Mom continued cutting slices of cake, and soon

everyone was happily shoveling it into their mouths. I took small bites of mine every now and then, and gazed around the room. I couldn't believe that Chase Cunningham was sitting on our love seat. I felt a pang of envy. I'd always dreamed about this moment, and now my dream had finally come true. Unfortunately he was with my best friend. Strike One.

"Wrenn, if you aren't eating, why don't you open your presents?" Mom suggested.

I put my cake plate aside and began picking through the stack of presents. I noticed Tabitha's first. I carefully removed the bow and placed it on the coffee table. Beginning at each end, I used my fingernail to break the tape, then pulled off the wrapping paper without tearing it.

"At this rate we're going to be here all night," Zoe predicted. "Open them the real way." I laughed with everyone else, but it wasn't like me to rip the wrapping paper to shreds. I liked to savor the experience. To me, anticipating what was inside was almost as much fun as receiving it.

Inside the box, hidden by tissue paper, was a brand-new shirt. I checked the size.

"Wow, this is great! Thank you so much, Tabitha."

"Yeah, I figured you would need some new clothes now that spring is here," she said.

"That was very thoughtful. I don't think she'll be able to wear anything in her closet from last year," my mother commented. I noticed a hint of concern in her voice when she said this.

My thoughts drifted to my last birthday party. It was so unlike this one. My mom had convinced me to have a girls' night. It was only me, Karly, and Zoe. And even though I despised them, I suffered through manicures, facials, and makeovers. We capped off the night with a chick flick, and Zoe and I stayed up late talking about guys like Chase Cunningham. It wasn't a terrible way to spend a birthday, but I hated the girl I remembered. She was dark and fat, and she was way too happy with all of that pizza she was eating.

I brushed a strand of blonde hair off my face, making sure the length and the darkness were gone. It was almost as if by merely thinking about the girl I used to be, she could come back—just that quickly. I pushed her out of my mind.

Someone handed me another present, and I snapped back to attention.

I opened each gift as meticulously as the first, driving Zoe absolutely nuts. In a moment, I just knew she was going to jump up and tear into them for me. She and Chase had chipped in for some new piano music and a CD; Karly gave me a gift certificate to my favorite store; and Mom and Phil had purchased a new, more modern "bed in a bag" set for my bedroom. It was black and pink, and had a Parisian flair. It was something I could see in Bree Donnelly's room, and I smiled when I saw it. Everything else around me was changing, why not my bedroom?

Steven's present was at the bottom of the pile. I could feel everyone's eyes on me as I unwrapped it, and my cheeks flushed with embarrassment as I opened the small gray jewelry box.

My heart leapt into my throat, and I honestly strug-gled to find words. Nestled inside was a silver I.D. bracelet. "Wrenn" was engraved in a fancy script. It was unique, and the prettiest gift I'd ever received.

"Wow, this is beautiful, Steven," I choked. "Really."

"Hold it up," Tabitha demanded. I removed the bracelet from the box and lifted it so everyone could see it.

"That's very nice!" my mother exclaimed.

"You did a good job, Steven," Zoe agreed. "And they say guys can't shop." Everyone laughed, and it was Steven's turn to blush. He looked at the floor in embar-rassment.

I flipped the bracelet over. The etching on the inside caught my attention. "Happy 16th. Love, Steven."

So simple. I could imagine him standing at the jew-elry store counter, debating over what should be engraved. Should he show his romantic side? Be sentimental? But for some reason, the words he'd chosen said enough.

"That's not fair. I want someone to buy *me* an I.D. bracelet," Karly chimed.

I looked at her in astonishment. Karly? The blonde-haired, blue-eyed most popular girl in the eighth grade, ac-tually wanted something that I had? She was jealous! The thought was worth its weight in platinum.

"Here, help me put it on," I said, turning to Tabitha. Everyone watched as she fastened it around my wrist. A perfect fit. "Thank you, you really didn't have to."

"It's no problem," he replied, with a shrug.

My stomach flip-flopped. I suddenly felt completely guilty for not wanting him at my party. Zoe was right.

Steven was a sweet guy—he was sweet to me even when I didn't deserve it. Forget types. If anything, I wasn't good enough for *him*. What was my problem, anyway?

"Thank you for everything, guys. All these gifts are incredible."

We sat around talking and laughing, and when it was time for them to leave, I made sure I walked Steven outside.

"Where did you park?" I asked, looking for his car. The street had been empty when I'd returned from the store.

"Your mom told us to park down one of the side streets so you wouldn't see the cars," he said.

My heart filled when I realized how much trouble everyone had gone through for me. "I'll walk with you," I said.

Steven shook his head. "You don't have to do that," he said.

"No, it's okay," I said with a shrug. "I want to."

We walked down the street in silence for a few moments. I struggled to find something to say. I decided to play it safe, and comment on the weather.

"It feels great out here, doesn't it?"

"Yeah, I'm not a big fan of winter," he confessed.

I wrinkled my nose. "Me either."

"It must be nice to have a birthday this weekend. You know, the return of Spring and all."

I stared at the pavement as we walked along. "Yeah. As a kid, I didn't really understand the concept of months and years, but I always knew that when the daffodils started to bloom, then my birthday was just around the corner. And I knew once my birthday was here, everything would begin to turn green again, and then there would be more flowers, and warmer weather."

"New beginnings," he said, shoving his hands in his pockets.

I looked at him, and nodded. "Yeah...exactly."

We walked a few more steps, and Steven cleared his throat. "Well, here I am."

I saw his Jeep in front of us. "Right. I, um, guess I'll see you at rehearsal tonight?"

"I'll be there."

"Good. And thank you again for the bracelet. It's incredible, really. It's the best thing I got today."

Steven shook his head. "You don't have to say that."

I smiled. "No, I'm serious. It's perfect."

"I'm glad you like it," he said.

His eyes caught mine, and for a few moments I couldn't move, or think. He had amazing eyes. They were blue and clear, and I couldn't for the life of me figure out why I hadn't noticed them before.

I blinked, then looked away. "I, ah, should be going. I'll see you later."

I quickly turned on my heel and headed down the street, back toward my house. *What was wrong with me?* I wondered. Now I had feelings for Steven? That was ridiculous. No. I shook my head, trying to remove the idea. I felt the weight of the bracelet on my wrist. *It really was beautiful*, I thought, gazing at it again.

"So what was the best part about today?" Phil asked,

as I opened my bed-in-a-bag set in my bedroom. The camera was still attached to his hand.

"Go away," I said, hiding my face.

"Come on, don't be such a spoilsport. What was the best part about your birthday?"

"Being able to share it with my friends and family," I said, with more than a hint of sarcasm in my voice.

"So the presents weren't nice?" he prompted.

"I didn't say that." I stood up and walked into the kitchen. Phil followed me.

"What about the cake?"

"Why are you doing this to me? I asked. Phil snickered.

"I just wanted to know if you liked the cake," he replied.

"I loved the cake. Now turn that thing off!" I turned my back on him and walked into my bedroom. He continued to follow me.

"I can't. Not until you sign off," he explained.

Ugh! The Channel 8 News Nerd! He wasn't even a real cameraman. He just sold air time.

"Signing off," I muttered, rolling my eyes.

"Say, 'This is Wrenn Scott on her sixteenth birthday, signing off.'"

I repeated the words, without much enthusiasm.

"Now say, 'And this is just the beginning.'"

"And this is just the beginning," I stated. I thought about the words. It was like I was preparing for battle or something, and as a beginning, I wasn't exactly sure if the best or worst was yet to come. But the words definitely implied that something greater loomed beyond the horizon; it wasn't over yet.

Phil finally hit the Stop button and I watched the little red light dim until it disappeared.

"Wrenn, I wanted to thank you for letting me come today," he said. "I really enjoy spending time with you, your mother, and Karly."

I turned my back to him and began shuffling papers around my piano, trying to appear busy. "No problem."

"I, uh, hope that there'll be more birthdays in the future, and that you won't mind my spending them with you guys."

"Sure," I muttered, only half-listening.

"Well, Happy Birthday," he called as he left the room.

I looked up. "Thanks," I said. But he was gone, and I didn't know if he had heard me or not, or if it even mattered.

I threw myself onto the bed and stared at the ceiling, thinking about Steven, the bracelet; thinking about Chase and the entire afternoon. My stomach began to hurt. I sat up—too quickly. I felt dizzy—a bit lightheaded. All the cake and sugar I'd eaten made me feel positively wretched. I was going to throw up.

I ran to the bathroom and sat down by the toilet. But even though I tried, nothing came up. Defeated, I opened the top drawer and took out a laxative package. I was just swallowing it when the bathroom door flew open.

"What are you doing?" Karly demanded.

I began to choke. "N-Nothing!" I stammered. "What is your problem?" I asked, slamming the drawer shut.

Karly pushed past me and opened it. "What is this?" she asked. "For fast, effective relief—Wrenn, what is this for?"

"For fast, effective relief," I repeated. "I wasn't feeling well."

"Why are you taking these?"

I pushed her away from the drawer. "Don't talk so loud," I hissed. "Someone will hear you."

"I'm going to start yelling if you don't tell me what's going on," she replied, lowering her voice.

"There's nothing going on."

"Then why were you taking these?"

"My stomach hurt. I ate too much cake and I thought I was going to be sick. Okay? Are you happy?"

Karly shook her head. "You're lying," she said. "You're lying and you know it. This is what you were hiding when you came home the other day. You're using this stuff to lose weight!"

"I am not! I only took one."

"Then why are they in your drawer? Huh?" she asked. "If you only needed one, then why do you keep a whole box here, in your drawer? Why isn't it in Mom's medicine cabinet?"

A feeble "Because that's where I want it" was all I could manage.

"This is ridiculous," she continued. "You are such a liar. I knew you were losing weight too fast. Your whole diet and exercise routine wasn't enough? So now you're starving yourself and taking laxatives to speed up the process? You are so stupid! It's not safe to lose weight this way, Wrenn. Even I know that!"

"You have to keep your voice down," I begged. "Mom will hear you."

"I hope she does hear me," she said. "Because if she doesn't, I'm going to tell her what you're doing."

My hands were shaking, and I could feel my eyes filling with tears. "You don't understand."

"Exactly. And if I don't understand, I know Mom won't understand, either."

"She's not going to find out, because you're not going to tell her."

"Don't think that I won't," she tempted. "Get rid of this stuff! Stop using it or I swear I'll tell Mom."

I rolled my eyes. "You are such a brat."

"Get over it."

I grabbed the box from the drawer and threw it in the trash can. "There."

She folded her arms across her chest, and remained planted firmly where she stood. "No. Get *rid* of them."

I felt like screaming. I reached down and grabbed the package out of the trash can and began popping pills out one by one, dumping them into the toilet bowl. When the entire box was empty, I flushed and watched them disappear.

"Are you happy now?" I hissed.

"Yes, I am," she replied.

I stormed past her, knocking her against the sink.

When I returned to my room I threw myself onto the bed and began to cry. I don't even know why I was crying: Was it because I was upset about nearly getting caught, or was it because now I didn't have any backup pills? I wiped my eyes, listening to Bree's voice in my head. "What doesn't stay in your body can't make you fat," she sang.

I jumped up and grabbed my running shoes. I'd had enough. I was never going to be fat again. *Never!*

Chapter

Eighteen

"Okay, people, this is it! We have less than two weeks till show time. Work with me!" Mr. Pike yelled. "Let's start this scene over." The music was cued and the dancers began their routines.

I sat by myself in the back row of the auditorium, trying not to fall asleep. It was way past lunchtime and my throat hurt. We had been rehearsing nonstop since eight in the morning. We were in an intense, two-day rehearsal phase that began yesterday after school, ended at midnight last night, only to start all over again, first thing this morning.

According to Pikey, we were doing this nonstop rehearsing to fine-tune the "rough spots" in the show. By this afternoon, all the wrinkles would have to be ironed out, because there were only a few more days until our dress rehearsal. Costumes were already fitted and hanging backstage, we'd memorized our lines and solos; after months of endless rehearsals and bouts of laryngitis, it would all be over in only two weeks. It would be bittersweet, of course, and I wasn't sure if I was happy or sad that the play would be over.

It seemed like a million years ago that Zoe first handed me the flyer about auditions. Yet the time had passed so quickly. I thought about how dramatically things had changed since then; and how much I had changed, too. Not all my changes were physical ones, either. No way could a before and after photo comparison ever capture it all.

I checked my watch, then flipped through my dog-eared script, silently rehearsing scenes in my head. My stomach growled. I checked my watch again. It was after two, and we were due for a lunch break—overdue, in fact.

Looking around the room, I saw Bree and Tad on stage, both looking pretty irritated. Mr. Pike was behind them, weaving through the chorus members, placing people, adjusting arms, and tilting heads. He made everyone repeat the scene three times. And by the time they were done, I was sure Bree was ready to go postal on him.

Tabitha was offstage, lying on the floor. Erica and Jared were sitting together up front, looking bored. Steven and a few others were scurrying about in the background, completely oblivious to everyone else.

"Mr. Pike, I am seriously about to starve. Can we go to lunch now?" Bree finally begged. The director checked his watch. By his expression, it was clear that he had no idea it was so late. With only a few precious hours left to rehearse, he suggested we continue until four, and then leave an hour early.

A chorus of "no's!" reverberated throughout the auditorium.

"Fine, but be back in forty-five minutes. We're behind, people. If this show is going to be a success, you'd better get back here on time and ready to work." But no one was listening. Everyone was grabbing jackets and running for the doors.

"Hey," Tabitha called on her way out of the room. "We're going to Andy's. Did you want to ride with me?"

"Sure," I replied, getting up from my seat.

"Come on, I want to get out of here before Bree sees us."

"Why?"

"She's in a mood today. And I'm sick of her."

We hurried out and headed to Andy's, where the entire cast and crew had assembled. Everyone congregated toward the back, filling up half the restaurant. Tabitha and I grabbed a booth, only to be joined a few minutes later by Bree and Erica.

"I swear, Tad is such a jerk," Bree growled. "I mean, who doesn't sit with his girlfriend when he goes to lunch? You'd think he would have saved me a seat."

No one responded.

"And I am so sick of hearing Pike's nasally voice," she continued. "I thought I was going to lose it on stage when he kept making me switch places, like, a thousand times. I mean, did you see him? How unprofessional is he? He should really think about retiring."

Tabitha pretended to be intrigued by the burger she'd ordered, and I only picked at my French fries, eating a small piece every now and then.

When no one offered a response, Bree changed the subject. "So, Wrenn. How are Zoe and Chase?" she asked.

"Fine, I guess," I replied with a shrug.

"Well, I wanted you to know that I'm thinking about calling him—just to straighten things out. I think the way he ended things was a mistake. No offense to Zoe, but I really think we could still be friends."

I nodded. "Good."

"Oh, and plus I'm still wondering about this whole 'Zoe and Chase' thing," she said with a sneer. "I think I have a right to know the truth."

I didn't look her in the eye. "Uh, hmm," I agreed, as I shoved another fry into my mouth.

"I mean, don't you think their whole relationship is a bit strange?"

Karly was right; I needed to come clean with Bree. If, by chance, she did talk to Chase and he told her he was talking to Zoe before they broke up, then she was going to point the finger at me. On the other hand, I didn't want to cause a scene. I finally decided that if I told her what I knew, it would have to be in private.

"I guess," I answered. "I don't know."

Tabitha coughed. "So, how much more of this torture do you think Pikey will put us through?" she asked.

I exhaled. *Thank you, Tabs.* "Hopefully not too much more," I replied quickly. "It sounded to me like we'd be done by five today if we decided to take a lunch."

"I don't know about you, but I really needed a break," Erica added. "Last night I went to bed and all I could hear were those songs, over and over again. They're like, drilled into my subconscious. I know I didn't fall asleep until like, three in the morning."

"I know. I've heard of these kinds of intense rehearsals before, but this was more like boot camp," Tabitha said. "I could hardly keep my eyes open on the way home last night. I crashed the second I walked into my bedroom."

We continued to complain about the physical pain and mental anguish Pikey was putting us through, and how relieved we'd all be when it was over.

"I don't know what I'm going to do with all my free time once we're done," I stated. "This thing is my whole life right now."

I felt a hand on my shoulder. I turned around in my seat and saw Steven.

"Hey, what's up?" I asked.

"Nothing. I just wanted to see if you needed a ride this afternoon or anything."

"Actually, since she and Phil were going out, Mom let me drive her car here," I told him.

"Awesome," he said. "The perks of having a license! Okay, well, I just thought I'd ask. I guess I'll see you back at school."

"Okay, thanks." I watched as he carried his tray to the front and dumped his trash. When I finally turned my attention back to my friends, Bree was glaring at me.

"What?" I asked her.

"What? *What?* Come on, Wrenn. Steven James? Tell me you can't do better than Steven."

"What are you talking about?"

She lowered her eyes and stared fiercely at me, with

a look that could only be described as complete disgust. "Do you actually *like* him?"

The silver I.D. bracelet slid down my arm as I lifted my drink. "He's just a friend. I mean, he's nice. We talk every now and then."

Bree clicked her tongue. "And here, I actually thought you'd changed." She picked up her trash and carried it away, with Erica hot on her heels. The bells on the door jingled as they left the building.

"Don't worry about her," Tabitha said, reaching out to touch my arm.

I crunched the ice in my drink with the straw. "He's just a friend," I repeated.

⊛

"What am I supposed to say, Zoe?" I asked her on the phone that evening.

"Why do you have to tell her anything?"

"Because she asked me! She thinks you and Chase were seeing each other before they broke up."

"You know we weren't. And why does it matter anyway?"

I hated that Zoe was being so nonchalant about the entire situation. This was a borderline crisis. If Bree knew I lied to her...."Because technically, you were."

"Is this about me and Chase? Or is it more about you and Bree?" she asked.

"What are you talking about?"

She breathed heavily into the phone. "You are so ob-

218

sessed with that girl! First you wanted to *be* her, now you're scared of her. What, do you think she isn't going to like you anymore because your best friend talked to her boyfriend while they were still dating? I mean, I didn't even know who he was when we were talking online."

"I'm not scared of her. I just don't like all the drama, that's all."

"With Bree Donnelly, *everything* is drama. You shouldn't worry about her, Wrenn, honestly."

"If she finds out that you two were talking behind her back, she'll blame me for not telling her. Then she'll go ballistic. Chase knew you before you knew him. He was at Andy's that night, remember? He was there. He knew who you were, and he was still dating Bree at the time." I let out a sigh. "This is all his fault."

"I am *so* not going to listen to this," Zoe said, her voice rising. "Chase is a great guy and I love him. I don't care about Bree Donnelly, and you shouldn't either."

I didn't know how else to explain myself; what I could say that would make her understand. This *was* a Big Deal: for me, it was much bigger than she realized.

"You know, I hate what this play has done to you," she continued. "You've changed. You aren't the Wrenn I used to know, and I'm tired of playing these little games with you."

I felt the blood rush to my head. Zoe was absolutely right. I *had* changed. And if she didn't like it...if she had a problem with it, then it was *her* problem.

"Well, if that's the way you feel, then maybe we

shouldn't be friends anymore." I didn't wait for her to respond. Instead, I hung up, then threw the phone onto my bed. When it rang a minute later, I didn't bother answering it.

Chapter

Nineteen

The next morning, I grabbed a bottle of water from the refrigerator. It was early—too early, in fact. I hated being awake early on a weekend. It was bad enough that I'd been up at the crack of dawn yesterday for rehearsal; now I couldn't even sleep late on Sunday morning.

The problem was that my mind was reeling. The things Zoe'd said last night on the phone really had bothered me. First they made me mad, then I got upset because she was normally my best support system. I still wanted to be her best friend. I hated that she was disappointed in me. I'd thought about her words over and over in my head for half the night, when what I really needed to do was sleep.

Now, here I was, bags under my eyes, hair in tangles, wrapped in a terry cloth robe, and no better off than before Zoe told me how she really felt: "You aren't the Wrenn I used to know."

Well, I decided I was glad about one thing: I didn't want to be that Wrenn anymore. I wanted to be the thin and popular Wrenn. That was my goal. And since I'd joined the cast of *Grease*, I'd done a complete 180. I was on my way. Why couldn't she see that this was my dream? My great dream, my one wish? A true friend would have been happy for me, not critical.

What was her problem anyway? I wondered. She and Chase were the happiest, most disgusting couple on earth. If anything, *she* was the one who had changed—for the worse. Now that she was dating Chase Cunningham, she wasn't the same "Zoe" anymore, either. So what gave her the right to criticize *me*?

Enough of this, I thought, taking a swig of water. I needed a hot bath.

For the next half hour I soaked in the tub, my hair piled on top of my head, facial cream on my face. It was a complete "girl's morning," and it was just what I needed. I felt relaxed, even semi-rejuvenated.

When I finished, I wrapped myself in a towel and opened the door. When I went into the hallway, something didn't feel right. I knew I wasn't alone; I felt like I was being watched. I turned my head, and out of the corner of my eye I saw it: a tall, dark figure, standing in the corner. I stepped back, knocking my elbow into the wall behind me, and screamed.

When Mom's bedroom door flew open, I finally realized what was going on. We all just stood there, with surprised looks on our faces, unable to move.

Remembering I was wearing only a towel, my face turned red with embarrassment, then hot with anger.

"No freakin' way" was all I could muster.

"Wrenn, please. Let me explain," my mother began.

"No! There's no need to explain. This," I said, pointing back and forth at them, "doesn't *need* an explanation."

They remained glued in place; caught in the act: Mom in an oversized shirt, and Phil wearing only jeans. Yuck. My mother and Phil, "together." Could my life *get* any worse?

I stormed into my bedroom and slammed the door. Moments later I heard Phil start his SUV and pull out of the driveway. Not long after, Mom knocked on my door and asked if we could talk.

"We are *not* talking about this," I argued.

"I need to talk to you."

"There is nothing to talk about. I don't need an explanation. I don't *want* an explanation." I pulled my red nail polish out of my drawer and began to paint my toenails.

"Wrenn, open this door."

I didn't answer, trying to ignore her completely.

"Open it!" She turned the knob back and forth, trying to push it open. "Open the door, Wrenn!"

"No! I'm not opening the door!" I screamed at her.

"If you don't let me in, I'm going to take it off the hinges," she threatened.

"Bring it on!"

I heard her walk away, but she never pulled out the power screwdriver. She just left, like a dog with its tail between its legs. She was wrong and she knew it. And we weren't going to talk about it until I was ready.

It was almost lunchtime when Karly finally came home from her night at Joy's. Perfect. The ultimate payback. Karly would freak out when she heard about what went down last night. If there was one person I could count on to take my side in this situation, it was Karly.

I waltzed into the kitchen and found Mom flipping through a magazine. My sister sat down at the counter and began eating a banana. I asked Karly how her night was. She furrowed her brow, completely confused.

"It was fine, why?"

"Oh, I was just wondering if more than one of us had an exciting evening, that's all."

"Wrenn," Mom pleaded.

"What are you talking about?" Karly asked.

"Well, my evening was completely uneventful. But that's okay, because it seems that Mom had a good enough time for both of us."

"Mom, what is going on? And why is Wrenn acting psycho?"

She didn't answer.

"It goes like this," I began. "I was soaking in the tub this morning. It was pretty early, so I didn't think anyone was awake. Well, imagine my surprise when I walked into the hallway and found Phil standing there, half naked."

"Half naked?" she repeated, her eyes wide open.

"Shirtless," I informed her.

"Shirtless? No way. Mom? Tell me he didn't stay the night," Karly begged.

No answer.

"Well, judging from the fact that he wasn't wearing a

shirt, and Mom wasn't wearing her usual pajama shorts—yeah, I'd say he spent the night. It looks like we aren't the only ones who enjoy slumber parties." I turned my attention toward my mother. "You should have invited us all, Mom. We could have had a 'girls' night,'" I threw in.

"Oh that is just so disgusting!" Karly cried. "You're sleeping with Phil? That's like, so gross!"

"It's not gross," Mom said.

"Ewwww!" Karly said, scrunching her face in disgust. She threw her unfinished banana on the counter. "I can't even eat this anymore. I'm going to puke."

Mom folded her arms across her chest in defense. "You know, I don't have to explain myself or answer to you girls. I'm an adult. My decisions are my decisions. You're just going to have to get over it."

"I know," Karly whined. "But Phil? Come on, you could do so much better."

"I love Phil."

"Oh, so now you *love* him?" I asked.

"Yes, I love him. Would he have stayed the night if I felt otherwise?" she asked.

"I don't know, why don't you ask Karly's dad?" I shot back.

The color drained from my mother's face, and I watched as Karly's eyes filled with tears. Immediately, I regretted those words. I felt positively horrible. "This—This, it's not about you, Karly, I swear," I stammered.

"Then what is it about, Wrenn?" she asked. She got up and stormed out of the kitchen. The door to her bedroom slammed shut with a bang. I jumped.

My mother glared at me. "Don't you, ever, EVER bring up my personal mistakes again," she shouted, her eyes tearing. "I love your sister very much. And you know what? I love you too, Wrenn. But I don't like you very much right now. And that's my prerogative." She turned on her heel and marched toward Karly's room to smooth things over and clean up the mess I'd made.

When I woke up hours later, my eyes were dry and my body felt sticky. The afternoon sun poured through my bedroom window, and the pink bedspread reflected onto the walls. It felt like a sauna and I was hot. I sat up and ran my fingers through my hair. The first thing I noticed was how quiet it was. I didn't hear the television or any voices. Nobody was walking around. I was alone.

I walked into my mother's room and grabbed a pair of shorts and a T-shirt from her drawer. The bed was never made anyway, but today it looked…well, more lived in than usual. For the first time in years, I noticed that two pillows were rumpled instead of only one. I felt like throwing up.

Grabbing my tennis shoes on the way out, I sat down on the porch steps and slipped them on, taking in the smell of dirt, and flowers, and Spring. *New beginnings*, I snorted. *Yeah right.*

I walked down the driveway and turned onto the street. Then I began to run. I jogged down the road, listening to the sound of my feet striking the pavement. I cleared my mind. I didn't want to think about Phil, or my mother, or Karly. I didn't want to think about the musical, or rehearsals, or Bree, or Zoe.

I was on the last stretch of my run, sweating and breathless, when I saw Steven. Just ahead of me, he was walking a golden retriever. I quickened my pace, hoping to catch up.

"Hey, Steven!" I called out.

Steven stopped walking and turned around. "Hi," he replied. He immediately introduced me to his dog, Rusty. Steven had decided it would be a nice afternoon for a run, so here they were. I was actually surprised by his look. He was wearing a basic T-shirt and athletic shorts. I'd never seen him wear anything other than flannel shirts and jeans. He looked completely different without his geek gear and he looked...normal.

"You're not trying to run to the ends of the earth again, are you?" he asked, smiling.

I smiled back. "Yeah, that was my intention. The way things have been going lately, running to the ends of the earth doesn't sound like such a bad idea."

"Anything you want to talk about?" We walked in step down the road.

"Where do I even start?" I said with a laugh.

He furrowed his brow. "The beginning is always good."

"Of course," I muttered. "The beginning. Well, for one, my best friend hates me."

"Zoe? Why would she hate you?" he asked.

"Because she thinks I've changed. She says I'm not the same person any more," I explained.

"Have you? Changed, I mean."

We turned the corner and continued walking down the street, with Rusty leading the way. "Do you think I've changed?"

"Yes, but not necessarily in a bad way. You look different on the outside, but deep down I still think you're the same person you always were."

"So she's wrong," I said.

"No, I didn't say that. You can still be the same person and misguided at the same time."

I felt a pang of hurt and sadness in my chest. "So you think I'm misguided?"

"I can't decide that. That's up to you to figure out," he replied.

He was talking in circles. Nothing he said made any sense at all, and thinking about it was giving me a headache.

I took a deep breath. "Okay, so the outward changes—was I misguided there?"

"I thought you were beautiful to begin with," he said without hesitation. "But nobody should make you feel bad about who you are, inside or out. If you need to make changes, nobody should try and stop you." He shrugged his shoulders. "The important thing is that you're happy. I mean with who you are. Never mind anybody else."

We walked in silence for a moment. I drank in my surroundings; the colorful houses, the freshly mowed grass, an occasional child playing in a backyard, and I wondered about the fact that Steven thought I was "misguided."

"So what else is bothering you?" he asked, finally breaking the silence that had fallen between us.

"There's more?"

"I don't know. You tell me."

"Well, I'm kind of annoyed at my mom. She and Phil are getting way too serious."

"But that's good, right?"

"Oh yeah, it's fabulous," I replied, sarcastically.

"What's the problem with that?"

I debated whether or not I should go into all this. But I knew Steven, and he wouldn't tell anyone or make fun of me. I knew in my heart that I could trust him with this horrible episode. So, I explained how Phil and my mother were always going out, and that he was always at our house. I told him about the night before, and how embarrassed I'd been earlier that morning, finding Phil in the hall. How I didn't think that Phil was my mother's type.

"Well, it's not really your decision," Steven said, after I'd finished my spiel. "Even if you don't think Phil is 'her type,' it doesn't matter, as long as she does. You never know, he may not be her type, but that doesn't mean he isn't exactly who she needs."

"But that doesn't mean I like what she did," I added, realizing he had a valid point.

"You don't have to like it," he said, smiling. "You just have to deal. You know, the world would be a better place if people concentrated on themselves—on making themselves better, rather than worrying so much about what everyone else is doing."

I sighed. Of course, he was right. So not only was I

misguided, but I worried too much about other people and what they thought or did. I glanced at Steven. Before looking away, I noticed he had such a nice smile. I listened to the sound of our feet crunching the gravel. Rusty padded along in front of us.

"So what do I do about this whole Zoe thing?" I finally asked.

"Talk to her."

"I can't talk to her. I don't want to. She doesn't understand."

"Why not?"

"Because she just doesn't. She thinks all I want is to be popular," I told him.

"Why would she think that?"

I thought about my birthday wish, all the diary entries, and all the daydreams I'd had about being in the same group as Bree Donnelly; how I wanted everyone to know who I was and envy me; how I wanted to be skinny and beautiful, and to have a hot boyfriend and be able to drive my own car. "I guess because that's all I've ever wanted," I confessed.

"Really?" he asked, disbelieving.

"Yeah. Haven't you ever wanted to be popular?"

"Maybe. When I was in the second grade," he replied with a grin.

I nudged him with my shoulder, smiling. "This is serious," I informed him.

"I'm sorry. It's okay, I'm serious now." He made a serious face. "So enlighten me. What's so great about being popular?"

I kicked a rock with my tennis shoe. It skipped several times before landing a few yards in front of me. "I don't know. It's the life. I mean, look at Bree Donnelly. Sure, she has her bad days, but for the most part she has the perfect life: lots of friends, a cool boyfriend, everyone loves her, and the people who don't are just jealous. People wake up in the morning and go to school just to see her."

"Wrenn, have you ever really looked at Bree Donnelly? I mean really stepped back and taken an unbiased look at her? She actually believes that people wake up in the morning to see her. But I can tell you for a fact, that's not true. I can't imagine why anyone would want to hang around her, or be anything like her for that matter."

"But it's not just Bree," I explained. "It's all popular people. I like the way they get to live their lives. The friends, the parties…that's just the ultimate to me."

"Being popular isn't always such a good thing, you know. With all those friends come just as many enemies, if not more. You really never know who's on your side, or who's going to turn his back on you, or stab you in the back. You have to keep up your image all the time or else you can lose it—just like that," snapping his fingers. "I mean, what's the point, really? Personally, I'd rather be backstage. There's a lot less drama back there. No pun intended."

I giggled.

"The truth is, Wrenn, I know I'm never going to be popular. And that's okay. I have my friends. I like them and I know they like me, too. There's nothing pretentious about anything or anyone. I am who I am. Like me or hate me, ignore me, make fun of me, whatever. I'm happy with who I am. And the way I see it, if someone isn't willing to get to know you for who you are—popular or not—then they aren't worth having as a friend, period. In the grand scheme of things, I would pick a Zoe over a Bree any day of the week."

We turned the corner and were back on my street. I could see my house in the distance. "Well, thank you for walking with me, and thank you for the advice. You've given me a lot to think about."

"I was just giving you my opinion. Take it for what it's worth. And, um, I think you were the one walking with me," he replied.

Oh. He was totally right. I was the one who'd gone after him—for once in my life. My cheeks flushed with embarrassment. "Well, thanks anyway," I said hurriedly. "I guess I'll see you at school tomorrow."

I walked briskly up the driveway, not stopping until I reached the front door, where I turned briefly to watch Steven and Rusty jog away.

Inside I found Mom in the kitchen, finishing the last of the dishes. I took a deep breath, trying to find the strength to say whatever came next.

"I'm sorry," I finally blurted out. "Phil is a nice guy. And if you like him, and want to date him or..." I swallowed hard, "...whatever, then don't let me stop you."

She turned to look at me. "Thank you, Wrenn. That's very adult of you."

I folded my arms across my chest. "I'll give Phil a chance, but you have to promise to warn me the next time you plan a sleepover."

"Fine."

I walked to my room, feeling part of the burden lifting off my shoulders. I grabbed the phone from my nightstand and dialed Zoe's number. It rang four times and no one picked up. I left a message. "Hey, Zoe, it's Wrenn. Give me a call when you get this message. We really need to talk."

I rehearsed my solos for the remainder of the afternoon, thinking occasionally about my earlier encounter with Steven. I smiled when I thought about his shaggy hair and the way he flailed his arms about when he was excited. Steven wasn't so bad, I decided. Popular or not, I kind of liked him.

When Zoe didn't return my phone call by dinner, I knew she wasn't in a forgiving mood. Still, I had to get this out. I walked over to my desk and turned on the computer. Neither she nor Sk8trGuy were signed on, so I decided to compose an email instead.

Zo—

I know you're upset, and totally disappointed in me. You're right, this show has made me crazy, and it was so stupid of me to worry so much about Bree. I don't care if she finds out about Chase, because my friendship with you is so much more important. I shouldn't have been so concerned about her in the first place. I thought that by get-

*ting a part in the musical I would become popular. But
someone told me that I didn't need to change; that I was
just fine the way I was. I guess it's time I accepted that.
So, I'm sorry for hanging up on you. I promise from now
on I'll be a better best friend. Hopefully I'll talk to you
soon.*

I read and reread the email before finally sending it
out into cyberspace. I didn't know if Zoe would get it right
away, or even if she'd call me at all, but at least I'd made
the effort. I only hoped that she would forgive me.

Chapter

Twenty

"I'm going to freak out. I can't do this, really."

"Wrenn, calm down. You'll be fine," Zoe assured me. "You deserve this!" She and Chase stood backstage with me before the musical was about to begin.

After all the rehearsals, the singing, the sore throats, and the stressing, it all came down to this one performance. Tonight I would prove to everyone that I could be a star.

"I'm sorry," I blurted out for the hundredth time. "Things just got so crazy."

"Don't even think about it now. Think about your acceptance speech the first time you win an Oscar, and how the only reason you're there is because your best friend convinced you to try out for the school musical in the tenth grade."

I frowned. "I'm not so sure I should be thanking you at all."

She waved her hand. "Of course you should. Now, we need to go before all the good seats get taken. Don't be nervous," she added, giving me a hug. "You'll be great."

Just as they were leaving, my mother, Phil, and Karly approached me from behind. "Wrenn, you look absolutely fabulous!" Mom exclaimed.

I looked down at my fifties-era Rizzo costume, which had to be altered at the last minute because it was too big. I'd lost even more weight since we were measured last month. Staring at myself in the mirror, I didn't look like myself at all. Between the makeup and the short dark wig, it was a wonder that even my mother recognized me. I was a completely different person. The only thing reminding me of my actual identity was the silver bracelet dangling from my wrist.

"So, are you nervous?" Phil asked. His camcorder was in hand, once again. I swear, the thing was permanently attached.

"Yes, I'm nervous. I'm about to die," I told him, looking directly into the camera.

"What has been your most memorable moment?"

"I don't know. Ask me later," I said, swallowing hard. "You're making me even more nervous than I already am."

"I'm just trying to prepare you for all of your future interviews."

I rolled my eyes. "Phil, I don't have anything to say."

"Is there anything you want to tell those at home who may be watching?"

I thought about this for a moment. "If I get through this night without throwing up I'll consider myself a success."

"And there you have it, folks," Phil commentated. "Wrenn Scott: Budding Starlet." Phil turned the video camera off and put it back in the bag hanging from his shoulder. "I'll be filming all night, so you can watch yourself later."

My mother smiled, and fingered the curly black wisps of my wig. "You've worked so hard for this. You'll be terrific," she said, stealing Phil's favorite word.

"We need to get our seats, Kerri," Phil reminded her. "This place is beginning to fill up."

"Don't tell me that!" I cried, covering my ears with my hands.

Karly folded her arms. "There are tons of people out there, and everyone will be watching you. If you pass out on stage, then you'll never live it down," she taunted, smiling.

"Karly," Mom chided.

"That's okay, because you're just jealous," I retorted.

She frowned. "If I was, I'd never admit it."

"All right, we're going," Mom said. "Meet us in the lobby after the show. Phil's treating us to dinner."

"Okay."

"Break a leg!" Phil called as they disappeared.

Everyone was running around in a state of panic. Bree's mother, her spitting image and looking more like an older sister, was working on her daughter's makeup. Tabitha was standing in front of a mirror, teasing and spraying her hair.

I checked my watch. Ten minutes until show time. I powdered my face—again, and added more eyeliner and mascara. I felt like a clown. Stage makeup was *so* not becoming.

Before long, I had another visitor. "How are you holding up?" asked Steven, just as I finished adding another layer of lipstick. He leaned down on one knee next to my chair so that we were eye to eye.

"I'm nervous. I think I'm going to die."

"The odds of you dying on stage are slim. So don't worry about that. And being nervous is a good thing; it'll keep you focused. Don't worry, Wrenn. You'll be great."

I sucked in a huge breath. "I hope so. Is everything all right on your end?"

He adjusted his headset. "Yeah," he replied. "We were having sound trouble earlier, but I think we've taken care of everything."

"That's good to know."

"Anyway, I just wanted to wish you luck. It's about to get really crazy around here."

I smiled. "Thanks for the tip."

Steven leaned forward, and, before I even had a chance to react, gave me a quick kiss on the cheek.

"Good luck."

The butterflies, which were already wreaking havoc in my stomach, went absolutely berserk as he walked away.

I turned back and stared at my reflection in the mirror. This time, however, I wasn't alone.

"Wrenn," Tabitha said with a sly smile, "what's going on between you and Steven? And why wasn't I informed?" She folded her arms in protest.

"Don't ask, because even I don't know," I replied, powdering my nose one final time.

"I'd ask if you wanted me to put in a good word for

you, but that's not even necessary. He seems to like you —
a lot."

"I know. But I can't even think about that right now.
How are you doing?" I asked, changing the subject.

"I'm good. You?"

"Totally nervous," I confessed. "The butterflies —
they've taken over my entire body."

She looked straight into my eyes. "Listen to me.
Being on stage is such a rush. Once you get out there,
you'll forget who you even are. You'll be Rizzo, and the
only way anyone will know otherwise is if they look at the
program to find out who's playing the part. And I'm telling
you, once the curtain goes up, you'll be addicted forever."

"I can't imagine being addicted to what I'm feeling
right now," I groaned.

"No, not right now, but once you hear the applause,
you'll know that you belong on stage. Wrenn, you're
amazing, and it's high time everybody found out."

Mr. Pike burst through the side door. "Five minutes
till show time, people! Five minutes!"

The electricity behind the curtain intensified. Cast and
crew members alike were running around like mad, adding
final touches to makeup, checking wires, taking that last
trip to the bathroom. Everyone was preparing for this, our
opening night.

Minutes later the music began, the cast took center
stage, and the curtain at last went up.

I was hot, and my makeup streaked where beads of

sweat were running down my forehead. *I need some air,* I thought, as I pushed open the heavy double doors, hoping that the cool April night would breathe some new life into me.

Inside the auditorium, the play was winding down. I had one final scene, after having nailed my solos and dances. Of course, Bree was stealing the show. The crowd seemed to feed off her every time she was on stage. But Bree was like that, though, no matter what she did.

I inhaled deeply but it didn't feel like enough. It felt like I was drowning. I breathed in again. I gave myself a few more seconds outside before returning inside and backstage. It was unbelievably hot, even with the doors wide open. I sat down on the seat where I'd earlier put on my makeup. I began to blot the sweat from my forehead, and then repowdered my face.

Suddenly I felt nauseous. The girl in the mirror disappeared, and the lights began to twinkle. My head felt heavy, and my entire body seemed to melt. I leaned forward, knocking over the case of powder, spilling it across the desk. I reached out blindly, feeling for my water bottle. I took a long drink, then closed my eyes, hoping the woozy feeling would go away. When I finally opened them, the world had righted itself. I breathed a sigh of relief and polished off the rest of the water.

I rushed back to the stage for the finish, and before I knew it, we were lining up for our curtain calls.

When the curtains rose again, the crowd went completely wild. It was unlike anything I'd ever experienced.

I saw Mom, Karly, and Phil seated a few rows from the front; Phil was still filming with his camcorder, watching me on the screen. Zoe and Chase sat across the room. I smiled at them, and Zoe took a break from clapping to wave.

Tad and Bree, starring as Danny and Sandy, moved upstage and took their bow. I watched them, remembering how badly I'd wanted to be Tad's girlfriend. Then I saw Jared the Chorus Guy bringing up the rear. I forgave Erica for stealing him from me—even though I never really had him in the first place. In the end, I think everyone ended up with the right person after all.

That's when I saw Steven. He was standing alone backstage, his headset on, clipboard in hand. He caught my eye and held my gaze until the red curtain swooshed to the floor, separating us from the crowd.

All at once people were laughing and hugging each other. Four months of hard work and endless hours of rehearsal were all wrapped up in this one night, and it was officially over.

For the next half hour we greeted people in the lobby. People who had never even spoken to me before approached me, commenting about the great job I'd done, and how they had no idea I could even sing.

Suddenly, a red light was in my face. "So, Wrenn, how does it feel to be a star?" Phil asked.

I took a deep breath. "It feels okay. I'm glad it's over, but it's kind of sad in a way."

"What are your future plans? Do you see yourself in any upcoming roles?"

"No, not any time soon—" Someone behind me touched my shoulder. I whirled around and was face to face with Steven. He was holding a pretty bouquet of spring flowers.

"Congratulations," he said. "You did great."

"Thank you." I wrapped my arms around him. I don't know who was more surprised—him or me.

"You're going to the cast party tomorrow, right?" He finally asked, pulling away.

I breathed in the scent of the flowers. "Cast party?"

"It's a tradition. The invitations are backstage."

"Well, I guess I am," I said. "But, um, if you don't mind, I could probably use a ride."

Steven looked at the floor, and ran his hand through his hair. "Sure. I'll call you."

I smiled. "That would be great."

"Okay, no problem. You really were terrific," he added. I smiled. Terrific. It was *such* an annoying word, but, coming from Steven, it didn't sound so obnoxious. It was tolerable, even. I turned around as he walked away. Zoe and Chase had joined the crowd, and they were all looking at me with expectant faces. The camera was still rolling.

"I thought he wasn't your type," Zoe commented.

"Oh, what do I know? I think it'll be okay," I replied.

Chapter

Twenty-One

Karly and my mother spent the entire afternoon helping me get ready for the cast party. Mom had arranged my highlighted hair elegantly in an updo, and thanks to Karly and her shimmery eye shadow, I had makeup to die for.

Since it was a semiformal affair, the little black dress that Mom had bought me months ago finally had a place to go. But the real surprise came the night before, when I tried it on and it hung like a burlap bag.

My mom had bitten her lower lip, examining my reflection in the mirror. She finally pulled out her old sewing machine and spent some time taking in the sides and shoulders so that the dress would fit perfectly. The results were spectacular.

Now this was my moment. I looked better than ever before. And I couldn't help but feel a flutter of excitement every time the dress caught my eye as it hung, freshly ironed, behind my bedroom door.

"Wrenn, you look terrific!" Phil exclaimed as I waltzed into the living room. Steven, early as usual, agreed.

I smiled at my escort. "Thank you. You don't look so bad yourself." Steven, wearing a nice blue suit, looked very stylish. His hair was spiked in front—like he'd gotten hold of some gel, and for once, it was out of his eyes. "Did you get a haircut?" I asked.

"Yeah, my mom insisted." Steven looked at his reflection in the mirror above the fireplace mantel.

"It looks really good. I like it."

He smiled at me and I looked away, hoping he didn't notice the blush in my cheeks.

"Oh, wow! What have you done with my sister?" Karly asked, seeing the finished product for the first time.

"What do you think?" I asked, twirling around with a newfound confidence. I never would have dreamed of feeling like this when I first tried out for the show.

She shook her head. "Who *are* you?"

"She's absolutely beautiful," Steven offered.

I smiled, blushed, and let out a nervous giggle. Mom came forward with her camera. "Okay, time for pictures."

"Mom," Karly muttered, "don't embarrass her. This is her first date, like, ever."

"Enough, Karly! Wrenn, just a few pictures, I promise. Please. Come and stand over here by the fireplace. You, too, Steven."

For the next few minutes, Mom positioned and repositioned us at least a dozen times, snapping photo after photo. And for once, I wasn't afraid of the camera. I wanted photographs of myself. For the first time in my life, I wasn't worried about my fat rolls showing or having to tilt my neck so that it wouldn't look like I had a double chin.

No, that Wrenn—the old Wrenn—was gone forever. She'd vanished into thin air, leaving behind a closet full of clothes that were way too large. My dress—once way too snug—proved it.

As we headed toward Steven's Jeep, I heard footsteps behind me.

"Wrenn?" I turned around and saw Karly. She was running down the driveway. I waited for her to catch up. "I just want you to know," she began, trying to catch her breath, "that I'm *so* jealous."

She smiled and I threw my arms around her. I had finally done something that was, by definition, "cool"; in her own way, I knew that Karly was proud of me.

"Thanks, Karly. That really means a lot." And it did—more than she would ever know.

At the cast party, I picked at my lasagna, pretending to take a bite every now and then, but mostly sipping water and laughing with everyone around me. The entire cast and crew of *Grease* were crammed into the banquet room at Benici's, an upscale Italian restaurant downtown. We spent the first half hour posing for pictures together at this, our last big fling together, to celebrate the end of the show.

With our meals finished and the evening winding down, we shared our most memorable episodes; we couldn't help but laugh hysterically about the "Hemorrhoid Convention."

Steven leaned closer to me. "Aren't you hungry?" he asked, quietly.

"Actually, I'm full. That salad was huge, really," I replied. "I'm just going to go to the ladies room to freshen up. I'll be right back."

I excused myself from the table and headed toward the restroom. When I pushed open the door, I realized I wasn't alone. Bree Donnelly was standing at the sink, reapplying her lipstick. In her designer gown and with a professional makeup job, it looked as if she'd stepped straight from the pages of *Vogue*.

"Hey," I said, opening my purse and pulling out my own lipstick. "I didn't get to tell you last night, but you did a really great job."

She rolled her eyes. "Yeah, like I haven't heard *that* a thousand times in the last twenty-four hours."

I ignored her and began lining my lips carefully.

"So, I guess you're like, Cinderella now, huh?"

I stared at her reflection in disbelief. "Excuse me?"

She turned toward me, her eyes flashing. "I just wanted to let you know that if you were going for the whole 'beautiful princess in disguise' thing, you should have chosen someone other than Steven James to be your Prince Charming."

My face burned hot with anger. "We're just friends," I shot back.

She snickered and it annoyed me.

"Besides, who are you to tell me who I should and shouldn't date?" I added, feeling a surge of power.

"Oh, please," she sneered. "You are in total need of guidance. People like you need people like me to give you direction."

"People like me? What is that supposed to mean? And what makes you think you're worthy enough to guide anyone?"

"It's like, a gift I have," she replied, coming closer. I took in everything—her dress, her curly blonde hair, her immaculate makeup and perfectly manicured hands. "I understand people like you, Wrenn. When you were fat and ugly, you wanted nothing more than to crawl into my skin and be just like me. People like you *need* people like me."

"Oh, that's right, Bree. You so figured me out. All I ever wanted was to be nasty, selfish, and bitchy. And— what else was it?" I brought my finger to my chin, feigning thought. "Oh yeah, to drive my own boyfriend to cheat on me," I shot back.

Score!

Bree's eyes narrowed. "I knew it," she snarled. "That girl is—"

"Zoe had nothing to do with it," I interrupted. "Maybe you should just accept the fact that Chase Cunningham is too good for you."

She came forward and pointed her finger in my face. "I can*not* believe you. You will be so sorry, Wrenn Scott. You'll be sorry you ever crossed me, because I'm going to make sure that everyone knows exactly what you are," she warned, her words laced with hatred. "A wannabe. A fake. You're nothing but a fat girl hiding behind a pretty black dress and a little bit of makeup. You're *nothing*. You *never* will be good enough. Not today, not tomorrow, not *ever*!"

I pushed through the door and returned to the banquet

room, leaving Bree ranting and fuming alone in the bathroom.

"Hey, are you all right?" Steven asked. "You look a little pale." I forced a smile and sat down beside him.

"I'm fine," I told him. But I wasn't fine. I was hot, and I was tired. And my stomach ached. The more I tried to pay attention to the conversation around me, the more flustered I became.

I hated Bree Donnelly. I *despised* her. I fanned my face and tried to cool my neck with the back of my hand. *I hated her. Who does she think she is anyway?* I wasn't the one who needed guidance. She did. What kind of name was Bree anyway? She was practically named after *cheese*. How ridiculous. At least *I* was named after a songbird.

I took a deep breath. Bree said I was nothing...I felt like I was going to throw up. In a rush, all of the negative thoughts I'd ever had, my frustrated dreams about everything I'd ever wanted to become, every bad feeling I'd ever felt for the last decade came crashing down on me. It was like a giant wave of emotion, and it was powerful enough to knock me over.

Now I was about to cry, and I was also about to be sick. I was tired of not being good enough—I was tired of hiding my insecurities behind highlighted hair and perfect eyeliner, when the truth was, I wasn't hiding anything from anyone. All I'd ever wanted was to be popular. I wanted to be pretty, and I wanted to be envied. I wanted Chase Cunningham and Tad Owens to fall for me. I wanted to be just like Bree Donnelly. And here I was: thin, with perfect hair, immaculate makeup, wearing a "to-die-for" dress, and I *still* wasn't good enough for Bree and Tad and Chase…or anyone else.

I had to get out of that room or I was going to hurl. I stood up too quickly, knocking my chair over behind me. It fell with a crash. The room was suddenly hazy; my head felt light and the sounds of laughter and voices seemed far away.

Steven asked if I was okay.

"I just need some air," I said. But my voice didn't sound like my own. It sounded like someone else, someone who was shaky and scared.

Everything began to blur. Taking a step, my feet felt like lead; it was like tramping through mud or deep water. I pushed my way through the crowd waiting for tables in the lobby.

"Wrenn, wait!" someone called. But I didn't stop. I burst through the front door. The cool air hit my face, but instead of feeling refreshed, it seemed that someone was strangling me from behind. I couldn't catch my breath, and everything was sparkling and bright—like it was all about to disappear.

"Wrenn!" the voice called again. I turned and took a step toward it. But now everything went silent; then the scene went from hazy to black. Then, there was nothing.

Chapter

Twenty-Two

"I told you. I'm feeling better. When can I go home?"

Once again I found myself sitting in front of Dr. Williamson. The past two days had been something out of a nightmare. The nurses watched me constantly. Together they whispered about me. They wouldn't leave me alone until I'd finished eating everything on my plate. They poked and prodded and injected. They followed me to the bathroom. And then they brought in Dr. Williamson.

According to her, I'd lost an unhealthy amount of weight in too short a period of time. I was dehydrated and my body was shutting down because of all the laxatives I'd taken. I might not have been skin and bones yet, but what I'd been doing made me a danger to myself. I was officially diagnosed with an eating disorder.

What?

It was bad enough getting this news, but the worst part was watching my mother as she crumpled into Phil's arms. She blamed herself—she kept saying this was all her fault. She should have said something sooner, she should have recognized the signs, she should have kept this from happening. I felt even more wretched than before.

"Wrenn," she said. "I've been talking with Dr. Williamson." She paused for a moment, struggling to find the right words. "And we believe it would be a good idea for you to go somewhere, to a place where you can get help for your eating disorder."

My body began to shake. "What?"

"It doesn't have to be for a long time, Wrenn. You can stay as long as you need," Dr. Williamson interjected. "But I'm recommending that you stay for at least eight weeks."

"I-I don't need to," I stammered, my eyes filling with tears. "I'm fine. I told you. Mom?" I looked at her, pleading with my eyes; silently willing her to change her mind.

Phil reached over and took her hand in support. "We just want you to get better, Wrenn. You're sick. You need help that I can't give you at home," she said.

My tears began to fall. "But I'm fine! I swear!" I cried. "It was an honest mistake! I will be so much better from now on, I promise." But no one believed me.

I stayed in the hospital for another day, and when my mother picked me up the following morning, I thought we were just going home. But then I saw my bright pink duffle bag nestled in the backseat. That's when I knew that from now on, things were going to be different. We didn't pass the familiar streets, where just days before I'd been somebody. We headed straight out of town.

"What about school?" I asked through tears.

"I've spoken to your principal. All of your teachers

have made arrangements for you to finish your work on independent study. You're such a good student that they have no problem with your finishing out the school year this way."

And I was a good student. Of course my teachers were willing to work with me. But the irony of the situation hit me at that very moment. I'd always been the fat girl, the one nobody noticed. And I had wanted everyone to talk about me because I was popular. Now I realized that on the Monday morning after the cast party, the halls at school were buzzing with conversation—and a lot of it was about me. But not because I was popular. No. They were talking about me because I'd passed out at the party, because I had an eating disorder, and because I was now headed to rehab. I wasn't Wrenn, the tiny, delicate songbird with the beautiful voice. I wasn't Rizzo, the star in *Grease*. And I wasn't fat—or just a nobody. No. Now I was someone with an eating disorder. I really didn't know exactly *who* I was anymore.

Seaside was a rehabilitation hospital on the coast, about an hour away from home and everything I knew. During the course of the ride, Mom kept talking about how great the place was supposed to be. It was right across from the ocean. I would be able to look out at the water every day. I would be with other people my age. There was counseling, and there were health classes: it was exactly what I needed...or so Mom told me.

As I walked down the sandy beige halls with my mother, bag in hand, I wondered if this was what it felt like to go away to camp…or to college. I'd never done either. We saw a common room, with couches and a television set. There was a communal dining area, an infirmary, and outdoor seating on the porch. All the rooms had identical twin beds, dressers, nightstands, and windows. And there were people. I could feel them watching me as I walked past them, my eyes lowered to the floor. I knew this time they weren't staring because I was fat. No. They were staring because they wanted to know why I was there.

Mom helped me unpack. She tried her best to make the tiny room feel like home. In addition to clothes and daily necessities, she'd bought me a journal and packed a few books and photographs. While I sat on the bed, she arranged the photographs across the dresser. There were a few family photos, some of me and Zoe, and a pack of new pictures. They were from the play. I didn't look through them right away. I couldn't bear to see them. Instead, I slipped them into my top drawer and ignored them. I wasn't ready to face that girl just yet; not when she had caused so many problems.

I cried when my mom left. Now I was all by myself, and I felt so alone. I cried when I looked out the window and saw the ocean sparkling nearby. I cried when my roommate waltzed in without a care in the world, and offered me a cheery, "Hey, what's up?"

I didn't leave my room for the next three days. They brought my meals to me—a staff member always stayed with me while I ate. Nurses came in to check on me regularly, and I could only assume that I was the typical "new kid"—dragged to rehab against her will. My roommate introduced herself. Her name was Rachel, and she invited me to every activity.

"Some of us are going to take a walk on the beach tonight. Do you want to come?"

I didn't answer. I kept my back to her at all times and tried to remain hidden under the comforter.

"Okay. Well, let me know if you need anything."

And first thing in the morning: "I'm going to breakfast. Do you want to come with me?" she asked. I pretended to be asleep.

"I'm heading to group. Do you want to walk together?" Lunch, dinner, television…she extended an invitation for everything.

On day three, I finally rolled out of bed and examined my reflection in the mirror. My eyes were red and puffy from all the crying I'd done. At this point there were no tears left. Even when I felt like crying, I simply couldn't; it was futile. I looked at my cheekbones, my thin neck, and my black roots that were finally beginning to show on my hair.

I took a shower and put on fresh clothes. I ate the breakfast the nurse brought in. I brushed my hair and put on a touch of eyeliner and mascara. When I finished, I made my bed and pulled out my schoolbooks. I sat down on the bed and began conjugating Spanish verbs. The work reminded me of Zoe, and I wondered what she was doing, and what kind of painting she was working on. They always meant more to her than I could ever understand. I felt a pang of sadness sweep over me. I continued conjugating my verbs.

I heard the doorknob turn, and watched as Rachel waltzed into the room. "Oh hey, you're up," she said. I noticed that she wasn't surprised at all when she said this. She seemed to be expecting it. "What are you working on?" she asked.

"Spanish," I replied.

She sat down on the edge of her bed. "What grade are you in?"

"Tenth."

"I guess they're letting you finish out the year on independent study, huh? That's what they did for me last year."

I raised an eyebrow, and looked at her.

"Yeah, it's my second time in a year. I know," she said. I didn't respond to this.

"I'm bulimic," she continued.

"Which means—"

She smiled. "Whatever you want it to mean."

I don't know what surprised me more: her admission…or the fact that she seemed okay about it.

"So how long will you be here?" she asked.

"Eight weeks. Unless I need more time."

"Do you think you will? Need more time, I mean," she clarified.

I shrugged.

She stood to her feet. "Well, it's almost lunchtime. Do you want to take a break and come with me?"

I checked the clock on the wall. I wasn't hungry, but I knew a plate of food was coming, whether I wanted it or not.

We walked toward the dining room in silence. The

area was small, with several round tables. I imagined the room couldn't hold more than a couple dozen people at a time. It seemed very private.

"We're like one big happy family," Rachel replied when I mentioned this.

By the time we grabbed our plates, several others had joined us. I followed Rachel to a table where some people were already sitting.

She made the introductions. "Guys, this is Wrenn. She's my new roommate. Wrenn, this is Dana, Ryan, and Tabitha."

I looked at Tabitha. She looked nothing like my Tabitha. This girl couldn't have been more than twelve years old. Her brown hair was straight and lifeless. She was all bone—her shoulders protruding from beneath a gray tank top, and her arms were wrapped in a sweatshirt. I watched her as she cut her sandwich into small bites with a plastic fork and knife, and then as she cut those bites into even smaller pieces. She finally brought a piece to her mouth and chewed for what seemed like forever. Then she began cutting again.

"She's anorexic," Rachel explained, when she noticed I was staring.

"Shut up, Rachel," Tabitha shot back.

"My, aren't we in a mood today," Dana said. Tabitha picked up her plate and carried it to the dining hall window. "I can't eat this," I heard her say. When she returned to our table, she had a different plate and a new sandwich. This one looked like ham and cheese. She began cutting again.

"So, what are you in for?" Ryan asked.

He looked older than I was, with brown hair and brown eyes. He was cute, with a nice tan and a few freckles splashed across his nose. His white T-shirt highlighted exceptional biceps. It was obvious that he worked out.

"I don't really want to talk about it," I mumbled, refusing to meet his eyes.

"Oh. I'm anorexic," he replied, taking a bite of his sandwich.

"Is everyone here anorexic?" I asked.

"I'm bulimic," Rachel reminded me.

"What's the difference?"

She sighed. "Basically we fall into two categories. We either eat too much and feel really wretched, or we don't eat enough and feel really wretched. Either way, we all do something about it."

"What do you do?" I asked.

"I make myself throw up," Rachel said.

I looked at Ryan. "I exercise," he replied. That explained the muscles.

"I did whatever I could to make sure I didn't gain weight," Dana added. "And Tabitha doesn't eat, period."

I looked back at Tabitha, who, again, was cutting small bits of sandwich into even smaller bits.

"Shut up!" she cried. The words were startling; they sounded more like the harsh cry of a seagull than a human voice. The occupants at the tables nearby stopped to watch the potential drama unfold.

I gazed at her for a moment. "Back home, I have a friend named Tabitha," I said.

Tabitha stared, eyeing me warily. "Where's home?" she finally asked.

"Amberson Heights."

"Oh." She turned her attention back to her sandwich. "That's strange. I mean, it's not a common name. I've never known anyone else named Tabitha."

"Me neither."

She thought for a moment. "I've never known anyone named Wrenn," she continued, finally eating a bite. "It's a pretty name."

"Thank you. My dad named me—before he died."

I listened to the conversations going on around me. On the outside it looked like any other day at a school cafeteria. But here I heard laughter, I heard crying, and I saw nurses and other attendants scanning the group, making sure everyone was eating. That was the biggest difference; unlike in school, here we were watched like crazy. I took a bite of my sandwich. It felt heavy in my stomach, and by the time it was half gone, I felt stuffed. I couldn't eat another bite, and didn't want anymore. As I set it down on my paper plate, I felt a hand touch my shoulder.

"Wrenn?"

I turned around.

"I'm Angela," she stated, introducing herself. "I was wondering if you would mind stopping by my office after you finish eating."

I shrugged. "Okay."

"It's at the end of the hall. Room 106. My name is on the door. You can't miss it."

"Okay," I repeated.

"So what's that about?" I asked, when Angela was gone.

"Individual therapy," Rachel explained. "Angela's great, though. She's new, but you'll really like her."

Ryan piled his trash onto his plate. "Well, Wrenn, let me be the first to officially welcome you to Seaside. I hope you like to talk—because they'll talk you to death at this place. And 'why' is their favorite word. Take it as fair warning." He grabbed his plate and got up to leave. "As for me, I'm going for a run. Anyone care to join me?"

Tabitha picked up her plate. Rachel immediately grabbed her arm.

"I don't think you're finished," she said calmly. Frowning, Tabitha sat back down. She resumed her picking and cutting.

"I'll go," Dana said. "I'm done here anyway. It was nice meeting you, Wrenn."

"You too," I replied.

After they left, Rachel interlocked my arm with hers. "Come on, I'll walk you to Angela's." We left Tabitha alone at the table to finish her meal.

Chapter
Twenty-Three

Angela's office was full of things — stuffed animals, inspirational posters that boasted photographs of mountains and sunsets, with phrases like "Keep Your Dreams Alive" and "Believe!" printed on them. The office featured a sitting area with a couch and two chairs, with a pale blue rug on the floor. The open window faced the ocean. It looked like it could be a teenager's room — I suppose that's the look they were going for — except for the rows of bookshelves full of psychology and self-help books.

Angela greeted us at the door. Rachel said good-bye, and Angela motioned for me to take a seat. I chose one of the beige chairs. She slipped off her shoes and sat down on the couch, tucking her legs underneath. She had short, stylishly cut, black hair, and smart-looking glasses. She couldn't have been that old; I figured she was fresh out of college.

"So how is everything so far?" she asked. "Do you need anything?"

I shook my head. I told her that everything was fine,

and I had everything I needed. She was concerned about my stay at Seaside…asked if I'd met anyone else, and so on.

"Just the people I was sitting with at the table," I replied with a shrug.

"And what did you think?"

"Everyone was nice. They seemed pretty normal, I guess." I thought about this for a moment. "Except for Tabitha."

"Everyone here is at different stages of their disorders," Angela said. "Some still need to do a lot of work; others are nearly ready to go home. Some we still have to accompany to the bathroom to make sure they don't throw up whatever they've eaten, while we give others more freedom. We try to trust our residents until they give us a reason to feel otherwise."

This made sense. Only, I didn't need watching; I wasn't like them. I nodded, and stared at the carpet.

"So what did you think about Tabitha?"

I thought for a moment. "I know another Tabitha. And she's nothing like the one here."

"Really? What's your Tabitha like?"

I cleared my throat. "She's a year older than me. She's pretty, and a lot of fun to be around."

"Is she one of your friends?"

"Yeah, but only for the last few months."

"How did you meet her?" she asked.

"We were in the musical together in school."

Angela adjusted herself in her seat. "Wow, that's

pretty cool." Then came all sorts of questions: what role
I'd played, what the experience was like, etc. It was easy
talking to Angela. It was almost like talking to a friend. If
I closed my eyes, I could imagine myself sitting on Zoe's
bed, confiding in her. I felt a pang of sadness, and wondered what Zoe was doing. Thinking of Zoe made me want
an orangeade.

After a half hour or so of talking, Angela checked her
watch. "Well, I have some things to do, but I was wondering if you'd come back tomorrow—you know, to let
me know how you're doing."

It didn't feel as if I really had a choice. There's no
telling what Mom's insurance was paying for me to stay
here. She may as well get her money's worth. Besides, I
didn't think individual therapy was optional. I nodded in
agreement.

When I went back to my room, my books were still
strewn across the bed. I sat down, made myself comfortable, then got back to conjugating my Spanish verbs.
Rachel interrupted only once, to let me know they were
going to watch a movie in the common room. "Did you
want to come?"

I shook my head. "That's okay. Maybe some other
time."

Rachel didn't push. "Okay, I'll see you later."

On Saturday, my mom and Karly came to visit me for
a few hours. I was allowed to leave with them for a while,
and we went to a local steakhouse for lunch. I ordered a
salad and a baked potato—sour cream only. Mom tried to
convince me to order a cheeseburger. I said no. She didn't
argue.

Between the two of them, the conversation flowed despite my lack of participation. I heard the latest Mitzi Monroe horror story, and Karly's usual middle-school intrigues. It felt like a typical meal at home. Phil had asked about me, Zoe had asked about me. They both wanted to come and visit at some point—if, of course, I was up to it.

I nodded. "Sure, that'd be fine." They didn't say anything about the one person I wanted to know about—Steven—and I didn't ask. Mom took several of my school assignments back with her: a few math lessons, an essay for history...whatever I'd managed to accomplish so far.

When they left I felt empty, but so relieved at the same time. I didn't like seeing them there at Seaside. They didn't seem to belong. But when I looked down the halls and watched Tabitha cut and pull apart everything on her plate before taking a bite, I felt like I didn't belong there either.

"Why?" Angela asked.

"Because I'm not like her," I answered. "She's thin and obsessive."

"You're thin, too, Wrenn."

I shook my head. "Not like her," I said.

"But you did lose a lot of weight. Maybe you aren't as thin as Tabitha, but who's to say you wouldn't have kept going? Maybe we just caught you before it got that bad."

I thought about this for a moment. "But I wouldn't have."

"How do you know?"

I didn't answer.

She sighed. "The thing about eating disorders is that they're psychological before they are physical. People with active eating disorders never feel good about themselves or their bodies, even when they lose weight and people comment on how great they look. They have to keep on losing. They always feel fat—that they'll never be as thin as they want. That's a downhill battle."

"That's crazy," I said. "Because no matter what you do, there is always someone out there who is prettier or thinner. I mean, no matter how hard I tried, there were always people who were better than me."

"Like who?"

I looked toward the ceiling, my eyes beginning to water. I took a deep breath.

"Bree Donnelly."

"Who is she?" Angela asked.

"Just a girl," I replied, shrugging my shoulders.

Angela leaned forward. "If she was just a girl, you wouldn't be so upset about her," she commented.

I thought about this. "I suppose not," I finally mumbled.

"So who is she?"

"Pretty, perfect, popular…take your pick."

"Is she one of your friends, too?"

My mind wandered back to the night of the cast party, standing with Bree in the bathroom. I'd felt so good about that night. I felt gorgeous—and thin. I felt like I could be popular; that people would actually want to be like me. I felt like I could be Bree Donnelly. Of course, Bree had realized that, too: *When you were fat and ugly, you wanted nothing more than to crawl into my skin and be just like me*, she'd said. And then I'd told her she was bitchy.

"No," I answered. "She's not one of my friends."

When I left Angela's office five minutes later, I had a stack of papers in my hands. I had them because I couldn't talk about Bree Donnelly. I couldn't find words or answers; I just didn't know what to say. So now, because I couldn't say anything about her, instead of talking, I was instructed to write. Angela told me to write a letter to Bree, telling her whatever I wanted or needed to say.

"I'll read it if you want me to, but if you don't, then that's okay, too," Angela explained. "And don't worry, she never has to read it or even know about it."

I trudged back to my room, the paper heavy in my hands. Rachel was curled up on her bed, reading a book. I sighed, then plopped down on my own bed, and stared at the blank paper in front of me. It was so intimidating. I didn't even know where to begin.

I wrote my name at the top of the page. Then I outlined it. I wrote the date. Then I stared at the page for a few minutes more, trying to think of something to say. I drew a tulip in the corner.

"What are you working on?" Rachel asked, looking up from her book.

"A letter," I replied.

"Oh. Who to?"

"The most popular girl in school."

"Cool," she said, without blinking. "Good luck with that."

She didn't hesitate, she didn't think twice. I sat up and stared at her.

"Why does none of this surprise you?" I asked her. "I mean, when I first got here, you kept asking me to do things with you when all I wanted to do was hide under the sheets. You knew I'd come to lunch, you knew I would go talk to Angela, and now the fact that I'm writing a letter to the most popular girl in my school doesn't even surprise you."

"Wrenn, you're forgetting about my seemingly continual involvement with this place. Trust me, Seaside is a lot easier to handle the second time around," she explained.

I thought about this. "So you had to write a letter, too," I confirmed.

She smiled. "Girl, I had to write dozens of letters."

I looked back down at the sheet of paper, which was still, for the most part, empty. "So what did you write about?"

"Whatever I wanted. Whatever I needed to get off my chest."

"How profound," I said, rolling my eyes.

She closed her book and tossed it on her bed. "Look, don't make it harder than it has to be. Just put 'Dear most popular girl in school,' and then tell her anything and everything you've ever wanted to say to her. The good, the bad, and the ugly. Tell her you adore her, tell her you need to be her friend, tell her you want to rip her eyeballs out of their sockets. Whatever it is, tell her."

I smiled. "You make it sound so simple."

"It *is* simple. She's not going to read it, is she?"

"No," I said, shaking my head.

"Well then, you have nothing to worry about! Just write whatever pops into your head." She gave her hand a little wave as she said this.

Whatever pops into my head, I thought. Rachel reached over and grabbed her book, then lay back down. I took my pencil and wrote "Dear Bree," just under my own name. Then I started writing.

I wrote and I wrote, and I filled up both sides of two full pages before it was time for our afternoon group session. We were going to the beach today, and I'd been looking forward to it all week. There was no time to finish the letter or proofread it, and glancing over the pages, I could see where I'd known just what to say—the words were sloppy and rushed, like my hand couldn't keep up with my thoughts. In other places I'd taken more time, with each word carefully thought out, and my handwriting neat.

Without another thought, I folded the letter and, on my way down the hall, I carefully slid it under Angela's door.

Chapter

Twenty-Four

Dear Zoe,

Hey girl. What's up? NMH. Well, there's actually a lot going on here. If anything, Seaside is interesting. There's a lot of talking, and a little drama, but in a way it's like its own little retreat. The beach here is gorgeous—I have a view from my room. My roommate's name is Rachel, and she's really nice. There are a lot of interesting people here, and I'm getting along okay. I'm sorry I haven't been able to talk to you. Mom mentioned you'd asked about me, and I wanted to thank you. I hope you can get over here to visit soon. If you can, please bring orangeades. I'm having serious withdrawal from them, and there's no therapy here for that sort of thing!

I drew a little smiley face beside this and read what I'd written so far before continuing.

I also wanted to thank you for being such a good best friend. I don't know where I would be without you—com-

pletely lost, I'm sure. I hope that what's happened hasn't affected our friendship. I know the last month or so before the show, I wasn't a very good friend. A lot of it was just moodiness, and a lot was just me being stubborn. I'm learning so much here—things about myself and things about other people. For instance, I've learned that you're really important to me, and I'm sorry for the way I've acted and the stupid things I've done. I hope that we can start over when I get home.

Thank you again for being a great best friend... even though I didn't deserve it. Tell Chase I said Hi!
Love,
Wrenn

Unlike Bree's letter, the ones to Zoe, my mother, and Karly got mailed the day after I wrote them—after I showed them to Angela. They weren't as intense as Bree's letter. In each one, I thanked them, said I was sorry, and told them I couldn't wait to get home so that things could get back to normal.

"What's normal?" Angela asked, after she read them all.

I shrugged. "I don't know."

"Do you think it was the most appropriate thing to say?"

"Maybe…maybe not."

"What was normal before you came to Seaside?"

I sighed. "Before I came to Seaside I went to school. I stopped at Andy's for an orangeade. I went home, did homework. Went back to school for rehearsal. Came home again and worked out. Then I went to bed."

She thought about this for a moment. "What kind of person were you at school?"

"A nobody," I replied.

"You were a good student, and you had your friends," she pointed out.

"But no one knew I was alive."

"So 'normal,' before you came here, was going to school and to play rehearsals and starving yourself and working out too much. Is that what you're saying?" she asked.

"I guess so."

"Is that normal?"

I frowned. "I guess not. I was just...misguided."

"That's an interesting choice of words," Angela stated, leaning forward.

I blushed. "They aren't mine. They're Steven's," I explained.

"Who is Steven?"

I fingered the silver bracelet on my wrist. "Now *that's* for a completely different session."

"Hey," I said, walking toward the concrete table and benches in the garden area.

Phil stood up and smiled. "I know you weren't expecting me."

I sat down at the table in the shade, the bench feeling cool against my legs. "It's okay."

"So how is everything going?" he asked, taking his seat once again.

I shrugged. "Fine."

"Your mom said you'd made some new friends."

I nodded, brushing aside a strand of hair blowing in the warm, sea breeze. "There's not really another option. But yeah, everyone seems nice."

Phil coughed, and cleared his throat. "I, um, hope this isn't a bad time or anything, because there's something I wanted to ask you." He reached into his pocket and dug around for a few moments. My heart flip-flopped in my chest when he pulled out a small, black jewelry box. When he opened it, there was the largest, most gorgeous diamond ring I'd ever seen nestled grandly between the black velvet.

"Oh, wow!" I cried, laughing. "Phil, that thing is ridiculous!"

He smiled. "I hope you mean that in a good way," he replied.

"Yeah!" I cried, taking in the massive, shiny rock reflecting the light back at me. Apparently selling media time was a lucrative business. "I guess she has no idea," I assumed.

"No. We haven't talked about it yet. I mean, we talked about the possibility in passing," he clarified, smiling. "But no. She doesn't know."

"When are you going to ask her?"

And without hesitation: "When you give me the okay."

For a moment, I forgot to breathe. I looked at him in

amazement. Tall, lanky Phil, the nerdy guy who had some-how managed to make my mother fall madly in love with him, was asking my permission to marry her. I struggled to catch my breath and find the appropriate words. "You don't need to ask me. I'm not the one who's supposed to say yes," I reminded him.

He gazed at the ring. "No, but you're Kerri's daughter. I love her, and I want to marry her, but this is your family, too." He looked at me. "And I think you have every right to have a voice in the matter."

I continued to stare at him in disbelief. Phil, the balding, air-time–selling, lunchbox collector, nerd gone crazy, was giving me a say in this huge decision. I thought about the irony of this situation for a moment. What was I supposed to tell him? *"No, I'm sorry, but I don't think you're my mother's type"?*

Steven's voice rang in my ears: *"You never know, he may not be her type, but that doesn't mean he isn't exactly who she needs."*

Looking at the ring and then back at Phil, and remembering how happy my mother had been for the past few months now that he was around, made me realize there was no way I could refuse. Maybe Phil wouldn't have been *my* choice of a husband for Mom, but most of the choices I'd made so far had backfired anyway—so what did I know, right? Even though I couldn't go back and change the things I'd like to, or even needed to change, I could start right now to try and make things right, and start making better decisions about things that didn't affect just me.

"Yes," I told him. "Ask her. You have my permission."

A huge smile crossed his face. "Thank you, Wrenn."

I laughed. "You're sweating! Were you actually nervous about asking me this?"

He shrugged his shoulders. "I wanted to make sure the timing was right. I didn't want to put any more pressure on you.... It was almost as bad as having to ask someone's dad for permission—maybe even worse." He pulled a handkerchief out of his pocket and wiped his forehead.

"Well, you did fine," I said, still giggling. "So what are your plans?"

Phil closed the little black ring box and stuck it back in his pocket. "I don't know. Do you want me to wait until you come home?"

"Nah," I said, shaking my head. "You could, but it would just drive you crazy to wait. You can ask her whenever you want."

We sat in silence for a few moments, listening to the waves as they crashed in the distance, and enjoying the warm breeze that was blowing off the ocean. "So," Phil began, finally breaking the silence, "do you have any advice for me?"

I thought for a moment. "No. She really likes you; I wouldn't be too worried."

I checked my watch. It was time for group.

"I guess I should get back in there," I said, standing.

"Okay. Well, it was terrific seeing you," he said. "We're all ready for you to come home."

At that moment I felt so completely horrible about everything I'd said and thought about Phil. He was a genuinely good guy. I mean, he'd driven almost an hour and a half to come see me—for ten minutes—just so he could ask me if it was all right if he married my mother. He hardly knew me, and yet he was trusting me with something so important—to him, and to my mom. He was ready for me to come home, and he was accepting me as part of the family he wanted to create with all of us. When it comes to stepfathers, you can't do much better than that.

We said good-bye, and I began walking toward the building. Something stopped me. "Phil?" I asked turning around.

"Yeah?"

"What would you have done if I'd have said no?"

"I would have waited," he replied, nonchalantly.

"For Mom?"

"No. For you."

I smiled and continued walking. I wished him good luck as he headed for the parking lot. He looked up and offered a little wave, then climbed into his SUV.

Chapter

Twenty-Five

I looked at the stars above me and wondered if I'd ever experienced a more perfect evening. It was a Friday, and Fridays always meant special activities. Last week we'd gone bowling. The week before, we'd gone to the movies. This week, our treat was a bonfire on the beach and toasting marshmallows.

Some of the counselors were there, keeping an eye on things, but for the most part we were on our own until midnight. Ryan, Dana, and a few others were playing in the surf. Tabitha was staying close to the fire, picking apart her marshmallows, and Rachel and I were lying in the sand, staring into space and listening as the waves crashed on the shore.

The sound was relaxing, and therapeutic, even. So when Rachel asked the name of the first guy I'd ever kissed, I told the truth.

"I've never kissed a guy."

"What?" I could hear the astonishment in her voice.

"I told you, I wasn't exactly girlfriend material. Guys

never paid me any attention, unless they were oinking, or pointing and laughing."

She frowned. "People *so* bite."

"Tell me about it. I did have a guy kiss me on the cheek, but that doesn't really count. What about you?" I asked.

"I had a boyfriend before I came here," Rachel replied.

I asked her to clarify which time.

"The first time. We dated for like, a year. After I came here, things just weren't the same between us. I was away from home for a few months and, I don't know — we grew apart."

"That sucks," I said quietly.

"I know. Believe me, I've written a lot of letters about him."

"About him or to him?"

"Both. I sent him the first few letters because we were still dating. I just told him I was sorry and that I missed him. You know, typical stuff. But he never wrote back."

I couldn't believe this. "And you never talked to him again?"

"I called him when I got home, to see if we could talk. He didn't want to; he said that I wasn't the person he thought I was, and that he didn't feel the same way about me anymore." She laughed. "He probably found someone else by then."

This made me so mad. Rachel was like, the nicest person I'd ever met. How could anyone drop her like that? Especially after what she'd been through. He should have been more supportive, and I told her so.

"Wrenn, the thing about Seaside is that while we are here, it seems as if our entire lives are on hold. We go to counseling and we do fun stuff, too, but everything is geared toward this one major thing: conquering our eating disorders. We tend to forget that while we're here, life goes on for everybody else. We may be stuck in this every-day world of talking, and thinking and trying to figure things out, but back home, everyone else is still working, going to school, and living their lives."

I remembered the day I first came to Seaside, when I knew that the school was abuzz about my being sent to rehab. I knew everyone would be talking about me. But then I didn't think about them anymore. Since then, the days seemed to blur together, and I found myself forgetting about time. One day I suddenly realized that school was already out for the summer—and I hadn't even noticed.

"So, what are you here for, anyway?" Rachel asked, interrupting my thoughts.

I smiled. "I was wondering how long it would take you to ask."

"Well, after a few group therapy sessions, most people are pretty comfortable with their disorder. It kind of becomes a calling card. 'Hi, I'm Rachel, and I'm bulimic.' Get me?"

"I know. But since no one officially asked—"

"You don't have to tell me if you don't want to," she said. "It's entirely up to you."

The longer I stared at the sky, the more stars appeared. They came out of nowhere; first dozens, then hundreds, then thousands. Looking up at them made me realize how small I was in comparison to everything that lay beyond. And still, I couldn't help but feel comforted knowing that there were people out there who cared about me.

"I'm anorexic," I told her. "I used to be fat. Well, I mean, I wasn't obese or anything, but I was bigger than I wanted to be. So, when I tried out for the school musical and got a part, I decided I needed to change. I cut out food pretty much altogether. I started skipping meals and only eating what I needed to get by—you know—like water and applesauce for lunch, or something like that. Then someone who I thought was my friend introduced me to laxatives. I figured they were just what I needed to take me down to the size I always wanted to be."

"What happened? I mean how'd you get caught?"

"My sister Karly found out I was taking the laxatives a few weeks before the musical, but I don't think she ever told my mom, even though she threatened to talk. They knew I was losing weight and that I wasn't eating enough. I exercised a lot, but I also kept really busy. I was at rehearsals several nights a week, and I kept telling my mom I'd already eaten, even though I hadn't."

I took a deep breath and continued. "The night of the play I felt really sick. You know, more than just nervous, but weak. There was a cast party the following night. I even had a date and everything." I smiled, thinking of Steven in his blue suit and his spiked hair. "I felt awful, so I got up to leave. And I hardly made it to the parking lot before I blacked out. I don't remember anything after that, but I know that Steven was there. He called 911 on his cell phone and rode with me to the hospital. I didn't wake up until the next afternoon. There were IVs and nurses force-feeding me the most awful hospital food you can imagine. I mean, I wasn't even eating normal stuff, like burgers and fries, and then they expected me to eat that crap?"

Rachel laughed. "Tell me about it. I know all about hospital food, trust me. You can throw that stuff up *without* forcing yourself."

I buried my feet in the cool sand, and continued gazing at the stars. "Why do you think we do this?" I asked. "I mean not just you and me, but all of us—here."

"Because we look in the mirror and we don't like what we see," she replied.

It was so simple, yet so profound. "Why did you do it?"

"I was a cheerleader, and when we did formations, I was always on the bottom—a base. It made me so mad. I wanted to be the girl who was hoisted up for everyone to see. When I got the stomach flu in the eleventh grade, I was amazed at how much weight I lost in twenty-four hours. I couldn't keep anything down. Every time I threw up, I got back onto the scale and watched as the pounds disappeared. After that, it just kind of became a habit. I came to rehab, straightened out my act, but I was on the squad again this past year, and I just couldn't take all the pressure. So I relapsed."

"I guess your parents'll never let you cheer again," I commented.

"No. But I don't want to anymore. It's so obvious that I can't handle it. I mean, I missed my graduation."

I looked at her. "Wow. I'm really sorry."

"It's okay. I'm dealing."

We continued to lie there in the sand, listening to the sound of laughter around us, and taking in the smell of burning wood from the bonfire nearby.

"So what happened to the guy?" Rachel asked, after a few minutes of silence.

"Steven? I don't know. I haven't talked to him."

"He hasn't written or asked about you?"

"Well, if he has, I'm not aware of it."

"That is so tragic," she commented.

"I know. I mean, I'd like to go home in a few weeks and be able to pick up where we left off. Things were just starting out...it was brand new."

She sighed. "Endless potential."

"Exactly. But I don't know if he'll give me another chance."

"Well, he should."

"Should he?" I asked. "I mean, I was just talking about him the other day. I thought about it and thought about it, and wondered...if he had done to me what I did to him, would I want to take him back? I can't honestly say that I would. I mean, I didn't listen when he told me he liked me for who I was. I didn't listen when he told me being popular wasn't everything, and I totally ruined our first date because I thought I was too fat. Would *you* take me back?"

"You should write to him," she declared. "It would be good for you. Say what you need to say, and see what happens."

I laughed. "Rachel, I've written 'Dear Steven,' at the top of hundreds of pieces of paper since I've been here, and not once could I complete even a sentence. I guess I'm just not ready to cross that bridge yet. I'm afraid of what'll happen, of what he's going to say."

"You should be more concerned about what you never gave *him* the opportunity to say," she replied.

We heard someone nearby calling our names. It was time to go. We stood up and brushed the sand out of our hair and from our clothes.

"There's one thing you have to remember about going through all this, Wrenn," Rachel said. "It's like one chapter of this huge book. If you make it through the next few pages, you know that this chapter will end, but that there's also a new chapter that lies ahead. There's always the chance for a new beginning. Don't ever forget that."

Chapter

Twenty-Six

I was never happier than when I saw that old Volvo pull into the Seaside parking lot. And when Zoe opened her door and climbed out of the car, two jumbo orangeades in hand, I wondered if life could get any better.

I let out a squeal and ran toward her. She set the two drinks on top of her car, lifted her sunglasses, and gave me a hug. "I'm so glad you're here," I said.

"Me, too," Zoe replied, pulling away. She turned and looked at the ocean, sparkling just a few feet away. "This is amazing. I could get used to this."

"Believe me, it's not just about all of us holding hands and staring at the sea," I said, rolling my eyes.

We unpacked her car. She'd brought provisions: snacks, a blanket, an extra pair of sunglasses for me, and a couple of magazines. I grabbed the orangeade and sneaked a quick gulp.

Oh, so amazing! I thought to myself. How I'd managed to survive this long without an orangeade, I had no idea.

We crossed the street and stepped onto the sand.

"I can't believe you get to do this every day," she remarked, as she spread out the blanket. I pulled out two individual-sized bags of Doritos, and sat down.

"Who says I get to do this everyday?" I asked, handing her one of the bags. "And I've only got thirty minutes."

"You're this close to the ocean and you can't even enjoy it?"

I shrugged. "It depends on the day, you know? Sometimes we come out here for our group session. And actually, I just got permission to go out in the morning. Some of the other residents run on the beach before breakfast. So I've been doing that the past few mornings."

"Running? Before breakfast?" she repeated. "They let you do that?"

"Yeah, but you can only get permission when you reach a certain point in your progress in rehab here. And you have to sign out and be back in half an hour. If not, they won't let you go again."

"Wow," she said.

"I know. It was really bad when I first got here. People were hanging over my shoulder and watching everything I did." I took a sip of my orangeade. "This is brilliant, by the way. Do you know how much I've missed these things?"

Zoe laughed. "I could kind of tell from your letter."

"You don't realize what you've got until it's all taken away."

We sat on the blanket together and stared at the waves crashing in front of us.

"So, you look good," she finally said, breaking the silence.

"Thanks."

"How do you feel?"

"Better."

"Good." She paused a few moments before continuing. "So what's it like here?"

I shrugged my shoulders. "It's all right, I guess. I mean, for what it is. I guess it's a lot like boarding school. I have a roommate, everyone eats together, we have health classes that we have to go to, and I have private sessions and group therapy. We do some creative projects, we have free time, and every now and then someone from outside will come in and give a talk about something related to our eating disorders and recovery. You know, like a doctor or therapist or something. I'm learning a lot," I added.

"I'm glad."

"So, how is Chase?" I asked, changing the subject.

Zoe grinned widely. "Absolutely amazing," she breathed. Apparently he'd gone with her and her parents to a recent gallery opening. Zoe was able to have a long conversation with the artist, and they exchanged email addresses. "He's really into abstract art. He actually said he wanted to see my stuff." She burst into a fit of giggles. "Chase and I got into this whole argument about the guy flirting with me. He was so jealous."

I began to laugh with her. "Guys are so paranoid!"

"I know!" she cried. "Anyway, we're supposed to go shopping for his dorm room soon."

Chase, like Steven, was headed to Northwestern.

Thinking about Steven made my heart flutter. I asked about him.

"Honestly? I haven't heard from him since school let out. I mean, he asked about you," she quickly added. "And when I got your letter, I let him know how you were doing. He seemed happy for you—that you were doing okay here."

"Really?"

"Yeah," she said, nodding. "He's a really sweet guy."

"I know. I feel like I totally screwed things up with him."

She thought about this for a moment. "Are you going to talk to him?"

"I'm not sure," I confessed. "I mean, yeah, I know I need to. I'm just…I don't know. Scared, I guess."

"Of what?"

"Of what he's going to say. Of what he thinks about me."

She rolled her eyes. "Wrenn, please. The boy was completely in love with you. You owe it to yourself to at least talk to him. He might surprise you."

I buried my face in my hands. "I am so completely stupid, Zoe. I finally get a good guy, and what do I do? I go and ruin everything."

Zoe put her arm around me. "If it's that important to you, then you should try to fix it," she said. "You both deserve that much."

I let out a sigh, knowing that she was right.

My half hour away from Seaside ended too quickly. Zoe and I hurried back inside and I checked in with the office, signed her in as a visitor, and then showed her around the place. She met Ryan, who was watching TV in the common area, and Tabitha, who had just finished her individual therapy and was in the ugliest mood, hardly pausing long enough to say "hi."

"Individual therapy is supposed to make you feel better," I whispered to Zoe, after Tabitha stormed back toward her room. "But I swear it brings out the worst in her."

And we finally ended up in my room, where I introduced Zoe and Rachel. The three of us sat down on my bed and began to flip through the magazines Zoe had brought. We sat together, commenting on the best- and worst-dressed celebrities, and drooling over A-List actors.

"Look at this," Rachel said, holding up the magazine for us to see.

I read the headline: "Is She Anorexic?" The article was about an actress who'd recently denied that she had any kind of eating disorder. There was a fairly large photo spread.

"Look at her!" she cried. "You can see the bones in her arm. That is so *not* healthy. I hate when magazines do this to real people. They're too busy snapping photos and gossiping about this girl to even think about getting her some help. 'Is She Anorexic?'" Rachel mocked, tossing the magazine aside. "It's like it's some sort of a joke or something."

We watched her as she continued ranting. Zoe pulled her knees closer to her chest, startled. "It's okay," I said. "She's fine."

Rachel snapped back to reality. "Ugh. I'm really

sorry. You must think I'm crazy. I'm not—it's just, this huge pet peeve of mine. I mean, unless you go through this, you don't have a clue. It bothers me that people are making money off someone when it's obvious they have a problem."

Zoe nodded, understanding.

Later, as I walked Zoe out to her car, I apologized again for Rachel. "It's still really fresh, you know? And this is the second time she's been here." But Zoe really did seem to understand. She liked Rachel, and wanted to come back to see me again soon.

"Is this just because I'm like, two steps away from the beach?" I asked.

She laughed as she got into the car. "You know better than that."

Chapter

Twenty-Seven

"You're going too fast, Ryan! Slow down!" I called.

Ryan slowed to a jog. It was a Saturday morning, and the sun was bright and warm, tanning my already dark skin. I was glad that, after passing the halfway point of my stay, I'd been given permission to do more on my own. I still had individual therapy with Angela, and went to group therapy with everyone, but while some of us, residents like Tabitha, were still required to stay on campus, I was allowed to leave once in a while. For the past week and a half, Ryan and I had made it a routine to go jogging every day before breakfast, with Dana joining us on the mornings she was willing to crawl out of bed early.

"I'm out of shape," I groaned as I caught up to him, trying to get my breath.

He turned to face me, jogging backwards. "You're out of practice. There's a difference."

Before coming to Seaside, Ryan was a track star. He'd even earned a track scholarship to Northwestern in the fall. He was fast, but he felt that in order to compete, he needed to be even faster. He began training hard—way too hard. He stayed on a very strict diet, ran every morning before school, went to practice in the afternoon, and then headed straight to the gym afterwards.

If there was one thing they drilled into our heads at Seaside—over and over again—it was that everything should be done in moderation. Nothing in excess. For Rachel, that meant not binge eating. For me, it meant eating well-balanced meals and staying healthy. For Ryan it meant eating right and working out only once a day for a limited amount of time, or he could have longer sessions but no more than a few times a week. For Tabitha, it meant eating all the food on her plate. I'd discovered that Rachel was right. The real issue was ourselves, and how we felt when we looked in the mirror. The worst part was that we were all suffering in different ways; ways beyond the physical and emotional damage our eating disorders had triggered. Rachel had missed her high school graduation. Ryan had missed the Regional competition, so he wasn't eligible for the State trials. For a while, he even thought his scholarship would be revoked. And I'd yet to determine what I'd lost in all of this.

"Are we done yet?" I asked Ryan.

"Almost."

He turned back around, but kept his pace steady with mine.

"So what happens when you leave this place?" he asked me.

"I don't know," I replied. "I know it's rehab, and it's not supposed to be fun, but I feel so good right now, I hate to think it's all going to be taken away."

"I know what you mean. It's kind of like its own little sanctuary," Ryan said, "cut off from the rest of the world. Of course, being at the beach doesn't hurt either."

We reached our halfway marker, then slowed to a walk.

"I just feel like for the first time ever, I'm around people who actually understand me," I confessed. "Everyone here knows what it's like to not feel good enough. It's like we're on the same level; no one's better than anyone else. I can be myself and not feel like anyone's judging me. Here, no one has to be perfect."

"Are you kidding me?" he said, acting offended.

I laughed. "Okay, Ryan. You're perfect; it's the rest of us who need help."

"It's a joke. I'm not perfect. And it wouldn't hurt you to realize that no one is — not here or anywhere else."

"I know," I replied. "It just scares me to think that, in a few weeks, I'll have to go back to a world that doesn't understand any of this. And what if I can't handle it, you know?"

"You can. Handle it, I mean," he clarified.

"Rachel ended up right back here a year later," I reminded him. "What's going to keep me and you from doing the same thing?"

"Wrenn, anyone can make mistakes; it's how you turn it all around that matters."

I sighed. "I guess this is my story, and nobody else's."

"Exactly. And the thing is…everyone has a story. The difference is that we're in a place that brings our stories together. So we can see that no one is perfect."

If only I'd learned that lesson a few months ago; I never would have found myself in this situation. "How did you get to be so smart, anyway?" I teased.

"Hours and hours of talking, and listening, and thinking," he replied, rolling his eyes. "Welcome to Seaside."

I took off my shoes and socks and began to walk barefoot. We made our way down the beach, enjoying the quiet summer morning. I completely focused my thoughts on how it felt when my feet sank into the wet sand, as it squished between my toes. Then I wondered how many more days I would have like this one. Maybe people weren't perfect, but these mornings sure were.

When I reached my room, I was sweating and in desperate need of a shower. I immediately grabbed my towel, shampoo, and face creams. When I emerged, I felt whole again—new clothes, dry hair, and a little bit of eyeliner, just for effect. As I walked toward my bed, I saw Rachel. She was packing.

"What's going on?" I asked.

"I'm going home," she said, smiling. She pulled off the pictures that were stuck to her mirror and put them in her bag. "My parents are coming to pick me up this afternoon."

"B-But, Rachel," I stammered, "what am I supposed to do here without you? I mean, I'm thrilled that you get to go home, but—" I shook my head in disbelief, not even knowing what to say.

"I know, I'll miss you guys, too," she said. "But I was given the okay, and I'm really ready for this."

I sat down on my bed, speechless. Just like that, and our time was up. In a few short weeks, Rachel had become such a good friend to me—one of my best friends, really. I counted on her. I needed her. I felt my eyes fill with tears.

"It's not going to be the same here without you."

She turned to look at me, and I saw that her eyes also were brimming. "I'm going to miss you, too."

"I would still be in that bed, bawling my eyes out if it weren't for you," I proclaimed.

She smiled. "No, you wouldn't. We all came around, eventually."

There was a knock on the door. I assumed it was Rachel's parents, but it wasn't. It was one of the nurses on staff. "Wrenn, your family is here."

I checked my watch. They were early. I hadn't been expecting them until lunchtime.

"You're going to be gone by the time I get back, aren't you?" I asked quietly.

"Yeah, I think so."

I ran over to my dresser and grabbed a blank sheet of paper and pen, then began to write.

"Here," I said when I was finished. "This is my home address, email address, telephone number...everything. Please write, email, or call me once in a while, okay?"

"If there's one thing I learned here, it's how to write a letter," she joked.

When I went to put the pen back in my drawer, something caught my eye. The pictures. I'd seen the packet a hundred times, and each time there was a reason I couldn't look at them.

This time I reached for the envelope and pulled out the thick stack. They were of the last nights I remembered before I came to Seaside. There was me as Rizzo, and singing on stage. There were several of me and Steven before we left for the cast party. The musical and the party seemed like episodes from another lifetime—it was as if years had passed since then. I saw Wrenn Scott in the photos, but it didn't seem like I was seeing the real me. I'd felt so alive and so beautiful that night, but now, looking back, I could see just how lost I'd been. I pulled one out, wrote my name and the date on the back, and gave it to Rachel.

"I guess I should go meet my mom and sister," I said. "I hate good-byes. I mean, really. I'm going to miss you so much."

Rachel came forward and squeezed me tight. "Not good-byes," she reminded me. "Chapters."

Chapter
Twenty-Eight

With Zoe's words to write to Steven ringing in my ears, and Rachel's encouragement just before she went home, I finally found the strength I needed to write my letter to Steven.

Dear Steven,

I wanted to thank you for what you did for me the night of the cast party. I'm sorry things didn't end better, but at the same time I'm glad you were there for me. It's difficult for me to explain my obsessions and the way I acted in the last few months. It seems almost silly now, but the truth is, I never believed that someone could like me for who I was. It just didn't seem possible.

I understand completely if you want to put all of this behind you and never speak to me again. After the way I treated you, I wouldn't blame you. If that's the case, I hope that, if we ever run into each other, I can smile and wave, and know that you were once my friend. Because you were, Steven. You were a great friend to me, even when I didn't deserve it. But if you can find it in your heart to forgive me, I'd really like the opportunity to see you again, so that I can prove to you that I'm a good person. Not long ago you asked me to give you a chance. Now I'm begging you for the same thing. Please give me a chance to make things better.

Thank you for everything you've done for me.
                        Love,
                        Wrenn

"But it's perfect," Angela informed me. "It says everything."

"I know!" I cried. "But maybe I'm not ready to tell him everything. Maybe he'll get the letter and see it's from me, and then throw it away. He might not even open it."

She nodded. "That's true, but how will you know if you don't send it?"

I fingered the silver I.D. bracelet: *Love, Steven.* I didn't know how I'd find the courage to mail that letter. It was important, and he needed to hear these things. And I needed to get them off my chest, but what if it backfired?

"Okay, let's go through a little scenario here," she said, straightening. "Let's say you get home, and you and Zoe head to Andy's for orangeades, and then Steven walks in. What do you do?"

"Freak out."

"Good one," she said, adjusting her glasses. "So you freak out, and then he walks over to your table to talk to you. What do you do then?"

"Freak out even more," I replied.

She rolled her eyes at me, and smiled. "So, after you are finished freaking out, what do you say to him?"

"I don't know," I said with a shrug. "That I'm sorry, that I wasn't myself, and I want to start over?"

"It sounds like a good plan, but isn't that everything your letter said?"

I thought about this for a moment. Then hesitating, I said yes.

"So why wouldn't you want to send him the letter now, so that he knows how you feel before that awkward situation comes up at Andy's or somewhere else?"

"You have a point," I said, considering the possibility.

Angela sat back in her chair and folded her arms. "I know I do."

That afternoon, I found Steven's address on that little slip of paper he'd given me like, a million years ago. I addressed the envelope and sealed it. I paid for a stamp at the front office, then returned to my room. I laid the envelope on the bed and stared at it for a while, debating about actually mailing it. I ran through all the possibilities in my mind—everything that could potentially happen by putting these feelings, scrawled on notebook paper, out into the world. But Steven needed to read this, and I needed to mail it. It was for the best. I carried it to the lobby, to the mailbox for outgoing mail. The letter felt like lead in my hands, but somehow I found the courage to drop it in. The envelope disappeared as the door closed with a bang.

Then I freaked. I yanked the door open, but it was too late.

It was ironic that my final independent-study writing assignment was an essay about what I'd learned, or what would be my legacy as a sophomore at Amberson High. Or maybe it wasn't ironic at all. It was just like my English teacher to go all philosophical on us for our final project, hoping that we'd take something away with us and apply it to our lives. I guess she was hoping that we'd somehow become better people by reflecting on these kinds of things.

I wondered who in my class had taken this assignment seriously. I wondered if the athletes had learned that, no matter how hard they tried, our football team would never make it to the state championships. I wondered if the science whizzes learned why Einstein was synonymous with "genius," while hardly anyone else was. I wondered if the cheerleaders learned that blue eye shadow was never really going to make a comeback—even if it was one of our school colors.

I assumed that my teacher was especially interested in my paper; that she was hoping to find me changed when she read it. My time spent in the play and at Seaside—and even my eating disorder—set me apart from everyone else in my class. I had a story that was mine to tell, and I knew that what I'd learned as a sophomore sometimes takes years for people to figure out. Some never get it at all. And so I began to make a list of the things I'd learned over the past year, especially over the last six months. When I was done writing, my essay looked something like this:

What I've learned so far:

I've learned that who I am isn't defined by the number I see when I step on the scale, or what I hear others whisper when I walk down the hallway. They don't determine who I am; I define myself.

I've learned that it's okay to be an "old soul" when it comes to music, and to not finish the songs I start to write. It's okay that I alphabetize my CDs and organize the shirts in my closet—by color and sleeve length.

I've learned that it is important to have a best friend who tells you like it is—even if you don't want to hear it, and even if you don't listen.

I've learned that life is too short to be spent worrying about what other people think.

I've learned that maybe I don't know who I am after all. And that's okay. Maybe I don't need to know just yet.

I've learned that life is like a book. Even if one chapter is ending, another one is about to begin.

And finally, I've learned that it's okay not to be popular, which was, in many ways, the hardest lesson of all.

I wrote my final essay and tucked it in the drawer of

my nightstand. The sun was pouring through my window. It was a gorgeous afternoon, and earlier we'd convinced the staff to let us have our group session outside, which was always a treat. I stood up, stretched, and glanced over at Rachel's old bed. A new occupant was hiding beneath the sheets. She'd just arrived yesterday.

For now, all that was visible was her black hair. I'd introduced myself the previous day, and listened as she'd cried most of the night. I asked her if she needed anything; she didn't respond.

"Dionna? I'm heading to group," I said. "Do you want to walk with me?"

She lay perfectly still. I gave her a few moments to decide, and then left the room, shutting the door quietly behind me. On the way down the hall, I passed a nurse carrying a tray of food.

"Up yet?" she asked.

"No, but she will be soon," I promised.

Chapter

Twenty-Nine

Angela and I were sitting on the couch in her office, going over plans of how I was going to take care of myself after I left Seaside.

"What's important," she'd explained, "is not falling into the same trap again. Dieting isn't bad, Wrenn. Working out isn't bad, you just can't take it to the extreme. It's okay to watch what you eat, as long as you eat sensible meals. And you don't have to cut everything out; it's okay to eat a candy bar every now and then." She smiled. "Chocolate itself isn't bad for you."

I nodded, understanding.

"It's not going to be easy," she'd continued. "Some people can't handle it, and they're the ones we treat again and again. It's not hard to eat when people are forcing you. What you need to do is apply the things you've learned in here, out there. It's important to have a support system ready, in case you feel yourself slipping. It's not physically safe for you to go back to what you were doing before you came here. You might not be so lucky the next time."

We were writing out a list of people I could talk to if I found myself relapsing—my mom, Zoe—when someone knocked on the office door. "Come in," Angela called.

It was one of the ladies from the front office. "Wrenn, you have a visitor."

I checked my watch. I wasn't expecting anybody, and my mom and Karly kept their visits to weekends. Angela told me it was okay to end our session early, and I followed the secretary to the main lobby. She picked up the clipboard and handed it to me. I signed my name on the sheet, along with the time I checked out.

"Thirty minutes," she reminded me with a smile.

I walked out the front door, and there he was, sitting on one of the concrete benches at the tables on the grassy lawn.

"Hi," Steven said, standing up.

I brushed the hair off my face. "Hi." We sat down across from each other.

"I'm, um, glad you came," I said. "It's a surprise. I mean, it's a surprise, but it's a good one." I looked down at my hands, and thought of Steven the last time I'd seen him—in that blue suit, as my date. Then I looked at Seaside, the building, and felt a pang of embarrassment— embarrassment for my even having to be here, and for Steven having to visit me under these circumstances.

"So how are you?" he asked.

"I'm fine." I paused for a moment. "How are you?"

"Fine," he said, nodding.

"Graduation?"

"It was good. Glad it's over."

301

"Congratulations."

"Thanks."

"So, um, what have you been up to lately?" I asked when he didn't say anything else.

He smiled. "I'm actually working. You know that internship your mom was talking about?"

"Yeah."

"Well, everything worked out, so I'm helping as a production assistant at Channel 8 this summer."

"Wow!" I cried. "That's amazing!"

"Yeah, it is. I like it—a lot." He cleared his throat. "I see your mom a lot, too."

My smile faded. So far, Steven had seen my mom more than I had this summer. That hurt. "Really? How is she doing?" I asked.

"She's okay, but you know, sometimes I can tell there's something on her mind, and I know she misses you," he said.

"Really?"

"Yeah."

I felt terrible, knowing that my mom was over an hour away, thinking about me and wanting me closer to her. It made me that much more ready to return home.

An uncomfortable silence fell between us, and, for a moment, I only concentrated on the sound of the waves nearby. "So, how is everything else?" I asked, urging him to go on.

"Fine, I guess."

This wasn't going as well as I'd planned. Angela was right; at some point I was just going to have to get this over with, so I sat up. "Look, Steven," I said, tucking my hair behind my ears. "I want to say I'm sorry. I mean, I know I really, really messed things up between us...."

"You don't have to apologize," Steven interrupted. "I got your letter. Thanks for writing it."

"Oh." I stopped. "You're welcome."

He sighed. "The thing is, Wrenn—"

At that point I knew exactly what was coming next. No matter how many times I'd daydreamed about Steven arriving at Seaside in his Jeep, sweeping me into his arms, and planting a kiss of forgiveness on my cheek, it wasn't going to happen. He was visiting for one reason and one reason only.

"You don't have to apologize because I'm not mad at you—not at all. And, really, this whole thing's not about giving you a second chance, or getting one. For me, it's only about you getting better."

"I'm getting better," I quickly confirmed. "I am! I know that what I did was so stupid. And it was getting out of hand. And that I'm lucky that when I came here I wasn't any sicker. Some of the people here...." I trailed off, looking toward the building, reminding myself of the daily struggles that went on behind those brick walls. "I've learned a lot in the last few weeks."

"I'm glad. But it's more than just that," he added. "I think you need some time to figure things out."

"Figure things out?" I repeated, not understanding. But I thought that's what I was doing at Seaside. That's what I was here for. I was figuring things out—I was! I felt warm tears fill my eyes.

He shrugged. "I think you need to find yourself. Figure out what you want to do, what kind of person you want to be, and I think that's something you should do on your own."

"You don't like me anymore," I confirmed, a tear spilling down my cheek.

"Wrenn, please don't cry," he begged.

I wiped my eyes with the back of my hand and laughed nervously. "N-no, I'm fine, really. I'm just...I don't know, sad—that's all."

"It's not that I don't like you anymore. If I didn't like you, I wouldn't be here. It may sound crazy, but it's the truth. I want what's best for you, and right now I really don't think that it includes me."

I was powerless to stop the tears. They fell faster and faster. "But you made me want to be better," I choked.

He pulled himself away for a moment. "Wrenn," he said softly, "what I saw these last few months wasn't you being better. Before the hair, the makeup and the weight—Wrenn, I liked you for you. I liked you because you were this amazing, incredible, talented person. I'd like to think that if you were sincere about my making you want to be better, none of this would have ever happened. To me, the old Wrenn was perfect the way she was."

The old Wrenn. The neurotic, chubby, wallflower Wrenn. I didn't speak, but only nodded.

"It's just—I don't know, I just don't feel the same way that I did before; you're not who I thought you were," he said, shrugging his shoulders. "Anyway, I think it's better this way."

Better for who? I wanted to ask. I continued wiping

my eyes, my mascara running. This wasn't better for me.
"I understand," I said, standing.

"Wrenn, please don't leave like this."

I laughed through my tears. "No, it's okay. Really. I don't have a lot of time, that's all. I'm only allowed to be away for thirty minutes."

He stood up. "Oh, I'm sorry...I didn't know."

"Yeah. The perks of rehab, I guess," I said, sarcastically.

"Yeah," he repeated. "I'm really sorry."

"It's no biggie," I lied, shrugging my shoulders. "I mean, we're still friends, right?"

"Yeah."

"Well, then, maybe I'll see you around."

I took a deep breath. As hard as it was, I stopped the tears long enough to say good-bye to Steven, but, when I heard the sound of his Jeep roaring to life, the tears started falling again. I wiped them away, sniffling as I walked back through the double doors and into the lobby. I took the clipboard from the front desk and scratched out my name, and noted my check-in time. I wiped my eyes again.

"Oh, sweetie," the secretary said. She reached over and pulled out a few tissues, handing them to me.

I took them, smiling at her through the tears. "Thank you."

I walked down the hall, trying to steady my breathing, and wiping the tears from my eyes. Tabitha passed me in the hallway.

"Wrenn, are you okay?" she asked.

I opened the door to my room, without bothering to answer. Dionna looked up from the book she was reading.

"I'm fine," I said, before she had the chance to ask. But that was a lie, too. Because I wasn't fine. I threw myself onto my bed and buried my face in my pillow and began to sob. That's when I felt it — a small hand touching my shoulder. I lifted my head and saw Tabitha sitting beside me. I sat up and let her hug me. Tiny, tiny Tabitha — so small and fragile that I felt she would crumble to pieces as we hugged. The salty tears streamed down my cheeks as I realized what I'd lost, and what this had cost me. I cried, and Tabitha held on, strong enough for both of us.

Chapter

Thirty

The morning sun poured into my room through the slit in the curtain. In my second week at Seaside, I'd tried my best to keep them closed tightly, even after Rachel told me it was futile: the curtains were too small for the window. The sun would always shine through the gap. Even when I safety-pinned them together one evening, when I awoke the following morning, there were two bright streams of light on either side. That's when I gave up. And when Dionna tried to do the same thing, I explained that it wouldn't work for her, either. And I knew that whoever came after me — and whatever her eating disorder — would also try to close those curtains. It would be like so many other things that connected us all at Seaside, something we'd each have to learn on our own: that no matter how you tried to hide it, the light would always shine through.

I rolled over and saw that Dionna was already awake and facing me in her bed. "I guess this is it," she said.

I smiled. "Yeah."

Dionna was still under house watch because she was

relatively new. Like Rachel, she was a bulimic, but that was just part of her story. She didn't protest when I walked over to my dresser and pulled out a pair of clean running shorts and a T-shirt, even though, like always, she would have to stay behind.

Ryan and Dana were waiting for me in the lobby on this, my last day in rehab, ready to embark on our final jog together.

"Good morning," Ryan said.

I breathed in the fresh air as we walked outside. "Isn't it beautiful?"

"That's the smell of freedom."

"I can almost taste it," I said, smiling.

"You're so freakin' lucky to be going home so soon," Dana said.

We crossed the street and stepped onto the warm sand, the ocean sparkling just in front of us. There are no words to describe the beauty of the ocean first thing in the morning—the sounds and the smells. It's just something you have to see to believe. No, there was no need to talk. So Ryan and Dana and I just ran, focusing on every step.

And at the same time, it was impossible to control my thoughts and feelings: I was both happy and sad. I was ready to return home, to play the piano, to sing. I was ready to be with my mom and sister. I was ready to see Zoe again. I was ready to discover what the rest of the summer had in store.

On the other hand, I'd made so many friends over the course of the last eight weeks—real friends. When Angela asked if I thought I needed more time at Seaside, I briefly considered saying yes, I did, just to get another week with them. But this was my story, and this chapter was ending. I knew it was time to face whatever lay ahead.

Back at the dining hall after our run, the staff fixed their typical "going away" sheet cake in my honor, even though it was breakfast. They did it because any time someone left Seaside, it was like a graduation: bittersweet. Still, as much as they cared for and had grown to love each of us, deep down I knew they never wanted to see us again, especially if it meant seeing us as we were when we'd first arrived—lonely, scared, and starving in so many ways.

I could never imagine why anyone would want to eat cake before ten in the morning, but we managed, and it felt great to be with friends. We passed around contact information so we could stay in touch. I showed everyone the pictures from *Grease* and the cast party, and when Tabitha asked if that was really me in the picture, I smiled and said, "No."

Because it wasn't. I didn't particularly care for the girl staring back at me in the photographs—her eyes were empty and hollow. As beautiful as I'd felt that evening, I could see that there was no sparkle in my eyes. I was sad, thin, and complicated. Still, the pictures served as physical proof of the transformation I'd undergone. They were a reminder, and I planned to always keep them close by.

I finished my breakfast and dove into the white sugar icing on my piece of cake. I watched Tabitha, who had already eaten most of hers. Her cheeks were pink; her tiny T-shirt no longer hung as lifelessly on her thin little frame.

She'd gained some of her lost weight back in the eight weeks I'd known her. She was eating, she was laughing, and she was truly beautiful.

After breakfast, Dionna watched as I gathered my things; she wondered aloud how she would manage without me. I told her exactly what Rachel had told me, which was probably similar to what Rachel's first roommate had told Rachel. We were all connected; our time spent behind these walls gave us something in common. It became part of our collective story and a chapter in each of our individual lives.

I packed my pictures and clothes, rolled up my comforter, and piled everything onto my bed, then I headed to Angela's office for one final conversation. When she asked me what I had planned for the rest of the summer, I shrugged my shoulders.

"I don't know," I said. "I'd just gotten my license before I came here. I was going to get a job to save up for a car. But now…I don't know."

Angela smiled. "That's okay. You'll figure it out."

We made plans to write throughout the remainder of the summer. Angela had a vested interest in keeping me away from Seaside, and the letter writing would act as a deterrent. She would offer advice from a distance for as long as I wanted, and if there was ever anything I needed to talk about, she was only a phone call away.

After we were done talking, I stepped out into the hallway and pulled her office door shut behind me.

Ryan, Dana, Dionna, and Tabitha met me in the lobby to say their good-byes. As I hugged each of them, I thought about chapters, beginnings, and endings. And I wondered what it all really meant, because part of me didn't want this chapter to end. And I realized that maybe it was okay. Maybe that was how it was supposed to be.

I brushed a stray piece of hair out of my eyes, then glanced at my reflection in the glass doors. I smiled when I saw her—the tiny, delicate songbird; the budding starlet; the daughter, and sister, and best friend. She was someone I knew very well, but had somehow gotten lost along the way—Me. And finding myself again was just as beautiful.

As my vision refocused, I noticed the ocean sparkling in the distance. And there it was before me: the rest of summer, full of possibility and endless potential, the next chapter just beginning.

I watched as my one wish was granted right before my eyes: my family, my friends—everyone who mattered most in my life—were all waiting outside for me to join them.

My heart felt like it would burst, and I couldn't help but laugh as I pushed my way through the glass doors and out into the sunlight.

Acknowledgments

To God: for the ability, determination and infinite possibilities.

Eric: for the support, the stamps, and for helping me to become the best possible version of myself. You've challenged me on so many different levels.

My family: for loving and accepting me *as is* and not trying to change who I am.

Robin Hardie: for assigning my first real creative writing project.

Gail Fletcher: for allowing me to stretch my creative wings.

Lee Fletcher: for the wonderful memories in the classroom and on stage.

Mrs. Ames, Dr. Cotugno and Dr. Rigsbee: for listening, understanding, and believing.

Dr. Clere: for introducing me to young adult literature.

Rhonda and Alanna: for the encouragement and enthusiasm.

My agent, Alison Picard: for giving me a chance.

My publisher, Evelyn Fazio, and her colleagues at Westside: for taking my story and making it better than I ever thought it could be.

To everyone who had a part in helping make my dream come true: this one's for you.